RISE OF THE FORGOTTEN

J. H. GATES

Joyce — Remember, you
can't do it alone —
God goes with you !
I. H. Gates Grandpa,
Joe Florancia

BOOKS BY J. H. GATES

Rise of the Forgotten
(Tales of Alarkin: Book One)

Coming Soon:

Through to the Dawn
(Tales of Alarkin, Book Two)

The Hinterlands
The Bloodlands

RISE OF THE FORGOTTEN

J. H. GATES

Raven's Breath
Press

Published by J. H. Gates in alliance with Raven's Breath Press

Characters appearing in this work are fictitious. Any resemblance to real persons, living or dead, is purely coincidental.

ISBN-9781096594215

Printed in the United States of America.

CONTENTS

Dedicated to my grandma, who was the first one to read the unedited first novel of a 14-year-old, book crazy girl – thank you for supporting me in everything I do!

And to my High Regium ... You are my inspiration.

PROLOGUE

A flurry of silk. Servants scurrying recklessly, scattering clothes, jewelry, and toiletries across the room. And a little baby girl, sleeping peacefully at Mariah's feet. Black ringlets framing pink cheeks, delicate fingers curled around her soft blanket. A perfect child ... and one day, a perfect queen. *My beautiful Princess Raven.*

Mariah allowed herself the smallest of smiles, enough to satisfy her motherly whim but not enough to invoke the wrath of her frenzied chambermaid. Synthia was hardly qualified to serve the Queen of Laynia, but Mariah hadn't the heart to reject the poor young woman on account of her propensity to fret.

"Oh, my queen, you're certain to be late," Synthia fussed, adjusting Mariah's pendant for the third time. "And King Wilgaun will have my head for allowing you to address the people in such a frazzled state! I suppose this will be the last time I see you, for tomorrow my head will be on a platter. That much I promise you."

Mariah laughed. Grasping Synthia's rough hands, she brought the maid to an abrupt halt. "Synthia ... dearest. I assure you that my husband – and the entire kingdom, for that matter – will have eyes only for my daughter. They won't notice if my necklace is a bit crooked. Besides," the queen added, appraising her reflection in the floor-to-ceiling mirror, "you have done a *wonderful* job preparing me for the ceremony."

Synthia snorted, planting her hands firmly on her hips. "Hardly, your ladyship. If you weren't so beautiful, I'd almost say you look a fright."

A timely knock rescued Mariah from any further admonitions. Smiling apologetically at her maid, the queen tiptoed across the cluttered floor, cracking open the heavy oak

9

doors.

Behind her, Synthia muttered anxiously about how queens oughtn't be troubled to answer their door, especially in the midst of a fashion-crisis. Without missing a beat, the maid ordered a few unlucky servants to start tackling the process of cleaning up the dresses scattered helter-skelter throughout the room.

Mariah was met by a very handsome – and very disgruntled – king. His frown was almost as prominent as the glittering crown upon his head. "*My dear.*" Wilgaun forced out the endearment, sounding more sarcastic than pleasant. "We will be late if you don't hurry … and to our daughter's own dedication, no less. Please tell me you're almost finished?" He tried to peek around Mariah to assess the progress, but she impishly planted herself in his line of sight.

"Is that all, *dearest*?" she inquired coquettishly, glancing up with an exaggerated flutter of her lashes.

The frown disappeared, and Wilgaun almost laughed. *Almost.* Instead, it was replaced by a benevolent – even tolerant – tilt of his head. "Yes, my lady. I'll wait for you in the throne room. Be there shortly, please?"

Mariah bit her lip, brushing away her disappointment with a practiced smile. "As you wish, my king."

Shutting the door, Mariah turned, fingers inadvertently wandering to her crown. The weight was still foreign and unnatural. How long had she been queen? Only a few years … years that had passed with excruciating monotony. She was an ornate book behind glass – gilt cover, illuminated letters, and fancy calligraphy, but never taken out of its case; a queen to be admired but not heard.

The servants, having witnessed the exchange, had ceased their activity and were staring at the floor, absently clutching half-folded garments. *They pity me. Servants, one and all, and yet they pity their queen.* Mariah clapped her hands, snapping them out of their daze. "Alright, that's quite enough fuss and bother.

Despite Synthia's notions to the contrary, I am perfectly presentable. You are all dismissed until after the ceremony ... and then we will deal with this disaster I've made," she added with a wink.

Pity was unacceptable. Mariah was queen; perhaps a nominal queen, but one who enjoyed all the benefits of royal life. And as queen, her place was to inspire good, not evoke sympathy.

Sympathy was only for the deserving.

℘

"My people, noblemen hailing from Laynia and across the length and breadth of Alarkin." With regal calm, King Wilgaun addressed the pompous crowd. "It is my honor and privilege to present my first child –" The applause rose, and he paused to allow the commotion to settle.

Glancing at his wife, Wilgaun tried to catch her gaze, but Queen Mariah stared demurely at the assemblage of nobility. Typical. He brushed off her apathy and continued his speech. He had rehearsed it to perfection – every word, every line, until it was absolutely flawless. *Or people would talk.*

Gossip was not limited to whispers between servants. The nobles were predators by nature, waiting to dig their claws in at the slightest provocation, and Wilgaun would not give them the satisfaction of one misplaced syllable.

"I give you ... Princess Raven!"

The gentry resumed their ovation with new vigor, gloved hands and ringed fingers colliding in a cacophonic rhythm. And amidst the pretentious applause, they concealed daggers of sedition, ready to strike.

"She will be a pride to my legacy and will lead this kingdo–"

A crash thundered through the throne room, rattling the crystal chandeliers and sending courtiers ducking for cover from raining debris. Outside the walls of Caritas, men began shouting and running; horses screamed as a tremor shook the ground.

Wilgaun whirled around, advancing towards the nearest

guard. "What is the meaning of this?" he demanded, finger inches from the guard's face.

The petrified guard could only manage an undignified stutter before a messenger rushed in. "The city is under attack!" he blurted.

An alarmed outcry arose from the crowd. They broke into a chaotic frenzy towards the nearest exits, tripping over each other's feet, skirts, and toppled chairs. Overall, a sight more befitting stampeding cattle than nobility in a castle.

The king stared at the absurd display. *Unbelievable.* He about-faced, sending the guard jolting back into attention. "Fetch my armor," Wilgaun ordered. The guard nodded and scrambled away.

"Noblemen, calm yourselves!" Wilgaun shouted. "This city has not been breached for –" Once again, his words were cut short as another *boom* cut through the air, followed by a vibration that echoed through the streets and castle flagstone.

"Wilgaun –" the queen started.

"Mariah," he interrupted, "the only thing that should concern you right now is getting Raven to safety!"

The last thing he needed was to answer the incessant questions of his wife; handling his own soldiers would be difficult enough. Women were fraught with emotion and liable to faint with the slightest distress, he was told. Personally, he had never seen Mariah faint, but he wasn't about to take that risk. Especially in front of his courtiers. Impatiently, Wilgaun snapped his fingers for a liveryman to fetch his horse.

A deep cracking, like the breaking of prehistoric bones, was a sure sign that the gates were crumbling against the onslaught of battering rams. The king muttered a curse under his breath. His gaze returned to Mariah, who hadn't budged. "*Go!*"

Mariah swallowed, tears forming in her eyes but never falling. "Be careful," she whispered, fingers tracing his jawline.

Wilgaun nodded curtly, pulling away from her touch. "Hide in the high tower; I'll send a guard up shortly." Mariah's gaze faltered, and her hand dropped away. Without another word, she was gone.

Wilgaun didn't have to be psychic to read her thoughts; like everyone else, Mariah was disappointed in him. She expected him to be like other husbands ... she didn't understand his duties as king. How could she expect him to show tenderness in front of his courtiers? His soldiers? He was their king – their commander in battle. He couldn't display even the slightest hesitation without risking the doubt of his people.

But what about the doubt of his wife? Wilgaun scowled, his self-justification brought to an abrupt halt by the one simple question plaguing his mind. Did Mariah doubt his love? All his wife wanted was his love, and yet somehow, he managed to push her further away every time they spoke. He certainly had given her every reason to believe in his indifference. In fact, the more he thought about it, the more he realized it was a miracle Mariah treated him as well as she did.

Wilgaun had hoped Raven would bring them together. That their relationship – more political than romantic in nature – might have a chance now that they had something in common. But yet again, something managed to tear them apart.

As usual, it was him.

∞

Mariah reached the staircase to the high tower and began her ascent. All around, the castle had exploded into a state of pandemonium. Servants raced through the halls, messengers ran to and fro, and noblemen fled into their rooms, bolting the doors behind them. But Mariah ignored them all; she simply cradled Raven against her breast, cooing and stroking the baby's delicate face. "You'll be safe. Daddy will be safe," she crooned. Raven watched her uncertainly, wavering between a crying fit and falling back asleep.

Mariah wiped another tear from her face. She may not have chosen Wilgaun, but he was still her husband; the least he could do was acknowledge her concern when his very life was at stake.

13

And since when had her affection ever been so ignored, so unwanted?

It took Mariah a moment to realize she had reached the top landing. Withdrawing a key from her pocket, she paused at a window, looking down at the courtyard; far below, a swarming mass of enemy troops hovered like carrion outside the walls of Caritas. "There are so many," she murmured. Dazedly, she unlocked the room, not bothering to latch it behind her as she set Raven's basket on the floor.

"There, my love," she said softly. "You're safe here."

A floorboard creaked in the back of the room, and the key slipped through Mariah's fingers. It landed with a hollow *thump* at her feet.

"Don't you know, Mariah?" The voice that drifted from behind her was disembodied and spectral, like a phantasmal shadow.

But the hand on her shoulder was all too real.

"You should never lie to a child."

ജ

Kisby stared mutely at the fighting that raged all around him. Bodies, pooling in their own blood, littered the cobblestones, and the cries of the dying pierced the air. King Wilgaun was in the middle of it all, shouting orders from his elevated position on his destrier. The Laynian soldiers immediately advanced but were cut off by a wave of hostile forces. Kisby grimaced, wishing he could close his eyes and go back to *before*. Before this strange army attacked, when he was nothing more than a simple foot soldier and no brave deeds were required of him. But where was the honor in that?

"Where did this army come from?" another soldier asked, panting as he swung at the nearest foe.

Kisby shrugged and kicked his attacker to the ground, finishing him with a quick thrust of his sword. That was three men he'd killed today ... three more than he'd ever killed in his life. But it was in defense of his homeland – a necessary evil.

Wasn't it?

"I don't know, Perin. Nowhere near here. Must be from the north," Kisby replied, forcing the last sentence out as he blocked a vicious downward stroke. The burly assailant cursed and resumed his onslaught; his attacks were sloppy but aimed to cut Kisby in half. Perin hacked on the enemy's side, and Kisby finished him with a swift blow to the neck. *Four.*

The archers on the wall were vainly trying to clear a path to the portcullis, but foes from the amassing army continued pouring in and thwarting their efforts. The king, surrounded by his personal guard, was nearly cut off from the other Laynian soldiers. Death was everywhere. *This has to end.*

Kisby growled, charging ahead of Perin. With a vengeance, he tackled the nearest invader to the ground. His sword rose and fell. *Five. Six. Seven.* As the numbers continued to climb, the pile of corpses around him grew; but he couldn't stop.

Block, slice, thrust. Block, slice, thrust. His actions became methodical, practiced. His muscles should have ached; his sword should have grown heavy. But Kisby felt nothing. Only a will to fight and kill any man who dared step foot inside the castle walls and threaten his people. "Try me, I dare you!" he shouted into the horde. "You won't take this castle while I'm still breathing!"

A grating laugh answered Kisby's challenge. Turning arrogantly, and immediately regretting it, Kisby took an inadvertent step back as he appraised his foe. Tall and unnaturally broad of shoulder, the new rival sneered down at Kisby; the scars marring his face were horrendous. With deliberation, he dragged his sword across the ground, scraping shingle and stone. To Kisby's ears, it sounded more like teeth on bone. Rolling his shoulders, a ripple of cracks moved up his spine. He refused to be daunted by this cur, no matter how loud its bark.

Appraising Kisby scornfully, one corner of the man's lip curled in distain. "You're right, *boy*. We won't take Caritas while you're still alive," he rasped, casually raising his blade. "But I rather look forward to burning it to the ground ... once you're *dead*."

Kisby snarled and charged recklessly. His opponent grinned, sidestepped, and sent Kisby sprawling to the ground with an outstretched leg. Kisby coughed, slowly regained his feet. *He could have easily killed me while I was down. The fiend is playing games.* Fuming, but more subdued, Kisby reevaluated his attack. He hesitated a split second before bringing his blade towards his adversary's head, then quickly redirected towards the midsection.

Effortlessly, the man deflected the slice and allowed Kisby's momentum to send him flying forward. A second later, a boot crashed into the small of Kisby's back. He yelled, whipping around and slicing at the man's legs. The tip of his sword connected; blood began to trickle. Kisby stood, smirking in challenge.

The man glanced at his leg, unphased. "You impress me – for a common foot soldier. Not many men can say they have fought General Gauln and lived." The general chuckled. "Actually, no one has."

"I guess I'll have to be the first," Kisby quipped flatly. They re-engaged, but as the fight went on, Kisby began to realize that Gauln was by far the better swordsman. Despite his confident words, Kisby was losing.

Kisby's sword flew into the air. A second later, his feet were swept from under him, and he crashed to the ground, body screaming, *breathe!* But nothing happened. A burning in his ribs dominated all other senses; blood dripped from his mouth.

Gauln knelt beside him. "Look at me."

Kisby blinked, gazed wandering. *My sword. I have to find my sword.*

"Look at me!" Gauln demanded, grabbing a fistful of hair. Finally, air rushed into Kisby's aching lungs, and his eyes met Gauln's. And then he saw his sword, trapped just out of reach

unmerited – rules.

Which brought to mind the king's request. Raven was to help entertain her father's guests – some visiting dignitaries from neighboring kingdoms – which required her presence at supper tonight. Supper, which started in precisely five minutes. *And the castle is a seven-minute gallop away!*

She sat bolt upright, leaping to her feet with a panicked, unladylike shriek. Freedom jerked his head up, crow hopped to the side, and resumed chewing the clump of grass that dangled from his lips in an absurd fashion. Grabbing his bridle, Raven dragged her horse to a rotten stump. It threatened to collapse under her weight as she launched off it and onto Freedom's bare back. She dug her heels in, and they raced towards Caritas.

Her hair was going to be a fright, but at the moment, her vanity was the least of her concerns. She could already see her father's disappointed frown. This would be yet another mark to add to her stained record. Why did she have to widen the gap between herself and King Wilgaun any further with her negligence and poor time keeping?

The outer wall of Caritas rose into view. To some, it was an ominous sight ... an imposing reminder of the power that ruled over the kingdom of Laynia. To others, it was a sense of security; a wall to hide safely behind. But to Raven, it was a prison. A physical representation of the dutiful restraints that confined her within those walls. Duty to her father. Duty to her kingdom. Duty to the mother she had never met.

"You're late."

Raven jerked on the reins and scowled, bringing Freedom to an abrupt halt at the portcullis. A young soldier casually leaned against the archway, face tinged with poorly disguised amusement.

The soldier – Tristan, Raven believed his name was – had begun his apprenticeship a few months ago. As of yet, Raven had experienced few interactions with him. Brogan, the senior gatekeeper, was normally the one to greet her ... and scold her for being out too long without guards or supervision. Like she was a child to have her hand slapped! If experience proved anything, this new gatekeeper would prove no different – and perhaps even worse. Old and cantankerous was bad enough. But young, inexperienced, and full of himself? And with the audacity to say she was late!?

Utterly insufferable!

"I thought you were the gate guard, not the timekeeper," Raven returned smoothly, dismounting and flipping the reins over Freedom's head. "Oh – excuse me. *Apprentice* gate keeper. An important distinction."

"I am, *Your Highness* ... but I also have spies in my employ. And they informed me that you were supposed to be at dinner, oh, about five minutes ago?" Tristan grinned impertinently. And something about his emphasis of Raven's title gave the distinct impression that he was making fun of her. The portcullis began its slow ascent, manned by an unseen figure.

Raven opened her mouth, then closed it again. Impertinent, just as she'd predicted. But was there also something refreshingly audacious about his straightforward manner? Sweeping past him, the Princess allowed herself a hint of a smile. "You should tell *your spies* they should mind their own business. Servants have no business gossiping about the royal family – especially if you insist on using their tidbits as blackmail."

Tristan laughed. "Fair enough, Princess," he acquiesced, giving a slight bow. "I'll keep that in mind."

The portcullis shut with a loud *clang* that could wake the dead. No dead were raised, however – just the senior gate guard, Brogan, who had been snoring contentedly for the last hour.

"What? Who's there?" Brogan demanded, scrambling to his feet. He sucked in his drool with an unsophisticated slurp.

"Just the princess, Master," Tristan answered casually.

Raven could feel his eyes boring into her back. She inwardly bristled at his use of *just* and *princess*, but refused to give him the satisfaction of turning around.

Tristan's last jibe almost broke her resolve.

"A very forgetful one at that."

∞

As soon as one of the stable hands had a hold on Freedom's reins, Raven was off and running – decidedly unladylike – towards the castle. Many guards and maids greeted her from their chores and posts, but she didn't acknowledge them, save a curt nod of her head.

How could I have forgotten about the guests? It was so simple – entertain boring courtiers and visiting dignitaries for a few short hours, then spend the evening with her obligation fulfilled and her father pleased for her efforts. At least, as pleased as he ever was. Now, she was about to bear the brunt of his well-deserved irritation for her tardy appearance.

The massive doors opened with a groan, loudly announcing Raven's presence in the great hall. *A little* too *loudly*. Plastering on a ridiculously fake smile, the princess curtsied deeply. "Good evening." Gliding to her seat, Raven ignored her father's glare as she lifted her skirt with practiced poise and slipped into her chair at the foot of the table.

The silence that followed was deafening.

Distracting herself from the courtiers' pointed stares, Raven observed the predictable entourage of servants. They brought in dish after dish of delicate entrées, tureens of steaming pottage soup, and platters of dark, yeasty rolls. Lastly, two man servants carried a wooden trencher displaying a roast pig with an apple in its mouth.

Raven fought the urge to wrinkle her nose as she waved away the pork; the wrinkled, pink skin and hideous snout was far too disgusting to eat even a bite. How the others managed entire platefuls was beyond her.

The visiting dignitaries resumed small talk amongst themselves; occasionally, one would strike up a trivial conversation with Raven. A few not-so-subtly dropped hints about their sons – all of which *happened* to be handsome, brave, rich … and completely unattached. It was a relief when the guests finished their meal and focused their attention on the troubadours and jesters – a respite from the boredom of politics.

A respite Raven wouldn't have the chance to take part in.

Wilgaun approached Raven, placing his hand on her elbow and firmly directing her from the room. The doors shut behind them, leaving the king and Raven alone in the hallway, with only two guards standing at the entrance to the great hall. They pointedly focused their attention on the far wall, pretending not to see or hear anything. Raven was sometimes tempted to test their stony indifference with some ridiculous stunt, but at the moment, the passive guards were the least of her worries.

Wilgaun whirled on Raven, his dark brows furrowed and mouth turned into an unpleasant frown. The king's broad, hulking stature was icing on the cake to his intimidating appearance. But worse than all these things were the narrowed slate-gray eyes, staring at her with … *disappointment*.

"Well?" he demanded.

"I – forgot," Raven confessed, lowering her head. *Like that will help my case.*

He groaned, shaking his head. "You *must* learn to take your responsibilities more seriously, Raven! You're nearly seventeen now, and as future queen you have to –"

"I know, set the example." If he'd said it once, he'd said it a hundred times. And this certainly wouldn't be the last, either. Why couldn't she make him proud for once? Better yet, why couldn't he see beyond her station as a princess to her true identity – as his *daughter*?

"Fine. Don't let it happen again." Wilgaun turned away and strode briskly towards the great hall. "Now return to our guests and mingle like a proper hostess, before there's even more talk."

Raven stumbled back a step and whispered, "Yes, Father."

∽

An hour and seven ballads later, Raven burst into her room,

slamming the door into the wall behind it. "He doesn't understand! I can't *always* be perfect … I'm human after all!" She flung herself on the bed and stared at the ceiling, silently fuming. Her only audience – a gray tabby dubbed with the unoriginal but apropos name *Smokey* – offered no sympathy. Rather, the cat kneaded her claws on Raven's stomach before laying down with a fluffy tail in the princess's face.

"Ugh! You're no help whatsoever," Raven groaned, picking her up and plopping her on the bed.

Muffled footfalls sounded from the hallway. Saush – Raven's Laynian shepherd – crept inside and sat timorously beside the bed, giving her tail a hesitant wag. Since she was normally discouraged from entering the castle, Saush almost appeared guilty, with her large brown eyes wide and mournful. Raven smiled, patting the floor in assent.

With a satisfied grunt, Saush plopped down next to her mistress; the dog's glossy black and tan sides rose and fell rhythmically, and before long, she was snoring soundly.

Raven laughed quietly. She lay on the bed for a while, daydreaming about knights and dragons – nothing more than idle procrastination, really. The history lessons her tutor had assigned her were staring Raven in the face, and she could only ignore them for so long.

Reluctantly, Raven picked up the first scroll, but soon her eyes wandered to the forest beyond the walls, basking in the golden light of the sun's westering rays. A swallow chirped as it lighted upon the stone windowsill, stretching its head through the open stain-glass window and pecking at Raven's ink bottle. *Who cares about boring old lineages of people who died long ago anyway?* Casting the parchment aside, Raven leapt off the bed, bare feet padding against the cool flagstones.

The swallow took flight as Raven neared the window; she followed it onto her balcony, which faced west and overlooked the breathtaking countryside of Laynia. Far off, a farmer in his wagon urged his team down the dirt road, sending up a cloud of dust in a futile attempt to beat the cloak of oncoming darkness.

Raven closed her eyes and envisioned him arriving home to a warm fire, being welcomed by his wife and children, then eating a simple home-cooked meal.

"I envy your children," she murmured. "They have what I cannot, even with all the riches I could ever want ... *freedom*. Freedom to dress practically, to talk to anyone – not only the pompous nobility – to run away when guests come. And to choose who they are going to be!"

If she could choose, what would she be? Outside the walls of the castle, infinite possibilities awaited. The famous words 'if only' had never been more on the forefront of her mind. *If only* she weren't a princess. *If only* she had the freedom to choose. *If only* ...

An intruding banging sent the princess flying across the room. She landed with a thump on her sofa, history scroll in hand and a false look of innocence plastered across her face. "Come in," Raven called demurely, adopting her best princessey expression.

Her chambermaid had already entered – without permission, and without apology. In that way, Synthia was totally predictable; she never bothered groveling to anyone, and rarely employed the manners befitting a servant, especially one in her prestigious position. Chambermaid to the princess was a highly coveted job, one that Raven thought would merit more respect. If her father knew how impudent Synthia could be, she would be working in the scullery.

But in memory of her mother, Raven could never bring herself to dismiss the maid.

"Ev'nin' miss," Synthia muttered. "I've brought hot water for your bath." She lugged a large jug over to a copper tub in the corner, pouring in the steaming water.

"You may proceed," Raven said sarcastically.

Synthia ignored her remark and began adding oils to the

water. A few other water-bearing servants deposited their loads, bowing profusely and muttering apologies for the intrusion before beating a hasty retreat.

Brushing a stray lock of dirty blond hair behind her ear, Synthia stood and stretched her back. "Will there be anything else then, Highness?"

"No, that will be all." Raven nodded her dismissal. But as Synthia turned to leave, Saush sat up and started wagging her tail, tongue lolling out in a doggish grin.

"Oohh-oooh!" Synthia gasped, her voice becoming progressively louder as she flapped her plump arms and hands. "What is *the dog* doing up here?" she demanded.

"*Saush* is here with my permission." Raven narrowed her eyes into a pointed scowl, daring the maid to challenge her.

Synthia wrinkled her nose in distaste. "Fine, but don't blame *me* if it soils something. A dog in the princess's room, *phfft*, if *I* were ..." She went on muttering as she yanked the door shut; her footsteps reverberated as she trudged down the hall and descended the staircase.

Raven shook her head, disrobed, and slipped into the bath. Sinking into the bubbles, she couldn't keep her mind from wandering back to her little game of make believe.

If only she weren't a princess ...

THE TOURNAMENT

Raven rose with the sun as it crested between the mountains, far on the east side of Caritas. Her room was still shrouded in shadow; outside, one pale star shown in the heavens. Throwing a shawl over her shoulders, she hurried into the hallway and up a turret's cold stone steps. She reached the doors and shoved them open, throwing her arms out. The wind swirled, cold tendrils pulling at her shawl and sending it dancing around her. Equally chilled and invigorated, she pulled her wrap tighter and absorbed the morning's hushed tranquility.

Thud. Shouts. The clattering of wheels on cobblestone.

So much for tranquil.

Raven peered into the castle courtyard below, leaning dangerously far over the parapet railing without a second thought, except perhaps that her aerial vantage might allow her to be seen by the milling castle staff. They stood, parchment and quills ready, as a covered supply wagon creaked to a halt in front of them. Five ladies of various ages filed out, some gaunt, others pudgy, but all dressed in rags more befitting of street urchins than servants to the crown. One of the youngest, who couldn't have been older than Raven, tripped on her skirt's ratted hem and stumbled out of the wagon.

More maids. Typical. Raven rolled her eyes, pushing away from the railing and making her way back down the turret. *Why do we even need more maids? We have plenty and then some ... but that's not my decision.* Raven shrugged away her criticisms; having a say in her father's decisions meant showing interest in *all* his decisions, a feat Raven had no desire to undertake. Even as King Wilgaun's sole heir, her duty would only require selecting her husband, who would assume the throne when her father was no longer able to fulfill its demands. She would be nothing more than a glorified hostess, welcoming guests and making small talk with politicians and noblemen. *Because you're doing* so *spectacular with that!*

Raven huffed, a dozen other excuses popping to the surface in her defense. She wasn't even seventeen. How could her father expect her to entertain *his* guests, when he didn't give Raven the time of day? Well, one thing was for sure - when she was queen, she would host far less insufferable dinner parties!

Dashing through the hallway before the servants began lighting the castle, Raven ducked into her room and quickly shut the door. That was her little game, dodging through the castle and avoiding being seen; a rather silly diversion, and one she was embarrassed to say even gave her a bit of a thrill. It was certainly the only source of excitement she could find in her monotonous life ... aside from galloping Freedom as fast as he'd go. Secretly hoping that one day, he might take flight and carry her away, far beyond her safe, predictable prison of royal life.

Raven flung open her wardrobe, flipped through the numerous dresses hanging in it, fingers lingering on a soft lavender gown. She quickly brushed past it. The informal gown was only suitable for everyday purposes; the sleeves were long and straight, and the bodice and skirt weren't form fitting or flouncy. It would be considered inappropriate for her role as both royalty and hostess – yet another point in which she failed to measure up to her father's expectation. And the entire court's, for that matter. Reluctantly, she donned a scarlet silk gown with gold embroidery and a matching thick belt; paired with her corset, the waist was constrictive, and the seams were acutely uncomfortable. But apparently fashion wasn't supposed to be comfortable.

Grabbing a comb, Raven assessed the state of her hair. As usual, it fell in lush, wavy black ringlets ... which were hopelessly unruly and impossible to tame without considerable pain. All the more reason for her to hurry and give it a perfunctory comb. If she didn't escape before Synthia arrived, she'd find her hair pinched into a tight bun that made her look like a drowned cat.

Satisfied that her hair met the most minimum requirements of decorum, Raven threw down the comb and rushed towards her only escape from Synthia's deplorable haute couture: the stables.

ഔ

"Hey boy!" Raven whispered as she approached Freedom's stall. He leaned over the half door and nuzzled her pocket, snuffling for a treat. She giggled, pulling her smuggled good out of her sleeve – the only possible hiding spot in such a conspicuous dress – and held out the carrot. "You know by now that I always have something tasty in my pocket, huh?" Freedom nickered eagerly as he lipped the carrot bit, devouring it with satisfying crunches.

Heedless of the scarlet silk, Raven plopped down on an old barrel to soak in the peace and tranquility of the stables. Here, tasks were done quietly and adequately; more importantly, no one would bother her. Smells of leather and horse wafted – better than any perfume or oil. Horses nickered and swished their tails as hay was brought in by the many stable hands, and the occasional clanking of bridles indicated trainers tacking up for the mounts' morning exercises.

"I suppose I had better get to breakfast before I'm late – *again*." Raven stood, already envisioning hours of mindless chatter, perfect posture, and impeccable manners … another opportunity for her to prove her inadequacy as Princess of Laynia.

Giving Freedom a quick rub on the nose, Raven reluctantly made her way out of the stables, crossed the yard, and entered the castle through the intricate oak doors that were manned constantly by guards. They seemed to be *everywhere*. She had a secret suspicion she was often followed under her father's orders, although she'd never been able to prove it. *So overprotective.* There weren't any threats to her in all of Laynia, let alone in her own castle!

Thoroughly riled, and lacking a target to vent her frustrations on, Raven slipped into the kitchen to casually observe the maids making breakfast and doing other rudimentary tasks. No one had entered the dining hall yet; nobles were predictably lazy, and often slept well past the normal breakfast hour. If it weren't for Synthia's sharp rebukes – followed by a slosh of cold water, when the maid was feeling particularly spiteful – Raven might also be sleeping. But the chambermaid insisted that rising early was most beneficial to mind and body, not to mention productivity. So, every morning, Raven was up at the crack of dawn; it had become an unbreakable habit, and now, she *almost* enjoyed it.

"Morning, Your Highness." Ella – one of the younger maids – gave a halfhearted curtsy, barely glancing up from her task of punching down an enormous ball of rye dough.

"*Good* morning, Ella – what's for breakfast?" Raven asked, stressing the 'good' with more cheek than strictly necessary. She began peeking in the bowls scattered about the kitchen. There was something about its perpetual state of disorder that was appealing.

"We have meat pasties, white rolls, sugar rolls ..." Ella lightly hit Raven's hand away from the bowl of sugar and spices as she continued, "meat omelets with biscuits, and pickled fish. And it's for *breakfast*, not snacking princesses," Ella warned, frowning with disapproval as Raven stole a sugary walnut and plopped it in her mouth.

"Is something burning over there?" Raven asked, pointing at the stove.

"What?" Alarm shot across Ella's face. She rushed over to the pot and yanked it off the fire ... only to discover the stew was barely even warm, and nowhere close to burning. She whirled around just in time to see Raven grab a spoon of sugar roll batter – delectable pastries that would be fried into small, light, sweet rolls, then dipped thoroughly in sugar with nuts kneaded in.

Ella grasped a handful of flour, preparing to hurl it in a halfhearted bluff.

Raven laughed at Ella's series of admonishments – a combination of scolding and threatening. But as soon as Raven slipped into the hallway, she donned a passive façade. Her father could *not* find out she socialized with servants – he wouldn't approve, to put it mildly.

Guests finally began to arrive in the dining hall, all stuffy, powdered, and primped for an equally stuffy breakfast. Raven slumped into her chair and stared moodily at the pompous spectacle.

"So, you're the princess, eh?"

Raven jumped and stared – rather rudely – at the snobbish looking young man sitting to her left. His curly, sandy-blond hair was wetted and brushed back tightly against his head, putting Synthia's drowned-rat bun look to shame. He had a mildly dished nose that flared at the end, and pale blue eyes that screamed self-satisfaction. He was clearly oblivious to his crooked, yellow teeth and fleshy lips, or he wouldn't have been so confident in his vanity. That was the only explanation Raven could come up with; surely no one could look so absolutely stuck up and not realize it?

"I'm *Sir* Fredrick Cambleworth, son of the duke of Roehn." His mouthful of a title was accentuated with a haughty sniff and straightening of his fancy embroidered collar.

I wonder how many times he rehearsed that, Raven mused, a sly smile creeping across her mouth. She made a pointed effort to suppress the urge of saying anything improper. Which was anything that included an insult to his face. Donning her most diplomatic expression, she replied with a grace that would make even her father proud, "I am pleased to meet you, *Sir* Fredrick." Well, except perhaps the sarcastic inflection of his title. But Fredrick obviously didn't notice, and her father wasn't here, so what was the harm?

"Do you enjoy jousting tournaments?"

Raven opened her mouth to reply, but he rambled on without pausing. "I've been in numerous. Of course, competing against those that share my – *ahem* – esteemed position ..."

Sir Fredrick *graced* Raven with his exploits through breakfast, and all she could manage were brief, half-finished comments. She couldn't help using the same adjective as she had originally thought of for the apprentice gate keeper, Tristan – *insufferable*. Except Sir Fredrick absolutely deserved the description. Tristan, on the other hand ... she just wasn't sure yet, but she wasn't ruling out the possibility that she *may* have misjudged him. A little.

When every breakfast course had been served, every possible subject of small talk exhausted, and every guest filled to bursting – literally – Wilgaun stood and lightly tapped a spoon against his glass, silencing the remaining chatter.

"Lords and Ladies, here is the announcement you've been waiting for!" Wilgaun boomed. "As you know, today marks the beginning of Laynia's Annual Summer Tournament. All of my knights and soldiers will have the opportunity to compete for your pleasure ... and a substantial prize. So please, join us under the pavilion as the minstrels provide entertainment."

Raven groaned, shrinking further into her chair. She couldn't help comparing herself to the minstrels – yet another part of an elaborate scheme to entertain her father's guests. It was sure to be a suffocating event. Not to mention unbearably hot. Despite Laynia's reputation for mild summers, the temperature had been rising, and silk gowns were far warmer than the casual dresses she normally wore outside.

Wilgaun proceeded to recite the history of the jousting tournament, which Raven had heard many times, and therefore felt little guilt for zoning out halfway through. Raven inconspicuously edged her way to the opposite door and away from the entourage of guests.

"Raven."

She froze at her father's voice. Only after his gaze began

boring a hole in her back did she reluctantly turn to face him.

"Yes?" Raven asked, feigning a ridiculous guise of innocence. Her father was clearly not convinced, though the only indication was the dramatic raise of one eyebrow.

"I would like you to entertain the visitors again today and give them a tour of the castle after the tournament ... which I know you *were* planning on watching." He somehow managed to raise the eyebrow even higher.

"Actually, I was –"

"They are honored guests, chosen to represent their kingdoms, whom we must respect in order to keep peace and diplomacy in the kingdom," Wilgaun interrupted. Raven could already see his temper rising. "I have invited them here for that reason, and I will *not* have the kingdom's trade and allegiance compromised. Not because some petty whim of the princess prevents her from entertaining ambassadors for a few hours!" Wilgaun finished by slamming his fist against the table.

Raven shrunk back. "Very well, I will see to your *honored guests*." Her words were meant to be biting, but they came out so quietly, she wondered if her father had heard her.

She could barely hear herself.

℘

Raven about-faced, keeping her chin up and head straight forward, just like she had been taught. Just like *he* had taught her. Wilgaun sighed, and suddenly his entire body felt heavy and ... *old*. His own teaching mocked him, reminding him yet again how every spare moment was used to insert a lesson or a reprimand. When was the last times he actually stopped to *listen* to his daughter, rather than scold her? Now, like many other times, he regretted the distance between them as he watched his daughter slip further and further away.

But no, he didn't have time for regret. He was the king.

℘

Raven struggled with a mixture of guilt and anger as she made her way towards the jousting field. She would never

34

admit it, but deep down, she knew the strained relationship with her father was as much her own fault as it was his. Sure, he may have started it, but it had become an unending cycle. He began raising his expectations of her and, in response, she began building walls. Whenever there was an opportunity to spend time with him, she always had some other place she needed to be, some lesson to attend. Any chance for conversation, she was the first to walk away. The first to close the doors on the king and his high expectations – expectations that she, as princess, *should* have been able to fill.

Should, but couldn't.

As a distraction, Raven forced herself to run through the order of her tour – a long, tedious, inescapable chore that was almost as painful to recite as talking to the guests themselves. She had barely gotten through the throne room section of her mental tour when Raven suddenly slammed into hard metal. Stumbling backwards a few paces, she executed a very graceless flop on her bottom. For a moment, she was too stunned to say anything or comprehend exactly how she had gone from standing upright to sitting, toddler style, in the grass.

"*Hey*, watch it – oh, erm, Your Highness." Raven stared as an armored competitor started to bow, reconsidered, and held out a hand to help her up instead.

"Tristan? *You're* competing?" Raven asked. She barely remembered to take his offered hand. It was hardly proper, accepting the hand of someone so far below her station, but it was less humiliating than remaining where she was. And goodness knew she couldn't stand without assistance – not in her voluminous gown and suffocating corset. Besides, the thought of snubbing societal norms was rather appealing. If only there were a few maids around to gossip about how the princess had held a commoner's hand!

"Yeah, why not?" he asked, flashing her a grin – a trademark quality, she was beginning to realize.

"Oh," Raven said lamely. She found herself staring,

momentarily put at a loss by his storm-blue eyes. What a contrast they were to Sir Fredrick's dull, pale ones!

Unacceptable. Princesses do not stare!

Raven shook herself out of her daze and pointedly began smoothing her skirts.

"You had best get back to your throne, Highness. This is the competitors' area, and I somehow doubt you wish to see men in various stages of … decency." Tristan's eyes twinkled.

Raven glanced around, alarmed. For the first time, she noticed the throng of men surrounding her. Some were clothed, others were shirtless, all shamelessly comfortable in their state of dishabille.

All staring at her.

Laughing awkwardly at Tristan, she shook her head. It took a concentrated effort to keep her eyes from lingering on one brute's bare chest. He was matted with thick hair from neck to navel, like the pelt of a great black bear. She'd never seen a man's chest before, but she'd never imagined it looking like *that*.

"No, I suppose not," Raven agreed. "Besides, I have guests to entertain. I'm sorry for running into you."

"Anytime. And the fault was all mine," Tristan added, though Raven knew he had only said that out of courtesy. He hadn't even been moving when she hit him.

Or maybe he said it because I'm royalty, and he has no other choice than to take the blame. Raven jerked her head in a quick nod, already starting to back away. "Right, well, good luck out there … you'll need it."

Tristan chuckled. "Thank you, Princess – I think!"

But maybe … maybe he said it because, despite our different stations, he actually – and sincerely – wants to be friends. The idea was preposterous – sincerity was not a common trait, especially when dealing with royalty. But there was something so forthright in Tristan's manner, with no attempt at guile, that Raven could think of no other explanation. Was she simply naïve, or was Tristan truly different than the other grasping men and nobility she'd met? And if so, why?

"Ah, there you are, princess!"

Raven almost jumped out of her skirts at Sir Fredrick's abrupt greeting, and she realized dismally she had arrived at the nobles' private tent. The guests surrounding Wilgaun were seated on a raised platform adjacent to the jousting field. The pavilion was situated at the center point of the roped off course so the nobles could see the clash from a short – but safe – distance.

The area was filled with peasants milling about the perimeter, although none were allowed within arms-reach of the king and his guests. *Because royalty interacting with peasants is so* disgraceful! Raven snorted to herself. She was beyond fed up with courtiers and their snobbery ... and she had arrived only seconds ago! Raven stiffly took her seat, which was inconveniently placed between her father and Sir Fredrick – one companion who wouldn't talk, and the other who wouldn't shut up. *Brilliant.*

Sir Fredrick barely waited for Raven to sit down, let alone gave her an opportunity to speak, before launching on his latest tirade. "A most excellent tournament I'm sure – a grand opportunity for me to learn about Laynia, exactly as my father wished. That is, of course, why my father sent me on this diplomacy escapade." And then – as Raven feared – he went on to explain the precise reasons of his coming, his father's wishes, and other equally monotonous subjects for the entire duration of the game.

Raven tried not to look as bored as she felt, but her hope for success was very slim. And it was miserably hot, which only added to her dour outlook on what was sure to be another mind-numbing day of endless politics and staged tournaments.

As a distraction from her own discomfort, she commiserated with the competitors who wore linen under-shirts and pants, woolen stockings, and heavy armor. Doublets were also a part of their expansive suit; a quilted coat stuffed with either linen or grass, depending upon the man's position and wealth.

Plus, they had to wear rags tied around their head under the helmets since they couldn't wipe away perspiration with their metal gauntlets. From what Raven understood, these *sweat rags* were nothing but glorified handkerchiefs; apparently calling them *handkerchiefs* was far too embarrassing for 'men of stature and might.'

A flash of silver caught Raven's attention. Another competitor had entered the course, bedecked in a blue and silver surcoat with an ecru emblem of a claw – the armor she had inconspicuously been watching for. Before the knight donned his helmet, Raven caught a glimpse of his face, framed with medium-length brown hair. *Tristan.*

His destrier – a stunning blue roan, uncommon in those parts – pranced nervously as the crowd's cheers began to escalate; they applauded each time another competitor entered, whether they knew him or not, and it was grating on Raven's nerves. But this time, despite her prior criticism, Raven found herself cheering along with them.

A quick sideways glance revealed that Sir Fredrick hadn't even noticed she'd been ignoring him; he was still prattling on without a glance in her direction. *I wonder what his* parents *are like!* Raven shuddered at the thought.

"Take your positions!" called the announcer.

The destriers mirrored their riders' tension, haunches tightening like a bowstring waiting to be released. The riders gripped the sides of their mounts with their knees, lances at the ready.

A horn sounded at the same time as the announcer's cry; "GO!"

The competitors spurred their steeds and charged, lances reaching greedily towards the oncoming opponent. Foam and spittle flew from the horses' mouths. Dust flew behind their pounding hooves. The riders clenched their shields ... and collided with a sickening scraping of metal.

Tristan's lance sent the other rider flying out of the saddle and onto the springy turf.

The crowd gave a standing ovation as Tristan raised his visor and lifted his shield in a show of victory. Raven found herself clapping enthusiastically ... until she realized that Sir Fredrick had finally discovered she wasn't listening.

"My cousin?" he reminded with a disapproving stare. And without a second thought, he continued chattering on for the rest of the tournament.

ɢ

"If you find it agreeable, I would be pleased to give you a tour of our castle." The words tumbled out of Raven's mouth before she lost her nerve and ran to hide in some remote corner. An appealing thought, though hardly practical with her father sitting right next to her, eyeing her for any evasive maneuvers. She hadn't employed any ... recently.

At the guests' collective nod, Raven led them through the expansive castle, adding tidbits about the different rooms and décor. To her dismay, she realized she was beginning to sound almost as boring as Sir Fredrick!

When the tour was finally done and they joined the king in the hall, minstrels took the burden of entertaining the king's guests, and Raven took the opportunity to scurry away towards her room. There, she could at last enjoy some peace and quiet!

I wonder if Synthia has – Raven hadn't finished her thought before something collided with her. She clawed at the air as she fell hard to the ground, accompanied by stacks of white bed linens and cloths. Her second time falling in a matter of hours – and this time, it was on hard flagstone, not dirt!

"Oh – Your Highness! I'm so sorry!" a maid gasped, scrambling to her feet. She began tossing sheets off Raven and quickly helped her up, fretting all the while. "Are you alright, Princess?" Her face was beet red, although that did nothing to hide the freckles dotting her nose and cheeks.

"Uh, yes ... I'm fine."

The maid sighed and bent down to retrieve the scattered linens. "I'm *so* sorry! I was busy working and not watching where I was going, and –"

"It's fine. Really. You'd be surprised at how many people I've run into today." Raven hid a smile. "What's your name?"

"I'm Breeanah, but you needn't call me that – I mean, you don't have to do anything – I mean, for me ..." she stuttered, then fell into an awkward silence.

"Well, Breeanah, I'm pleased to meet you." Raven curtsied, and Breeanah followed suit, smiling shyly.

"And you, M'lady."

Lost in thought – though considerably more aware of any potential persons she might run into – Raven snickered at the fit her father would have if he knew she'd been knocked off her feet not once, but twice today. And by her inferiors, no less! *He'd probably cancel my seventeenth birthday party next week and hire a new tutor to train me how to be aware of my surroundings.*

She groaned at the reminder of the upcoming fanfare. Everyone tittering on about how the grand event was *planned in her honor*. The spectacle was branded in her mind:

Old men and their stories.

Young men and their bragging.

Old women whispering secret judgements.

Young women flitting about, attempting to dance with every suitable beau from sixteen to sixty – as long as they had money.

And Raven, there in the middle of it all. A proverbial Maypole, festooned with colorful garlands, slowly wound to the point of suffocation.

All the talk throughout the castle made it nearly impossible for Raven to push the event from her mind, even for a second. If she thought there was the slightest chance of escaping the ball, she'd take it.

Angry king or no.

WHEN OPPORTUNITY KNOCKS

A rapid succession of banging on the door disturbed Raven from her book. Trying to hide the irritation from her voice, and not caring much if she failed, she called, "Yes?"

"Raven, I need to talk to you." Wilgaun's request – which sounded more like an order – left no room for argument.

Suppressing a sigh, Raven shut her book and reluctantly opened the door. She was in no mood to tolerate a lecture, especially since she'd been uncharacteristically well-mannered for the past few days – even enduring a few endless monologues from Sir Fredrick – and therefore couldn't imagine what her father could find to scold her about.

Wilgaun quickly entered the room, brushing past Raven and sitting on the settee. A few seconds later, he stood and began pacing. If Raven didn't know better, she'd almost say he was … *nervous.* The thought made her uncomfortable, but she sat down on her settee and waited, poised and patient – exactly how he taught her.

Finally, he began, "I have decided that it would be a good thing for you to become better acquainted with the other kingdoms in Alarkin."

Raven stared at him blankly, trying to mask her disappointment. She wasn't sure what she had expected – and this was better than another lecture – but it certainly wasn't anything great. *Another boring tutor to teach me another boring subject that I've already learned a million times.* But she didn't say any of that. Instead, she nodded mutely.

Wilgaun finally ceased his pacing and precariously perched on the edge of the settee, as far from her as possible. He may not have noticed, but Raven did … and another part of her heart closed off from him.

"It has been brought to my attention that many noblemen's children, such as Sir Fredrick, have been sent on ambassadorial trips to neighboring kingdoms, learning more about culture through diplomatic visits. I would like you to go on a trip of your own." He spoke quickly, as if he expected to be interrupted at any time, but Raven offered no reaction. "You will travel by carriage, accompanied by Ambassador Kirgan. You may take a personal maid and a companion. I will arrange all of the, erm, *security*."

"You mean ... I'm leaving the kingdom? I get to travel?" Raven asked, barely breathing.

"With a contingent of armed guards, of course," Wilgaun reassured her hastily.

Needlessly. Safety was the least of her concerns.

A grin crept over Raven's face. "When do I leave?"

"A fortnight after your party. Be sure your chambermaid has packed all that you need by then," the king added, exhaling with audible relief.

Had he really thought Raven would be so difficult to convince? *Yet another example that demonstrates how little the king knows his daughter.* She forced a stiff smile. "I'll tell Synthia to prepare my things. And as for my companion ... do I *need* a companion?"

Any relief at Raven's compliance immediately vanished. "Yes!" Wilgaun nearly snapped. He took a deep breath and continued in a calmer tone. "I do not trust some maid to be your only female escort. You will find a suitable companion – *of my approval*," he added emphatically, "at the party. I will see to the formalities."

Raven crossed her arms. "I don't need a companion."

Wilgaun groaned, running a hand over his face. "Raven, you have much to learn. Just – see to it you're ready." Wilgaun stood and strode out the door, not glancing back once as it slammed behind him.

Pushing away her annoyance at her father getting in the last word, Raven rushed over to Smokey, interrupting the feline's bath and swinging her in a circle. "*Finally*! I get to *go* somewhere – *do* something! A sense of freedom!" Raven exclaimed, squeezing her cat tighter.

Unamused, Smokey struggled until Raven put her down. She began cleaning herself, oblivious that her mistress's world had been irreversibly changed for the better.

ॐ

Wilgaun couldn't take his mind off Raven, despite her easy acceptance of the proposal. Had he been too stern? Was he doing the right thing, sending her away? Would Raven's companion fulfill her duties adequately? Raven was headstrong, and impossible to predict – the complete opposite of her mother. With a grunt, he realized that – in temperament, though certainly not in looks – Raven bore a closer resemblance to him. That being the case, was it wise to allow her so much free rein?

Nonsense. He was the king, and his decisions were rarely mistaken.

Once, though, he had been unforgivably wrong...

ॐ

Raven was curled up on her bed, pretending to read but actually imagining a rather dramatic version of her trip, when a knock came from the door.

You've got to be joking. Again? This time, she made no effort to hide her irritation at being disturbed. "What?"

Breeanah, the maid Raven had literally run into earlier, was waiting patiently in the doorway. "I've come to change your bed sheets, M'lady, if it's convenient," Breeanah explained.

No barging in? Asking for permission? That's new. Raven waved her permission. "Sure. Where's Synthia?"

"She wasn't feeling well, so I'll be serving you until she is – if that's alright with you," Breeanah added hastily. She busied herself with the bedsheets, avoiding eye-contact.

"Fine with me," Raven said with a smile. She scooted off the bed and plunked Smokey on the floor. The cat protested with an

43

annoyed meow.

Breeanah smiled back, quickly changing the sheets. "Will you be needing anything else?"

"No that's –" Raven stopped mid-sentence. *Why not? It might be a nice change from Synthia bossing me around.* "Actually, I have a favor to ask you. More of a request. In a couple of weeks, I'll be going on an ambassadorial trip – uh, keeping the peace –" she clarified at Breeanah's confused expression, "and I need a chambermaid. I was wondering if you would like to accompany me?"

"Oh, yes! I'd like nothing better!" Breeanah exclaimed, nearly dropping the old sheets. "Uh – Your Highness," she added, fiddling with the used bedsheets. "I hope you won't think me impertinent for asking, but … why do you *request* me to do things? You could simply *order* me. You being the princess and all."

"Would you prefer that?"

"No – but I'm only a servant. What I prefer doesn't matter."

Raven thought she saw Breeanah's head lower a fraction; it made her uncomfortable, so she forced a laugh. "I'm no tyrant."

Breeanah followed suit and laughed as well, a bit more hesitantly. "'Course not, Princess. When the time comes, I'll see to packing your things. And Princess?"

"Yes?"

"I think you'll make a great ruler," Breeanah said shyly. "Goodnight." She bobbed a curtsey, then quietly exited and shut the door.

Raven sat dumbfounded. *What I prefer doesn't matter,* Breeanah had said. What kind of masters did she serve before coming to Caritas? The rift between social classes was absurd, with nobility throwing their weight around and serfs cowering under their dominance. Why couldn't people just get over their differences and treat each other as equals?

"Because of me," Raven whispered. "Because of useless royals like me, who rely on servants to do everything."

It was her fault.

Another thing to add to the growing list.

Pomp and Circumstance

The castle bustled with activity as maids readied for the party; their hurried footsteps sounded from the hall, rushing back and forth in a cacophonic pattern. Raven, however, couldn't see any of their bustle. Instead, she sat with excruciating stillness, locked away inside her chambers, while Breeanah styled her hair.

Sneaking a glance downward, Raven appraised her first birthday present of the night: a regal dress of deep purple. The gown tapered at the waist, where it was tied with a gold braided belt, then flared with an impressive amount of fabric down to her ankles. The neck was adorned with dozens of tiny amethysts, which ran up the thin sleeve on her right shoulder; her other shoulder was bare. A long, gauzy train added an air of elegance, as did the gold glitter that had been sprinkled on Raven's skin.

Breeanah finished Raven's hair, securing it onto her head in a loose bun with many tiny curls hanging down around her face. As a final touch, she added the princess's crown – a delicate tiara made of interwoven vines and flowers of purest gold. One of the few Raven owned that didn't give her a headache or look like a giant hunk of metal perched on her head.

"You're all ready," Breeanah said cheerfully.

Raven smiled her thanks, impressed with the young maid's work. Unlike Synthia's torturous process and horrifying end result, Raven actually found that Breeanah was fairly gentle, and *much* better at styling. *Too frivolous,* Synthia would say.

But tonight was the night for frivolous.

At her father's knock, Raven glided out of her room and took her place at his side, hand tentatively resting in the crook of his arm as they made their way towards the ballroom. Behind them, the clink of guard's boots was yet another reminder of the few moments of peace and quiet Raven enjoyed with her father.

She cleared her throat, breaking the silence. "The dressmakers really outdid themselves this year. The imported silk taffeta fabric makes all my other dresses look plain."

Wilgaun glanced over, pausing longer on her face than her dress. "You look very beautiful."

Raven was the first to look away. "Thank you." They resumed the awkward silence until they reached the balcony overlooking the ballroom.

"Ladies and gentlemen, presenting Princess Raven Rivanstar, firstborn and heir to the throne of Laynia, on the event of her seventeenth birthday!" the announcer called out. The guests clapped with polite enthusiasm, if such a thing was possible.

"Keep an eye out for a companion," Wilgaun reminded – not for the first time.

All flattery at his compliment was gone. "I know!" Raven returned testily. "Must you repeat it at every turn?" Descending with grace that belied her tone, she sashayed from the balcony, curtsied, and continued to the polished mahogany floor of the ballroom. Raven felt her face growing warm; the air was overused with so many people, and the political agendas of those attending was even more stifling. As she greeted distinguished guests and self-proclaimed friends, Raven fought the urge to make a desperate escape.

The announcer – under orders from Wilgaun – rapped his staff, drawing the crowd's attention. "We will now have a dance in honor of the princess, in which she will lead us with a partner of her choice."

Raven glared up at her father. *Choose one of these strangers to dance with and be up close – and … step on my feet?! I think not!* With a decisive huff, she whirled around to face the crowd, poised in exact imitation of the numerous tutors who'd taught her to walk like she had a rod stuck inside her back. "I have decided, as it is my birthday, to have a country dance!"

Confused mutters drifted through the crowd, but none dared contradict her. She was, after all, the princess.

Cuing the minstrels, Raven took hold of a random man and woman. They each, in turn, grabbed a partner, who then grabbed more partners, and soon there was an all-inclusive dance, making a large square around the room. Wilgaun was shaking his head in bewilderment, probably wondering how his daughter had managed to turn a gaggle of stuffy courtiers into a twirling mass of clapping, stomping, rowdy dancers – some more begrudging than others.

Raven couldn't hide an impish smile.

After the dance finished, everyone gathered around the table to eat the first course. Raven sat at one head of the table, waiting for everyone to be seated. Wilgaun would sit at the opposite end; hardly conducive to conversation between father and daughter, but it was tradition. Besides, what would they say to each other? Comment on the various dishes or note which dignitaries had chosen to attend?

Raven could smell the tantalizing dishes wafting around the room … roast birds stuffed with berries, savory pot roast, fluffy rolls, and many other delicacies were laid out on the table, and all the goldware sparkled next to porcelain plates. A large stone table in the corner was piled high with presents in elegant wrappings, and the entire castle was lit by hundreds of candles.

"Countess Burina, allow me to introduce my daughter, Princess Raven."

Raven jumped at the sound of Wilgaun's voice behind her. As she stood and turned to greet his latest guest, she found herself staring into mesmerizing green eyes that left her at a momentary loss. The young woman – who Raven now realized was the Countess Burina - stood out from the other guests, with pale, creamy skin and cascading golden curls framing her face. High cheekbones, thin but shapely lips, and a delicate nose all complimented her stunning eyes. Beautiful, certainly, but to Raven, it was like looking at a mask … a refined, polished elegance which hid her true nature, whatever it might be. For some reason, Raven was oddly intimidated. Not a normal feeling.

"I am pleased to meet you, Your Highness," the countess purred, curtsying deeply.

Raven snapped herself out of her daze. "Pleased to meet you as well, Countess," she replied. She mirrored the curtsy.

The countess laughed; a charming, airy sound. "Oh please, Your Highness, call me Farah." She touched Raven's arm convivially, and Raven almost recoiled.

Instead, she feigned a smile and replied, "Then you must call me Raven."

Wilgaun nodded with approval, clearly oblivious to Raven's discomfort. Leaning close, he whispered, "The countess would make a fine companion – she is the right age and comes from a respectable and sophisticated family."

"Well, *Raven*, I so look forward to getting to know you ... I hope we shall have the chance," Farah said. If it weren't for her guileless smile, Raven almost would have thought the countess knew more about Raven's trip than she was letting on.

"Likewise. And on that subject ..."

For the remainder of the meal, Raven talked with the countess about becoming her companion; with little persuasion, Farah readily agreed. In fact, she was so eager, Raven thought it a little odd. But the conversation ended, and Raven shifted her focus from the countess's puzzling enthusiasm to simply surviving the night.

When it came time to open her gifts, Raven marveled at all the foreign inventions and trinkets she received. There were items ranging from glass kittens to gold-woven scarves ... exotic trinkets from across Alarkin, and perhaps beyond. They were perfectly useless, but diplomacy prevented Raven from saying so. And after all, was it not a sign of wealth for a princess to own an assortment of beautiful – albeit impractical – fineries?

Just when Raven thought the last of the endless line of

courtiers had ended, and all the gifts taken away by attendants, another man stepped up to present her with his gift. He was graying, almost sage-like; among the colorful gowns and silken shirts, he looked utterly out of place in his plain frock. Raven tilted her head, trying to place the odd man. He clearly wasn't a courtier, and Raven didn't recognize him from any diplomatic embassies. But there was definitely something familiar about him ...

Gently taking her hand, the old man placed a small, crudely wrapped bundle in her open palm. Raven couldn't help noticing the tremor in his worn, wrinkled fingers. "You must keep this with you at all times," he said softly. "It will save someone's life ... though you may never discover how."

And then he vanished into the crowd, leaving Raven at a loss. When she tried, she couldn't even recall his face; the only thing that testified to his existence was the small parcel resting lightly in Raven's hands. She tucked it into a hidden pocket to open later. *Very strange.*

When the guests had finished eating, they milled back into the ballroom, awaiting the next dance. A few minutes later, a waltz began. Raven groaned. This was a scheme of her father to get her to slow dance with some handsome, dull-witted noble's son! Fuming, she grabbed the closest one – an unfortunate young duke whose shy nature was only made worse by Raven's refusal to acknowledge his existence. The moment after the dance ended, he made a hasty retreat.

Good. It was unwise to flirt with an angry princess.

∽

As soon as she had waved farewell to the last guest, Raven dashed upstairs and flung herself on her chaise lounge. She'd dismissed her servants, so she had the rest of the night alone – thank heavens. She'd had more 'unalone' time than she cared to have in a lifetime!

Her hand slipped to her pocket, fingertips touching an unfamiliar lump. *The gift.* She yanked the parcel out, pulled at the string, and watched the cloth fall away, revealing a small red hinged box. Slowly, almost reverently, Raven opened it.

Inside was a small glass bird. It had black eyes and its whole body was crusted in pale green gem fragments, no bigger than grains of sand. The wings and tail were white, and larger white gems adorned the back and traced the wings.

Raven stared, livid. "How in *Alarkin* is this supposed to save someone's life? It's just another pretty trinket to sit on my desk!" Jumping to her feet, she slammed the bird down, slipped into her nightgown, and flopped into bed.

After a few minutes of tossing and turning, Raven reluctantly peeked over her covers at the little bird. She was almost surprised it hadn't turned its head to stare at her. Even if the man's words were folly, how could she risk leaving the trinket and being wrong? And at the expense of someone's life! She groaned, slipped out of bed, and stashed the bird with a handful of other baubles she'd set out to bring on her trip.

It never hurt to be over-cautious.

THE JOURNEY BEGINS

Raven couldn't believe it. Today was finally the day – the day she would leave all that she knew and journey into the unknown beyond the borders of Laynia. No more safe, stifling castle walls, no more stuffy tutors and endless lessons – at least for the foreseeable future. A taste of freedom, however dampened by the presence of the contingent of guards. Not to mention the watchful eye of Countess Burina.

Ever since agreeing to accompany the entourage, Farah's presence within the castle walls had constantly haunted Raven's every step. The countess hadn't even bothered returning to her home after the ball; instead, she had sent for her luggage to be brought directly. Farah had spent every spare minute talking with either Raven or her father, the topic ranging from politics to courtiers to parties. All equally boring and monotonous subjects, but somehow, the countess made them seem more interesting than they really were.

Farah's throaty laughter and easy countenance drew the attention of everyone in the room; her unchallenged influence made Raven squirm, but what could she do? She'd already agreed to let Farah join her, and Wilgaun would *not* let Raven go back on her word. And there was absolutely no reason for Raven to dislike Farah – the countess was interesting, conversational, and slightly less intolerable than the average noble.

So why did Raven feel she was being suffocated?

Caught in the *almost ready to go but not quite* stage of preparations, Raven observed the dreary activity of guards and maids bustling with last minute details for the trip. Occasionally, one would glance up at the dreary sky, as if to determine whether it would rain or not, then scramble back to their tasks. Wilgaun had bid Raven farewell with an awkward kiss on the cheek before he left to attend to other duties. Farah hadn't made an appearance yet, leaving Raven alone except for Saush, who sat diligently – albeit mournfully – by her mistress's side.

Raven stroked Saush's head, whispering the occasional encouragement into her drooping ears. Although she'd miss her faithful companion, Raven had the consolation of bringing Freedom. She had insisted on her stallion's presence – *in case.* In case she was able to ride – which was very unlikely, but a good excuse to bring at least one of her animals.

The countess suddenly materialized behind Raven, making her jump. "Is that your dog?" Farah asked, gesturing to Saush. Raven answered with the barest nod. "She's charming, though I prefer cats myself." Farah's smile was borderline patronizing.

"Dogs are more loyal and understanding. Cats are fickle," Raven said sharply. Her words were far too defensive; why did such a simple comment put her on edge? Letting out a slow breath, Raven added in a calmer tone, "But I like cats as well."

The smile never dropped from Farah's lips, but something in her gaze told Raven that her defensive tone had not gone unnoticed. With a gracious nod, Farah conceded, "To each their own."

Clearing his throat, the head of Raven's security approached and gave a quick bow. "We are ready to depart, Your Majesty." With short cropped brown hair, interspersed with gray, and restless eyes, Sir Kisby was one of the most respected knights in the King's army. Not only had he earned his rank as third in command, he had earned the men's loyalty – a far more valuable feat. Raven rarely interacted with him, but from what she could tell, he was a straightforward, diligent commander, just as his station demanded.

Now, however, he appeared slightly annoyed, though he masked it well. He nodded towards the latest addition to their entourage – a gaudy, bejeweled coach with a pair of matching white horses and servants outfitted in red livery. "Ambassador Kirgan has brought his own carriage, though I informed him –"

"I insist, I absolutely insist," Ambassador Kirgan interrupted, taking each of the ladies' gloved hands and kissing them in turn.

"Welcome, Ambassador," Raven said with a curtsy. Kirgan – well known for his popularity among the ladies, despite being closer to forty than twenty – was Laynia's chief diplomat. Raven had always made a point to avoid him; his suave, borderline flirtatious personality irritated her.

"Ambassador Kirgan, I am *so* pleased to see you again!" Farah gushed, also welcoming him with a deep curtsy.

"You've already met?" Raven asked disinterestedly.

"Yes, although it has been far too long." Kirgan exchanged a knowing look with the countess. He clapped abruptly, startling Raven to attention. "I have done everything in my power to make this a comfortable trip. If there is anything either of you lovely ladies need – from a golden broach to a cup of tea – *please* let me know," he enticed with a broad grin.

Raven rolled her eyes discreetly. "Thank you, Ambassador, we will."

"On your lead, my ladies." Kirgan gestured grandly towards Raven's carriage, beating the footman to the door.

Raven nodded, stepped inside. This was it. She was finally leaving. Her first step in a journey across Alarkin. And who knew what adventure it might hold?

଺

As the carriage wheels started turning on the cobbled streets of Caritas, Raven's gaze drifted out the window. Once they left the castle grounds, they passed house after house, each fairly similar to the other but always with a touch of the owner's personality: a pot of pink flowers, a few items flapping on the clothesline; bright checkered curtains hanging in the window. Raven had just taken note of a particularly bright yellow shop when a guard in her peripheral caught her attention. Her eyes drifted to his steed – a blue roan – and it clicked.

54

Tristan was accompanying her as a ... guard?

He flashed her a grin before resuming the vigilant watch of a soldier; back straight, eyes ever scouring the road ahead and surroundings for potential threats.

"Quite charming, is he not?"

Raven's neck literally cracked, her head whipped around so fast. She gaped at the countess. "*What*?"

Unfazed, Farah nodded toward Kirgan. "The ambassador."

"Oh." Raven nodded with a little too much enthusiasm. "Yes, he's always been very ... beguiling," she finally managed. *Beguiling? Really?* She cringed. The countess was starting to rub off on her.

"Has your father arranged a marriage for you, or have you already found someone?"

Raven blushed, caught off guard by the question. She hadn't been expecting the countess to broach the topic so soon after leaving. Couldn't Raven get a moment's peace without hearing blather about marriage and suitors?

Her attention suddenly riveted on the seam work of her skirt, Raven mumbled, "Neither – I'm not ready to be married." Why did the countess insist on talking about suitors? No one else did, and her father *certainly* never mentioned such things. The entire idea made her uncomfortable.

And it was even worse after thinking about Tristan as *charming*!

Farah patted Raven's hand, smirking. "You may want to change your outlook – I'm sure your father will have you arranged as soon as you return. That is why he sent you, naturally."

Her words implied that such a fact was obvious; it sent a rush of panic through Raven.

"What do you mean?" Raven asked slowly. Her throat had suddenly filled with cotton.

"Oh, you have not guessed?" Farah tutted. "You poor naïve thing – the king sent you on this mission for one reason and one reason alone. To meet *all* the eligible suitors!"

Raven stared, aghast. "Y-you mean ..."

"Dearest, don't be so alarmed. It really isn't all that bad. I was arranged with a marriage, too – I marry in the spring. And Duke Wilbore is really a darling. Why, he would get me practically *anything* if I asked him. Although," she added as an afterthought, "he can sometimes be a bit ... monotonous."

A fancy word for boring. I wonder if that's where his name came from. Raven involuntarily shuddered at the possibility of such a fate.

"He is away presently, so I am getting my 'last breath of freedom' before I marry." Farah flashed a smile at Raven, then faltered, laying a hand on Raven's forehead. "Goodness, you look pale. Are you feeling well?"

Raven didn't doubt that she looked paler than usual, but she brushed away the countess's concern – and her hand. "I'm fine. A little anxious about leaving the castle, that's all." A twinge of guilt nagged at her; she wasn't in the habit of telling white lies. "Anyway, I hope my father puts my ... *marriage* ... off for a few years; I'm only seventeen, after all." Her last few words raised in pitch – a desperate plea for the countess to play along with her fantasy.

It was too much to ask.

Farah's next words left no room for doubt. "Don't get your hopes up to simply have them crushed."

Raven swallowed back a wave of sickness as she played the countess's words over and over again in her mind. *You have not guessed? You poor naïve thing! All the eligible suitors ... last breath of freedom ...*

Shutting her eyes against the barrage of thoughts, Raven deliberately focused on every minute detail of the scenery outside the confines of the carriage.

The caravan was traversing a well-maintained road through the Laynian countryside. Vibrant green leaves contrasted the gray sky that stretched forebodingly over the land; a breeze rustled the trees' foliage and rippled the surface of cattail-ringed ponds. In anticipation of the oncoming storm, most of the birds had retreated to their nests, not daring to sing.

Sure enough, within the hour, rain began pattering on the carriage roof. Farah occasionally attempted small talk, but Raven was content to let conversation die. Watching the rain drizzling was more interesting – and safer – than anything the countess wanted to talk about. Besides, the weather didn't constantly remind Raven of the arranged marriage awaiting her at the end of the trip.

The travelling party ate a lunch that consisted of meat sandwiches with cold cider, sliced cheese, and smoked fish. The servants ate in their carriage, or anywhere dry, while Kirgan, Sir Kisby, Raven, and Farah sheltered under a small tent. The guards – including Tristan – stood outside forming a perimeter, forced to eat in the rain.

Raven remained silent as Kirgan and Farah prattled on about the latest styles and fashions of Sirap, home to many of the most stylish designers in the kingdom of Laynia. Kisby, at least, had the good sense to keep his mouth shut. A half-hour later they were on their way again, pushing to arrive at the Aspen Inn by nightfall and, hopefully, outdistance the worst of the storm. However, with the progress slowed by multiple wagons and the pace kept moderate to avoid excessive bumps, Raven found herself in the midst of both the storm and the night.

She huddled for the next few hours in the cold, dark carriage. *Maybe it would be better to be back in my tower, curled up with Smokey in front of a roaring fire.* A bolt of lightning lit the sky. *No maybe. I* would *rather be back in my tower.* Raven snorted. This was *not* the kind of excitement she had bargained for! She hugged her arms tighter around her waist and frowned at the rain dripping down the interior carriage walls.

"I can see the inn!" someone called from the head of the procession.

Raven peeked out the window, fairly sighing with relief at

the cheery light streaming out from their destination. Then a wave of guilt struck her. Here she was – dry, if not entirely warm – in the enclosed coach, while the drivers and knights faced the raw, bitter elements. If she were a guard, she'd have mutinied by now.

Once inside, they were greeted by the innkeeper's wife – a cheery, stout woman named Claudia – who showed them to their rooms. The place was completely empty except for the staff; Wilgaun had probably arranged it ahead of time ... for a hefty price, no doubt.

"Come on down to the dining floor whenever you're ready to eat ... I left wash basins in your rooms, if you feel the need to freshen up," Claudia informed them, happily bustling away to ready dinner. Raven noticed her slipping a generous tip from the ambassador into her apron pocket.

Raven thanked a servant for delivering her luggage, observing her quaint room. Large timbers supported the roof above her, and a dark wood made up the wall planks. A cozy fireplace was positioned on the left side of her log-framed bed, and a small desk and chair sat by the window. Lastly, the bed cover was a rich purple dotted with golden flowers – Raven's favorite colors. Synthia had probably sent it in advance before she'd taken ill. Overall, it was a cozy place, though certainly not as grand as the lowest guest room in the castle. Still, Raven could get used to the charming simplicity.

A light knock came from the other side of the door. "M'lady? It's Breeanah." At Raven's permission, Breeanah cracked the door, her slim form easily fitting through the small opening. Raven caught a glimpse of a guard standing post at her door – an annoying necessity.

Breeanah curtsied before assuming a hunched posture with fingers intertwined and knees pressed together, like it was the only way they could support her unnaturally thin body. "Is there anything you need, Princess? I just came to check and see before I headed down to supper."

"No, but I'll walk down with you, if you don't mind."

"Oh – um, of course, M'lady."

They exited the room – trailed by Raven's guards – and had begun the descent down the staircase when they nearly ran into Tristan. He seemed to be focused on playing a game that involved how many stairs he could take a time. Halting a few inches in front of the young guard, Raven drew in a sharp breath. No one, other than gentry, had dared to stand so close to her – ever. She hated to admit it, but Tristan's proximity was unnerving.

Appearing to come to the same conclusion, Tristan took a step backward and grinned. "Oh, excuse me, ladies," he apologized, giving a quick bow.

"Why is it that whenever I see you, we're running into each other?" Raven forced a laugh, trying to dispel the sudden awkwardness. Or maybe it was just her – neither Breeanah nor Tristan seemed uncomfortable. She inwardly growled. Tristan was a soldier; she shouldn't feel uncomfortable, or awkward, or *anything* around him. He was below her station, which meant he was below her feeling anything for him.

But that didn't explain the way her face was burning.

"Perhaps I'll have to purposely find you somewhere and *not* run into you," Tristan teased. He gave another quick bow, first towards Raven and then Breeanah. "Princess … M'lady."

The two curtsied, then continued on in silence. Breeanah glanced at Raven with sly smile – which Raven pointedly ignored – before the maid parted ways and went to sit with the other servants in the kitchen.

Claudia served a hearty country cottage pie; a homemade crust stuffed with eggs, meats, potatoes, and cheese, followed up by mulled cider, light wafers, and nut pasties. The company settled into silence, each person exhausted from the long journey and bleak weather. After eating their fill, they retired to their rooms.

And Raven listened to the heavy downpour drum on the

roof, trying not to think about arranged marriages ... or friendships with those far below her station.

༄

Claudia slipped through the halls towards her room – an impressive feat, she thought, considering her well-stocked girth. She took great pride in being able to tiptoe about 'no louder than a ghost' when her patrons had gone to bed; maybe that's where the stories came from about the inn being haunted. With a shrug, Claudia's hand slipped into her pocket, grasping the hefty coin the ambassador had gifted her. Pompous royals or not, she had made a lovely profit.

A barely audible voice drifted from beneath the ambassador's door. Pausing, Claudia leaned closer, trying to discern words. One voice came from a woman, followed by a man's low timbre.

"Wonder what they're talkin' about at this late hour?" she muttered, catching something about a Nimrooden fellow. Normally, when a man and a woman were alone in a room at night, there was less talking and more –

The door opened abruptly, sending Claudia scrambling backwards when the countess emerged. Seeing Claudia, she stopped abruptly and pinned the matron with a stare that could cause a specter to shudder.

"What are you doing here?" Farah demanded. "Spying on the ambassador and his guests?"

"I'm just goin' to my room, Mum – nothin' more," Claudia answered, chuckling nervously.

The countess nodded, eyes narrowing. "I see. I trust, should anyone happen to ask, you saw no one tonight?" Farah grabbed Claudia's hand and not-so-subtly pressed a silver coin deep into the pudgy flesh.

The matron's eyes widened. "Course not, ma'am. I'll be silent as the grave I will," she assured, dropping the coin down her blouse and patting it. "Silent as the grave."

From the look Farah gave her, Claudia was convinced that –

if she didn't keep her mouth shut – she *would* end up in a grave, and it *would* be her ghost haunting the inn.

BURGLAR VALLEY

Unlike the previous day, the morning dawned temperate. The sky boasted a glorious blue, and swallows lighted on the carriage as they sang in the new day.

And Raven would be stuck *inside* the carriage for the rest of the day, unable to enjoy it.

The countess had absolutely forbade her from riding Freedom, stressing that it would be absurd for a princess to be seen on horseback. Especially when there was a "perfectly comfortable seat" inside the carriage. Raven wondered if every spark of adventure had been drilled out of Farah, or if the countess was simply born that way.

"How far until the first stop?" Raven called to the driver, leaning her entire upper body out the window. She could feel Farah's disapproving stare but opted to ignore it.

"We'll stop fer lunch in a few hours or so, I reckon," he replied with a drawl.

Raven frowned and rephrased, "How long until we arrive at *Trythe*?"

"Oh uh, another few days, I reckon."

Raven rolled her eyes and slumped.

"You really shouldn't slouch – it will ruin your back." Farah's charming smile did nothing to improve Raven's plummeting mood. If anything, it made it worse.

Raven muttered a reluctant acknowledgement and sat up. They'd left the Aspen Inn a day ago, and the monotonous schedule had repeated itself; eat at an inn, travel until noon, eat lunch, and then travel some more. Raven's back was beginning to ache, and if she had to sit still any longer, her legs might lose permanent feeling.

"Stop the coach!" Raven banged on the wall until the driver complied. Seconds later, she was out the carriage door and breathing in the fresh air, every muscle screaming in relief at the newfound freedom.

"Where are you going?" Farah demanded. Her attempts to grab Raven's skirt had failed, and now the countess's hand hung suspended in midair like a dead spider on its thread.

"I am sick and tired of this stuffy coach. *I need air!*" Raven declared. Hiking her dress hem up, she waved the driver forward and began walking along the dusty road, easily matching the horses' leisurely pace. Raven noticed Tristan watching her from his roan, unreadable emotions playing at the corner of his mouth. She deliberately turned her gaze away and walked a little faster.

"Stay close to the carriage ... you don't want to be carried off by some rogue band of ruffians," Farah said, sounding more annoyed than concerned.

Raven ignored the countess and closed her eyes, inhaling the fragrance of pine needles baking in the warm summer sun. For a while, birds serenaded the procession, but after a while they faded. Even the other animals that had been present in abundance – deer, turkey, and livestock – were nowhere to be seen. All was silent ... eerily silent.

"Does it seem ... unnaturally still?" Raven asked, glancing at the deserted countryside.

Tristan shifted in the saddle, glancing around. "We're nearing Burglar Valley – you may want to get back in the coach."

Raven's mouth twisted into a sarcastic smile. "That sounds inviting."

"Is there no way around?" Farah asked with a frown.

Kisby rode up beside the carriage, also taking in their surroundings, but with a casual air that belied any concern. "Not unless you want to waste a day skirting the perimeter. Don't worry, Countess, they won't attack carriages surrounded by an armed escort," he said with a firm nod.

Despite his confident words, Kisby still insisted that Raven continue in the safety of her carriage. She reluctantly complied, crossing her arms and staring out the window in what must've looked like a ridiculous pout. Not exactly manners befitting her station, but neither her father nor any one of a dozen tutors were there to correct her. After fifteen minutes of strained silence – which Raven figured was enough time to convey her displeasure – she leaned out the window and addressed Tristan directly, trying to fluster him into telling the truth. After all, if receiving unexpected attention from his princess didn't fluster him, what would?

"What, *exactly*, is in Burglar Valley?" Raven asked. "And if this place poses any threat to the royal family, why hasn't it been taken care of?"

The corner of Tristan's mouth lifted slightly, but much to Raven's chagrin, he appeared otherwise unruffled. *So much for flustering him.* "Exactly what the name implies, Princess ... burglars. Petty criminals and thieves come here to hide, hoping to escape justice since this land technically isn't under Laynia's jurisdiction. Sir Kisby has been planning to clear this place out – unofficially, of course – but other, more ... *pressing* ... issues have demanded his attention."

Raven raised a questioning eyebrow, but Tristan didn't elaborate, and she refused to give him the satisfaction of asking.

The further they went, the more Raven began to notice the crude features of Burglar Valley. For one thing, plants *literally* grew out of the shacks these people had the audacity to call houses. For another, the washed-out roads were completely unattended, sprouting with patches of grass or pocked with pond-sized puddles. The carriage frequently hit large rocks and potholes, jostling Raven and sending her grasping for a handhold.

Men guzzled tankards of dark ale at tables outside the local tavern, laughing raucously and pointing at the procession of guards and carriages – even at Raven. She turned away with a haughty tilt of her chin. It was only mid-afternoon, and they were already inebriated. *More disgusting than exciting.*

Tristan trotted his roan up to the carriage window, forming an effective barrier; his eyes never once left the road. "This place isn't suited for royalty to see ... you should close the blinds. Besides, it will hide you from prying eyes." He raised his eyebrow significantly, as though Raven should know exactly what he meant.

She did know, though that didn't mean she would give him the satisfaction of validating his concern. In fact, she had half a mind to oppose him. But as soon as Raven opened her mouth to protest, Farah pulled the curtains closed with a snap. Raven glared, though it was too dim inside for Farah to notice. *Unbelievable.* The moment the countess turned her back, Raven snuck a peek through a crack in the curtains.

Although everything about the place was revolting, Raven was equally fascinated and disturbed. It was one thing to read about poverty and crime; seeing it for herself was entirely different. Beyond the pages of a book, Raven had always found it difficult to imagine people living in hovels and vying for scraps off the street. Here, it was an unpleasant but undeniable reality. Was this, in any way, her fault? Her father's?

"What ya got in that carriage there, eh?" The raspy voice belonged to an equally pathetic gutter rat, who seemed to be having difficulties maintaining his balance. He flailed clumsily, barely managing to catch his balance on the flank of Tristan's roan. The stallion pinned his ears and crow-hopped away, nearly sending the drunkard sprawling.

Tristan's hand drifted to his sword hilt. "None of your business. Get moving before there's trouble."

The drunk sniggered. "What kind of trouble would *that* be, eh ... *boy*?"

Tristan withdrew the sword an inch. "Stay any longer and you'll find out." The man's eyes widened before he scuttled away.

Raven stiffened, any sympathy disappearing as the situation became more apparent. These men weren't victims; they had chosen their life of crime. Their fate was no more than they deserved.

The rest of the village was mostly the same; dilapidated buildings, poorly tended plots of land, and darting figures lurking in the shadows. Even if the territory wasn't under her father's authority, Raven had no doubt that Kisby could arrest these men in a heartbeat. Interference with an official Laynian escort gave him just cause to mete out punishment accordingly.

Another figure darted across the street, door slamming behind them. If Raven were him, she'd be hiding, too.

∽

As they moved away from the town, Tristan forced himself to ease the death grip he had on the reins. Destiny had begun to pick up on his nervousness and was acting up. Running his hand along the stallion's neck, Tristan scanned around him. The houses had finally begun to thin out, diminishing the number of locals out and about.

Diminishing their chances of trouble.

In spite of Sir Kisby's assurances, Tristan hadn't let his guard down for a second. Whatever misfortunes or bad decisions had led these people to seek refuge in Burglar Valley, there were few who wouldn't jump at the chance of stealing a few extra coins. Perhaps even hostages. None would dare attack the princess, but if they thought an insignificant nobleman was within their grasp, any number of would-be criminals could easily convince themselves that ransom was a good idea.

The princess. Just thinking of her was dangerous. Tristan's suggestion to shut the curtains was for more than the ladies' benefit. Having Princess Raven within sight was a distraction, and in combat, distractions got people killed. That's what all the seasoned warriors said. Not that he expected combat … at least, he hoped there wouldn't be any.

But the group of men that appeared from the foliage, creating a human blockade across the road, was *not* a good sign.

Kisby cantered to the front of the procession, face twitching with displeasure at the interruption. "Out of our way. This entourage is on official Laynian business. If you think we will be dissuaded by a bunch of drunken miscreants, you are sorely mistaken."

The tallest of the bunch – apparently the leader – stepped forward. A ragged scar ran from his hairline to nose, and the affected eye drooped hideously. "There'll be a fee for passin' through 'ere," he said. The other men laughed, elbowing each other's ribs like he'd cracked a witty joke.

Kisby frowned, clearly not amused. "Absurd. This is a public road that can be used –"

"It don't matter what the fee's for. Basically what we're sayin' is t' give us money," the leader interrupted with a repulsive grin.

Tristan noted the man's teeth – those that were left, at least – were black with decay. An unfortunate whim of imagination left Tristan thoroughly convinced that the man's breath would smell like a rotting carcass. He almost reached up to plug his nose, but that wouldn't stop his make-believe senses.

"In short …" Kisby paused to draw his sword, and a few of the robbers flinched. "No." The rest of the guard – including Tristan – also drew their weapons.

"Come on," Tristan muttered under his breath. "*Leave.*" In spite of the thieves' avarice, Tristan still dreaded bloodshed. Taking the life of another – even when justified – wasn't as glorious as the tales made it out to be. There was always a cost. That he also learned from seasoned warriors. Warriors who knew the cost of taking a life.

Tristan refocused, waiting for the bandits' answer.

For a heart-stopping moment, the leader hesitated. And then a sneer crossed his face. "Boys … take 'em out."

ഇ

Take 'em out. The moment the words left his mouth, Raven dropped off her seat, skirtage billowing around her as she hastily flung the seat cushion up. In the compartment below lay the sword she'd stashed at the beginning of her journey.

Ignoring the countess' gasp, she gripped the handle with all her might, staring at her reflection in the polished metal.

Her face was white with terror.

Flinging the cushion down, Raven crouched, hands shaking with a mixture of fear and anger ... fear for her men, for her own safety. And anger for her cowardice.

Before the emotions paralyzed her and rendered her useless, Raven grabbed the door latch.

She was a princess, not a child made of porcelain. At her own insistence, she'd received extensive training in sword combat, hoping exactly for a situation like this to prove herself. So why couldn't she turn the handle?

Farah watched. Already knowing Raven couldn't.

"It's pointless, Raven." No pet name, no title, no frilly words. Just an unyielding firmness as the countess gave voice to the whispers of doubt floating in Raven's head.

"You aren't strong enough."

Raven looked away, bowing her head. Her fingers slipped from the latch. "But I want to help." It was more of a question, a yearning for affirmation. Someone to tell her she could.

Farah raised an eyebrow. "Do you? Or do you simply want to prove that you're not the soft princess that everyone believes you to be?" Raven flinched, and the countess softened her tone. "Let the men handle it, Raven. They're soldiers, it's what they're trained to do. You'll only get in their way."

Raven replaced the sword, huddled in the corner of the carriage, and waited, listening to the cries of dying men.

Hiding while others fought battles for her.

૪౨

Tristan took down the last man, finishing him with a sword pommel to the head. Wounded men – mostly bandits – lay strewn across the road, red stains seeping from mild to deep slashes. A few of them had stopped moving. Tristan looked away, focused on running a cloth across his blade. So much loss that could have been avoided. What kind of man risked his own life for a handful of coins and a warrant of arrest posted across the entire kingdom?

Kisby strode up next to him, thrusting his sword into its scabbard with a metallic clank. "Soldier, report."

Tristan snapped to attention, saluting. "A few of our men received minor wounds, but no fatalities. Five attackers dead, two severely injured, and the rest taken into custody, including their leader, who's called Brank. Sir," Tristan added, eyeing the prisoners. They were kneeling, heads bowed and breathing heavily as the knights bound their hands and feet.

Kisby nodded, appraising him. "And what did you say your name was?"

"It's Tristan, sir."

Grunting unintelligibly, Kisby turned and approached the line of prisoners. Reaching the leader, he crouched down in front of him and jerked the man's chin up. "Look at me, thief, and tell me honestly ... why did you attack our party, hmm? We have fourteen well-seasoned knights. Mostly," Kisby said with a sideways glance at Tristan.

He tried not to take offense to the comment.

"You, on the other hand," Kisby continued, "have only a pathetic band of ruffians armed with sticks and wooden axes. Where is your *possible* advantage? Are there more of you on the way?"

Brank spat. "You stupid castle mongrels – you think we'll come crawling to you, begging for mercy –"

A sharp strike across the face stopped him short.

"You had better cooperate, otherwise we will have to be more ... how shall I put it ... *persuasive*," Kisby said, eyes glinting. This was the closest thing to a smile that Tristan had ever seen from his commander. It was an alarming sight.

Ambassador Kirgan walked up behind them, stopped, and stared mutely at the interrogation.

Tugging against his bonds, Brank shifted uncomfortably. "You know why we attacked. As fer being outnumbered, we were assured an easy fight by –" He stopped short, eyes darting to the sides, searching for a threat that wasn't there.

"Don't stop now. Tell us who assured you an *easy fight*," Kisby intoned.

Brank remained silent, and Kisby pursed his lips. "This is an ornery one, eh – what's your name – Tristan? What is your remedy for this *uncooperative ruffian*?" A slight crinkle at the corner of Kisby's eyes gave away his intentions.

Tristan hid a smile. "Well, I suppose we could stab him and put him out of his misery." He knew perfectly well that Kisby had no intentions of impaling anyone, but a bit of humor at their captive's expense was fair play.

Kisby shook his head. "No, too quick. How about we delimb him?"

"Too messy ... not to mention time-consuming. We should probably just hang him from a tree, leave him, and go about our business." Tristan shrugged. "The black vultures will get him soon enough."

"Excellent idea; go fetch some rope."

Eyes widening, Brank lurched against his bonds like he could already feel the vultures picking at his flesh. "Wait, I'll talk!"

The man was a lunatic in his panicking. There were no such things as black vultures; they were harvest stories created to frighten children. With giant wings, red eyes, and poisonous breath, the predatorial birds could hardly be real. But Brank obviously didn't know that.

Kisby lifted one eyebrow expectantly.

Brank licked his lips, eyes still darting in and out of focus. "We were told some carriages and soldiers would be passin' through. We were promised all the spoils ... as long as we killed everyone."

Tristan flinched. Whoever had hired these bandits clearly knew they were coming, and their route was only known to a privileged few. It took more than a common ruffian to procure such clandestine information. Was someone intent on assassinating the princess? If so, why hadn't they sent a more sizable force? Anyone with a lick of sense knew these common thieves were outmatched. So why risk giving away their nefarious plan with a failed attempt?

"That doesn't answer the question. *Who hired you?*" Kisby demanded. The outburst was predictably followed by his signature frown.

When Brank failed to answer, Kisby turned to Tristan. "This man seems to have lost his voice. Maybe the vultures will remind him how to use it."

Brank relented. "Alright! But promise me something."

"No guarantees."

Ignoring – or not hearing – Kisby's remark, Brank leaned in closer, confirming Tristan's suspicion about his breath. It definitely smelled like a rotting carcass. "Protect me. If I squeal, he'll kill my men and punish me with a fate worse than death."

Kisby waved his request aside. "Very well, tell us."

"The man called himself ..." Brank lowered his voice even further, "*Gauln.*"

Kisby's face twitched. But if he recognized the name, he gave no further indication.

Brank rocked back on his heels. Reaching with his bound hands, he revealed a scar carved across his scrawny chest. The wound was still raw. "Last time he gave me this, and promised I'd have a thousand times worse if I failed again."

"Do you know what he looked like?"

"No, he wore a hooded black cloak," Brank said, shaking his head.

Tristan rolled his eyes. *Typical.* Every person the guard sought to identify wore some sort of a hood, conveniently masking their features. It made his job so much harder.

Looking to Kirgan, Kisby waited for a moment before turning back to Brank. "You have my thanks – you've been most helpful." He stood, drawing his sword.

And Tristan stared dumbfounded as Kisby thrust his blade

through Brank's heart.

Tristan shot to his feet, jaw clenched. "Why did you do that? You promised to protect him!" He tried to avert his gaze, but out of the corner of his eye, he could see the blood pooling around the dead thief's corpse.

"They're all the same, boy ... imbecilic, lying thugs who can't think for themselves. Each and every time, they will choose the wrong master because it comes with the highest profit." Kisby snorted, kicking the body's leg. "And I did protect him from this *Gauln* fellow. His death came at our hands."

"You mean at yours," Tristan said, glaring. "I take no responsibility on this matter." He turned to walk away.

Kisby's hand shot out and grabbed Tristan's shoulder, locking him in a vice-like grip. "You are only a boy who's training to be a soldier," he spat. "You must learn to respect and trust the decisions of your superiors!" He noticeably relaxed, then said, "I only want you to learn the easy way. If you keep dealing with criminals, you *will* fall into trouble."

"I understand, sir." Tristan glanced from Kisby to the ambassador, who watched from a few paces away. "But with all due respect, it's not right to break deals with anyone. If you make a deal, you should honor it." Tristan pointed at the cowering line of prisoners. "Otherwise, you're no better than them."

He walked away with Kisby's glare boring into the back of his head.

TRYTHE

"Take them to the roadside." Ambassador Kirgan's last words still rung like a thunderclap in Tristan's mind. The captives had broken into a panic trying to escape … and the guards hauled them into a ditch and slit their throats. Kisby had given the order without hesitation.

Murder.

That was the only word Tristan could think of that grasped the severity of the thieves' punishment. Yes, they may have deserved their fate, but killing was only justified during battle or after a fair trial. These men had been slaughtered like common animals, their bodies left for carrion.

And the ambassador had acted without Princess Raven's approval. At least, Tristan desperately hoped he had. The thought of Rav– *the princess,* he reminded himself – ordering such a heinous deed … it was unthinkable. She might be a royal, but Tristan refused to believe she would execute men without a trial, thieves or no.

But there was only one way to find out.

The entourage eventually pulled off to the roadside, allowing the company a chance to eat and relieve themselves. Raven sat, alone, munching on an apple and watching with an unamused expression as the countess and ambassador discussed menial logistics. Taking advantage of the rare opportunity, Tristan approached and cleared his throat.

Raven jumped and glanced up, eyes a startling blue, almost tinged with purple. Periwinkle, if he had to put a name to it. Beneath her dark lashes, the effect was … disconcerting.

Tristan bowed, using the moment to recover his composure. "Your Highness."

She also seemed to be recovering her poise, avoiding eye-contact and carefully placing the half-eaten fruit on a napkin. Finally, she nodded in acknowledgement. "Sir Tristan." The coldness in her voice was unmistakable, and Tristan took a half-step back.

"It's not *sir*, Your Highness. Just Tristan."

Raven blinked. "I don't believe you came here to discuss the minutiae of your title. Did you want something?"

Swallowing, Tristan inclined his head. "Yes, Princess. I came to make sure you were alright, after the attack. Such business can be … *unsettling*." He studied her discreetly, watching for a reaction.

If possible, Raven's expression grew even colder. "I see. I'm fine, thank you. Is that all?"

"No, actually."

Tristan's forwardness took Raven off guard, and her impervious façade faltered. "Uh, what?" She cringed, quickly correcting herself. "I mean, what else do you need, soldier?"

"I'm curious what you think about the thieves' punishment."

Genuinely confused, Raven's brows furrowed. "What punishment? I thought they'd all been killed in the attack or run off."

A wave of tangible relief swept through Tristan. *She doesn't know.* But that meant …

Sir Kisby strode up beside him. Tristan didn't need to see him to know Kisby was listening to every word Tristan spoke.

Tristan gave a perfunctory bow. "Good day, Your Highness." Turning on his heel, Tristan rejoined the other soldiers, who were cracking jokes through mouthfuls of food. Like they hadn't just executed half a dozen men earlier that day. How could these men laugh it off so easily?

And why was the princess suddenly so aloof? What had he done to incur her disapproval? Without her help, Tristan wasn't sure if he could expose Kisby. And even if he did, what could he say? He was only a lowly soldier. No one would listen to him.

Especially the princess.

೧

The carriage jostled back into motion, resuming the monotonous journey. They were due to arrive at the kingdom of Mieldren later that evening, giving everyone a well needed break from endless dust and ruts. But the reprieve of being on the road again offered Raven no comfort. If anything, it gave her time to think. And that was infinitely worse.

Why had she been so short with Tristan? It wasn't his fault – any of it. The attack, the needless killing. *Her cowardice.* And still she'd chosen to take it out on him, the only person who'd bothered to ask how she was. *Unsettled* had been his word of choice. Raven let out a sardonic laugh; unsettled didn't begin to cover her sentiments.

She traced her fingers along the carriage's interior fabric, marveling at the silky cobalt velvet stitched with elaborate gold vines and leaves. Such beauty … and all she could think about was death.

"Why do they do it?" The words had no sooner left Raven's mouth than she regretted them. But she hadn't been able to stop herself. Instead, she'd exposed her inner turmoil to the one person who she *didn't* want to talk to right now – Farah.

The countess let out a sigh. "I don't have telepathy, Raven. Why does who do what?"

Too late to take it back. Raven spoke slowly, trying to banish any emotion from her voice. She doubted she'd succeed. "Steal. Kill. All the horrible crimes outlaws commit."

"I can't say for sure, Raven." Farah gave a blasé wave of her hand, rings sparkling. "Money, power? Hatred?" She shrugged. "It doesn't really matter, does it?"

A shiver worked its way up Raven's spine, and she curled her arms tighter around her waist. "Maybe. But why would you hate? Stealing can be justified, and I suppose wanting power is understandable, but killing out of hatred …"

Farah laughed, making Raven bristle. "You're so adorably naïve. One day you'll understand how the world works."

"I am perfectly aware of how it *works*," Raven retorted. "I just don't understand the motives." It seemed at every turn, Farah took the opportunity to remind Raven how little she knew. Perhaps it was only so infuriating because, more often than not, the countess was right.

"We're nearly at Mieldren. You'd better fix yourself up ... and put a lid on that attitude. King Taungan won't take lightly to any slights – perceived or otherwise."

Raven bit back another retort. As usual, Farah was right.

଄

Trythe Castle overlooked the Geode Sea on the southeastern tip of Alarkin. Built entirely of dark rock, it almost looked like the castle was chiseled out of the same inhospitable cliffs that plummeted beneath the fortress and into the thundering sea below. The city of Trythe sprawled on the southern side of the castle in a mass of taverns, shops, and houses. The buildings were primarily made of stone with thatched roofs, coarser and less colorful than those in Caritas.

Further south, bordering the town, the cliff diminished into a sandy beach and a bustling ship port. Many shops were open despite the ashen sky; women even hung sheets out to dry. Like it would do any good with the perpetual misting. A salty breeze blew through Raven's hair, undoing any finger combing she'd attempted. For the first time in hours, she smiled.

"It's rather bleak here, don't you think?" Farah's observation was met with silence as Raven watched a herd of sheep. They stared back and bleated, shaggy wool billowing all around them in the most ridiculous fashion. Farah would think them repulsive. Perhaps for that reason alone, Raven thought they were rather adorable.

Children scampered about with sticks and a small wooden puck, but their game – and subsequent chatter – came to an abrupt halt. As one, they stopped to stare as the entourage of carriages bearing the crest of Laynia rolled past. Raven grinned and gave an encouraging wave for them to continue, and they smiled back. The game resumed, but many of the children dropped their sticks and raced alongside the carriage through the village, shouting and waving.

"How cute, they're giving us an escort," Raven said. She received an unenthusiastic '*mhm*' from the countess. Raven frowned. "Don't you like children?"

"Children are fine, in their place, when they are well-bred and well-mannered. *These* are common street ragamuffins," Farah added, and Raven could have sworn she gave a disdainful sniff.

They bumped across the drawbridge, moving further away from the swarm of children and closer to the imposing spires of King Taungan's abode.

It took that entire time for Raven to come up with a civil reply. "The only thing that sets them apart from us is what they were born into. Had they been noblemen's children, you'd never know the difference."

"Oh, and I suppose you could be a baker's wife if you were *born into it?*" Farah returned with unmistakable sarcasm.

Raven muttered something under her breath.

"You must accept your role, dearest ... some are born to be bakers' wives and some are born to be royalty." Farah rested her hand lightly on Raven's arm.

She fought the impulse to shake it off.

"Everyone should have a right to choose. If I want to marry a baker, or a blacksmith, or a soldier ... I should have that choice." The carriage came to a stop near the castle steps. Raven flung the door open, grateful for the cool wind to counteract the sudden warmth that had spread across her cheeks. Marry a soldier? Where had that come from? She groaned, trying to convince herself it had been a random example, instead of ... a not random one.

Led by the castle steward, a portion of Raven's company – which included herself, the countess, Kisby, and Kirgan – presented themselves to King Taungan, who lounged in an entirely uncomfortable looking throne made of thick, uncushioned wood erected in sharp ninety-degree angles. The king himself – as tall, imposing, and angular as his chair – tilted his head benevolently, stroking his trim onyx-colored beard.

Taungan took a long pull from his chalice. "Welcome, Princess Raven. I trust you've had a safe journey?"

Raven studied the ridged, undecorated goblet. Did everything in Mieldren resemble a block of wood, carved out only enough to allow functionality rather than any artistic taste whatsoever?

She started, realizing she hadn't answered. "Yes, thank you. It is most gracious of you to open your kingdom to us," Raven returned. Diplomacy had been drilled into her so thoroughly, it was almost automatic. *Almost* being the key word.

"Of course. It would be rude to deny your father's request," Taungan said. Raven wasn't sure if that meant he respected her father or didn't want her there but had no choice except to allow them for his reputation's sake. She suspected it was the latter – hardly a comforting thought.

Taungan waved towards the steward. "Horace, show our guests to their rooms."

Horace nodded and beckoned, leading them down a series of hallways in an odd, shuffling gait. After gesturing to their rooms, he half-turned to address them, keeping his eyes on the floor. Raven noted one eye was blue, while the other was brown.

"His Highness requests you join him in the great hall to relate your trip over supper," the steward mumbled. "Until then, you have the afternoon to rest and freshen up." He licked his lips. "I am at your service, should you need anything."

Raven thanked him, oddly amused by the eccentric fellow. Entering her high-vaulted room, she curled her arms around her midsection and shivered. The floor-to-ceiling window overlooked the stormy Geode Sea; far below, waves crashed against the craggy rock. If she went too close, she almost believed she could fall, plummeting past the cliffs and into the murky depths below. *Geode Sea*, Raven scoffed. *More like sea of storms.*

Edging her way around the interior wall, she made her way to the pile of luggage and dug through it, snatching her warmest cloak. The dark blue wool was coarse, but it would stave off the worst of the perpetual draft.

Everything about the castle was cold and hard, all mirroring its owner. Cold flagstone made up the majority of the floors, and what few rugs existed were dark and abrasive. The damp, gray sky seeped through every window; torches did little to dispel the gloom. The only thing they seemed capable of was creating eerie shadows in the spacious room.

After washing her face – the water in the ewer long since cold – and plaiting her hair, Raven hurried back downstairs and caught the arm of a passing servant, who directed her to the great hall. Farah and Kirgan had already taken their seats across from Taungan in a semi-circle around the fireplace. As Raven sat next to Farah, a servant handed her a steaming cup of wassail, which helped with the cold – a little.

They exchanged tedious pleasantries, but then the conversation stagnated, and Taungan appeared in no hurry to resume it. Even Farah, normally so adept at tête-à-tête, was at a loss for words.

Raven cast a sly glance at the countess. Fighting was hardly an appropriate subject, but when all else failed …

"Have you had any troubles with thieves?" Raven asked. Expression far too innocent, she took a sip of the mulled drink and waited. Farah's look of disapproval was unmistakable.

For the first time since they'd met, Taungan looked interested. "Trythe is far too formidable for any – *rabble* – to dare attack."

"Not the castle, naturally. Anyone can see that it is nigh impregnable. I was thinking more of the highways and byways," Raven amended casually.

"None at all. Why do you ask?"

Despite Farah's tightly pursed lips, Raven briefly related their incident in Burglar Valley, earning sidelong glances from her companions. She ignored them.

When she finished, Taungan leaned back and drummed his fingers on the arm of his chair. "Fascinating. And you said they all died in the fight?"

Raven frowned and started to answer, but Kirgan cut in. "Yes, unfortunately, none were left alive except the few who escaped. A pity; we could have questioned them."

The entrance of a newcomer brought the conversation to a halt. Taungan bared his teeth in a semblance of a smile and stood. "Perfect timing. Allow me to introduce my first-born daughter, Melodea."

For some reason, his commendation on *perfect timing* rubbed Raven the wrong way, and she stiffened. And indeed, if anyone resembled perfection, it was this Melodea. Smooth, glossy brown hair, wide blue eyes, and a perfect complexion. An expensive gown flowing gracefully over a comely figure – everything about her screamed perfection.

Following the countess' lead, Raven stood and curtsied.

Melodea's full lips curved into a demure smile, and she returned the gesture, glancing up through long lashes. "I am pleased to meet you, Your Highness. Countess Burina – Ambassador Kirgan."

"I have three other daughters, but they are still young and not ... comfortable with guests," Taungan said. He smiled tightly. "They are tending to my wife, who has taken poorly. Again." A loud sniff marked his disapproval.

It was rumored that the queen often took to her chambers, suffering from chronic illness. Now, Raven wondered if her poor health had more to do with avoiding her husband than anything else. She took another sip of wassail to hide her snicker.

"I also planned for Melodea to visit the neighboring kingdoms, you know," Taungan continued. "Unfortunately, she hasn't had the opportunity, due to lack of ... *suitable* ... company."

Farah suddenly spoke up. "I don't wish to impose on any plans you have, but why shouldn't Melodea join us? Why, I could send a missive to Wilgaun first thing in the morning ... this very night even!"

Eyes flashing, Raven whirled her head around to glare at the countess. Since when was her father plain *Wilgaun?* No title or deference for his position! And it wasn't Farah's place to suggest Melodea accompany them.

Even if it were, Melodea was *not* coming with them. "We wouldn't want to cause such an imposition." Raven's words were unnaturally even, spoken through gritted teeth. "I'm sure Princess Melodea is far too busy to go galivanting off at the last minute."

To Raven's surprise, Melodea agreed with her. "Indeed, I wouldn't want to –"

"Excellent!" Taungan interrupted. "This would be the ideal opportunity for her ... please write as soon as possible, Countess."

As Kirgan and Taungan launched into a full lecture on scheduled itinerary and other tedious formalities, occasionally joined by Farah, the two princesses listened in quiet dread. Raven refused to make eye contact with Melodea, choosing instead to stare into the crackling fire, watching the embers pop and dance in the hearth. It was going to be a long stay.

GUESS THE TRAITOR

Raven fiddled with her silverware. It was bad manners, but she hardly cared at this point; Taungan clearly didn't care a fig about decorum, and she was bored.

After the last detail had finally been ironed out, everyone was ushered to their places at the table. Even the heat from the large fireplace, which they had been gathered around moments before, barely reached Raven. A solitary iron chandelier – enormous as it was - offered minimal light, and somehow, the chairs were even more uncomfortable than they looked. In fact, everything about the castle was outrageously inadequate!

To make matters worse, Tristan was here. Taungan had invited Kisby and his men to dine with them – no doubt to alleviate Taungan's boredom with his guests. The men were all under strict instruction by Kisby to be respectful in the present company of royalty, but that hardly helped the churning in Raven's gut at the sight of Tristan. They hadn't spoken since their cold encounter at lunch, and the flicker of hurt and confusion in his eyes was unmistakable. Or was there more to his discomfort than her rude treatment? Raven frowned, continuing to twirl her fork between her fingers.

Taungan clapped, and servants streamed in with trays of food. One carried an entire stuffed peacock – a rather unusual display of hospitality and extravagance. Or maybe Taungan just had strange tastes when it came to meat.

"Sir Kisby, I heard you were waylaid on the road." Taungan raised an eyebrow expectantly.

Glancing uncomfortably towards Kirgan, Sir Kisby cleared his throat. "Indeed. On our way out of Burglar Valley, a dozen men waylaid us, demanding money. At our refusal, they attacked. The only information we could extract from their dying leader is that they expected an easy fight." He smirked. "The rest fled like the cowards they were."

Raven couldn't help noticing Tristan. His mouth was twisted into a frown as he stared at Sir Kisby. Even after the conversation wandered away from the fight, Tristan hardly spoke to anyone the entire evening. A mixture of guilt and indignation battled in Raven's mind. Logically, there was nothing she had done wrong; she had only treated him with the passiveness her rank demanded. And he was a grown man – he had no reason to pout over the words of a lady so far above his rank. But ... she still couldn't shake the feeling that she had been in the wrong.

The meal ended, and Raven excused herself.

She wandered aimlessly through the halls, lost in melancholy. The trip had been nothing like she'd imagined; for the most part, it was monotonous. And when there *was* action, what had she done? Hid in her carriage like a timid mouse. *Like a scared, helpless little princess.* Raven wanted to blame someone. After all, it was the bandits' fault for attacking; Farah's fault for telling her to stay in the carriage.

But ultimately, the decision to hide had been hers.

Suddenly exhausted, Raven turned toward her room. But before she'd placed one foot on the staircase, a hand shot out and grabbed her, pulling her into the shadows of a hidden alcove. The curtain fell closed behind her.

Pulse racing, she stumbled backwards, coming face to face with none other than Tristan. She wasn't sure if she should be relieved ... or even more nervous. "What –"

"Shh!" Tristan boldly placed his hand across her mouth, silencing her outburst. "I've bought us a minute away from your guards, but you need to be quiet. Remember Sir Kisby's account at dinner? About the bandit attack?"

Raven grabbed his hand, forcing it off her mouth; Tristan frowned but didn't try to replace it.

Arms crossed, she looked away. "What about it?"

"He lied."

Raven jerked back to look at him. "Huh?"

Pacing, Tristan gestured broadly. "We captured most of the men alive, except a few who died in battle or escaped, but none of the prisoners died from their wounds." Tristan's mouth twisted into a grimace.

A sickening feeling settled in Raven's chest. "What are you saying?" she asked slowly. "What happened to the other men?"

Footsteps pattered across flagstone, and Tristan pulled Raven further into the shadows as a gaggle of tittering maids wandered past. Tristan's hands rested lightly on her shoulders, and Raven detected the faint scent of leather and pine. She immediately stepped back.

His hands fell away.

Raven's words were a faint whisper, barely enough to penetrate the thick silence. "*What happened?*"

Tristan's eyes closed, forehead pressing against his arm that rested against the wall – as if he were trying to push away the memory. When he finally spoke, his voice was strained and husky. "We – *they* – killed them all. Under the ambassador's direction, Sir Kisby ordered the men to take them to the roadside. His falsehood at dinner confirmed my suspicion that began with our conversation earlier today: you had no knowledge of this order, did you?"

Another pang of guilt shot through her, but now was not the time to apologize. She pushed the feeling aside. "Why would Kirgan have them killed?"

Tristan shook his head slowly. "I don't know. The leader, Brank, mentioned a General Gauln who was behind the attack. His directive was to –" he faltered. His words became almost inaudible. "*Kill everyone.*"

Raven's mouth went dry. "So someone wants me dead? How could that be? What enemies could I possibly have – and why would Kisby lie?"

"I'm not sure. I don't have all the answers." Tristan glanced down the hallway.

With the slightest shift of the curtain, Raven followed his gaze and saw Ambassador Kirgan sauntering down the hall with Farah hooked on his arm, both laughing and talking like old friends. Which they were, of course ... although neither had mentioned it to her until *after* Farah had been arranged as Raven's companion. Her jaw clenched.

Raven waited until the two had disappeared; then she brushed past Tristan, pushing the curtains aside and exiting the alcove. "Do you honestly expect me to believe you?" she exploded, though she had the sense not to raise her voice *too* loudly in case someone overheard. "You, who I've known for a few days? You want me to take your word over all the guards, Farah, and the ambassador?" Stepping onto the first stair, she whirled around, glaring down at him.

Tristan fumbled for words. "I just –"

"No." Raven crossed her arms. "You want me to believe that my father's most trusted men are traitors? If anything, maybe *you're* the traitor!" Pivoting on her heel, she stormed up the steps, not bothering to see if Tristan was following.

After what she'd said, he'd be a fool to follow her.

∞

"Ambassador Kirgan, a traitor? How absurd! He may be too cavalier with his flattery, but to betray his kingdom? My father?!" Raven paced, fuming. "I thought I could trust Tristan, but apparently not. He must be doing this so he can – so I'll –" Raven stuttered, trying to think of a logical answer. After all, it wasn't like Tristan was telling the truth ... was it? How could such loyal men – her father's chief diplomat and a commander in Laynia's Guard – stoop to treason? Or whatever this was.

Breeanah, sitting quietly on the settee as she waited for Raven to finish venting, finally voiced her opinion. "Maybe you should talk to the other guards – ask *them* what really happened?" She packed another folded and laundered dress into Raven's suitcase.

"Kisby wouldn't lie in front of the entire company!" Raven

exploded. "One of the soldiers would have said something, surely." Her voice was muffled from behind a screen as she struggled to remove her golden gossamer dress. It had so many elaborate seams and ties, wearing it was similar to being caught in a fisherman's net. With a triumphant cry, she yanked it off her head and flung it on top of the screen.

"Maybe, like Tristan, they simply didn't want to contradict their commander in front of everyone," Breeanah returned calmly.

Raven gave a reluctant nod. "That's possible. Maybe I was too hasty ..." Now in her nightgown, Raven emerged from behind the screen and slumped next to Breeanah, burying her face in her hands with a quiet moan. "It just sounded so absurd at the time. And Tristan ..." Her voice trailed off into the stillness.

Breeanah tentatively rested her hand on Raven's shoulder. Her fingers were so thin; if Raven tried, she could easily snap one in two. Not for the first time, she wondered where this poor girl had come from ... and what hardships she'd had to endure before coming to Laynia.

"It's very easy to judge when we don't want to believe someone. Especially when the odds are against them. I guess we have to ignore our prejudices and learn to evaluate everything with truth."

Raven dropped her hands from her face, eyebrows raised. "Where did that speech come from?" she asked with a grin. She moved from the settee and plopped on her bed in a cross-legged position, wordlessly patting the space next to her.

Perching on the edge of the bed, Breeanah shrugged. "I – had a mentor who taught me a few things," she said haltingly. "A long time ago."

"What happened to them?"

Breeanah stiffened. "I don't know."

"I'm sorry – I didn't mean to pry." Raven's gaze faltered.

"It's alright." She smiled faintly. "I just ... wish I knew."

They fell silent, watching the moon dance between clouds over the crashing waves. Quietly, Raven began to sing, and Breeanah's lilting voice joined her. "*Return to me, on a starlit night, when the moon hushes the sea ...*"

PAST NIGHTMARES

Seventeen years earlier, after the attack on Caritas ...

A hooded figure strode through the nearly abandoned halls, shying his head away and retreating into the recesses of his hood at the occasional passerby. No one could recognize him. The success of his mission hinged on his anonymity ... and the quickness of his blade. The trap door opened silently, and he crept down the long, dark passage until it opened onto a crumbling balcony. Near the edge, a man casually sharpened his weapon.

The man Kisby had journeyed across Alarkin to kill.

"You came." General Gauln turned leisurely, clearly unconcerned with the arrival of his uninvited guest.

"I've been preparing for this day," Kisby said emotionlessly, flipping back his hood. "You left me for dead. Unfortunately for you, I'm very much alive ... ready to avenge the soldiers you and your men *slaughtered* when you invaded Caritas."

"Ever the self-righteous soldier," Gauln sneered. "But is that really why you're here?"

Kisby flinched, then quickly recomposed himself. "Of course."

"Really? You're sure you aren't here to kill me for ... personal reasons?" Gauln let the insinuation dangle. "Such as proving you're a better fighter than I am? Or that you've grown more powerful in your pathetic quest for revenge?"

"That's just a bonus." Kisby drew his sword, leveling it towards Gauln's chest. "Draw your sword, demon."

Gauln made no move towards his weapon. He glanced down at his chest, lifting his arms in a mock gesture of submission. "Go ahead. Kill me, if you think that makes you a better soldier. But if your motives are purely egotistic, at least be man enough

88

to admit it!"

Kisby's jaw clenched. Pulling the sword back, he poised to strike, and the tip plummeted towards Gauln's heart.

But it never reached its mark.

Instead, the sword hovered mere fractions away, with Kisby unable – or unwilling – to execute the death sentence. Gauln quirked an eyebrow, taunting.

Ramming the blade back into its sheath, Kisby let out a low expletive. "Fine. The only reason I came here today was to sate my own vanity. Satisfied?"

Gauln grinned. "Immensely. From the moment I saw you, I knew you were different. There wasn't that same squeamishness, that weakness of character. You had bloodlust in your eyes. I've waited for you to find me – you didn't think that peddler really helped you out of the goodness of his heart, do you?"

Kisby opened his mouth to protest, but Gauln waved it away. "I *sent* him to find you. He waited until you left, then took a faster route and informed me of your imminent arrival. He was well compensated for his trouble, I assure you." His low chuckle implied the compensation involved a more violent payment than the average reward.

Kisby frowned. "Why would you risk letting me find you? All I wanted was to run my blade through your gut!"

"Did you?"

"I don't know what you –"

"Did you kill me?" Gauln repeated.

Unamused, Kisby snorted. "As you're still around to voice your stupid riddles, I'd say you're still alive. For now," he added.

"Exactly my point."

Kisby fell into an uncomfortable silence.

"Do you understand now, boy? I *wanted* all of this to happen. You've played right into my hands, yet I still haven't killed you. Can you imagine why that is?"

"My name is Kisby. And no, I can't imagine."

Gauln recoiled derisively. "Oh no, that name won't work. We're going to have to change that – something that doesn't scream 'do-gooder-knight,' I think. Because when I'm done with you…" He ran his knife across his palm, ignoring the sting as it bit into his flesh. "You are going to be absolutely *wicked.*" Laughing, he grabbed Kisby's hand and drew the blade across his palm. Kisby flinched, but Gauln's injured hand shot forward and locked Kisby's in a vice-like grip.

Blood mingled and splattered across the flagstones, leaving a crimson trail – a symbolic homage to the trail of death their combined blades would bring to the world.

∞

Present …

Kisby gasped, hand shooting out and grasping the wound to stem the flow of blood. Except there was no blood … only a thin scar running across his palm. "Accursed dreams," he growled, throwing the blankets off his sweaty body. The wind brought an instant chill and tousled his sleep-matted hair as he stepped onto the balcony. The same balcony that connected with other rooms in this portion of the castle. Kisby drank deeply of the cool night draught; gradually, his head began to clear.

"What is troubling you?"

Kisby whirled around at the countess' voice as her ethereal form emerged from the shadows. Her white gown fluttered in the breeze and brushed over her bare feet, giving her a closer resemblance to a specter than a woman. Still, at least she *was* human … most likely.

Kisby groaned, allowing his muscles to relax as he ran a hand over his face. "Don't do that again."

"You didn't answer my question."

He hesitated only a split second, but it was enough to draw Farrah's attention. "I had a dream of – of when I joined. I keep waking up thinking my hand is bleeding," he muttered. It was a lame excuse, and they both knew it.

"The path we follow is not for those of frail constitution ... or commitment. Second thoughts are unacceptable." Farrah's words were even and measured but penetrated with unnerving precision.

The woman had insight, Kisby gave her that.

His knuckles rapped against the balustrade. "I know."

Her breath came dangerously close to his ear; a low, seductive whisper of evil portents. "*You had better.*"

Farah's fingers trailed along Kisby's shoulders, and a shiver ran up his spine. He waited until the whispering sound of her bare feet faded away before retreating to the safety of his room.

That woman!

That Woman

Raven's hand flopped to her side; the end of the last goodbye wave. With an additional passenger, it had taken hours to depart. King Taungan made sure *every* possible detail and situation was discussed in full, assuring Melodea – though more for the sake of his pride – that she would be safe.

Raven's conversation with the guards had produced nothing. They had all backed Kisby's side of the story before hastily excusing themselves. She hadn't been able to talk with Tristan, and if she was being honest, she didn't want to. What could she say? That he was a liar? But she couldn't bring herself to turn him in, either. If there was even the smallest chance he was telling the truth, or was simply misguided, she wouldn't be the one responsible for his punishment.

Gaze wandering, Raven discreetly studied the newest member of their party. Princess Melodea sat on the opposite side of the coach, staring out the window with her back straight and slender hands folded in her lap. Raven frowned. *Prissy.*

A second later, she straightened her own back.

∞

"This blasted heat!" Raven fumed. She paced back and forth, fanning herself with graceless flaps. "Why must we encounter every weather cataclysm?"

Farah, sitting next to Melodea on a blanket under a giant elm, swallowed a dainty bite of meat pie and dabbed the corner of her mouth. "Do try to control your temper, Raven dearest. Anger is not becoming … especially with your pale complexion," she tutted. "And you should eat something."

Melodea said nothing, deliberately preoccupied with her food.

"I thought you were my companion, not my governess,"

Raven muttered. Snatching a fresh roll, she hitched up her skirts and marched into the trees. Behind her, Farah called for her to come back, but Raven deliberately ignored her – again. Days spent locked in a carriage with anyone was bad enough, but someone as intolerable and self-important as the countess was … well … *intolerable*!

Out of breath from her brisk pace – not to mention the absurd heat and trying to walk and eat at the same time – Raven paused at a shallow forest pool that was fed by a trickling waterfall. Moss covered the outcropping of large, flat stones, but the water was kept fairly clean from the constant movement. Raven inhaled deeply, scents of musty leaves and pine filling her lungs and soothing her mind. A balm for the wretched blight she suffered from: Farah.

A loud crashing approached from behind her, followed by a desperate call. "Your Highness!"

Raven rolled her eyes. She'd known one of the guards would come for her, but this was sooner than expected. She popped the last hunk of bread into her mouth and sat behind a boulder to wait. The fool could keep bumbling about for all she cared; she wasn't about to make his job easy.

"Princess!" The man, more frantic now, came closer.

He'd find her, eventually. Either that, or they'd send in the entire troop, which would be as embarrassing as it would be time-consuming. With a sigh, Raven stood and made her way to the soldier. "I'm over here."

"There you are, Your Majesty!" The guard exhaled, resting his hands on his knees. "We were worried something happened to you!"

In two minutes? Raven was tempted to laugh at him but thought better of it and settled for a curt nod.

"The countess implores you not to go anywhere unescorted, for your own protection. Your Highness," he added at her scathing look.

"You may tell the countess I'll be there shortly. When *I'm* good and ready."

The guard kicked at the ground, refusing to meet her gaze. "I'm afraid you must come back now, Your Majesty," he said, licking his lips. "M'lady's orders."

Raven raised her eyebrow. "Orders? And since when is the countess 'your lady?'"

The guard shifted uncomfortably, gaze fixed on his boots.

Grunting, Raven shooed him away. "Let's go then. We wouldn't want to displease *her ladyship*," she taunted. Not waiting for a reply, she took off at a brisk walk, sending the man scrambling to catch up.

When she entered the clearing, the picnic was packed up and Farah stood waiting by the carriage. "Ah, there you are! I was beginning to worry you'd wandered off and gotten lost." Her simpering expression, hidden poorly beneath a façade of concern, was hardly convincing.

Raven brushed past her and swung into the carriage, sitting at the far corner from Melodea. "I was fine, Countess. Really. Besides, worry is not becoming, especially to your light complexion," she returned, ignoring the horrified gasp that came from the other side of the cab.

Farah shook her head and sighed, sitting heavily. "My dear Raven, why do you despise me so? Everything I do is only for your good!"

"I don't *despise* you, Farah." The carriage rolled into motion. "I just wish you wouldn't treat me like a child. You're here because my father wishes it, and propriety demands it. But I don't need your fawning and incessant … molly-coddling!"

Farah's gaze hardened. "Well, Raven, if that's how you feel, I suppose there's no changing your mind. All I want is to help you. But since you obviously don't want it …"

They sat in strained silence, broken only by Melodea's occasional attempt at small talk. Neither Raven nor the countess deigned to reply.

"All I will say is this, Raven." Farah stared at Raven,

unusually blunt. Her expression was flat, even cold. "If your father thought you were ready to journey on your own, he wouldn't have sent me. I am here because *you* –" she jabbed a finger – "are not ready to face the world on your own. You are still a child. So stop trying to act like a woman."

Raven bit back a retort, oddly unsettled. Farah's words brought back memories of Burglar Valley and ... *the attack*. She'd used that same, cutting tone, reminding Raven she wasn't enough. That she wasn't ready to face the world.

That she was still a helpless princess who was not, and would never be, ready to ascend the throne.

Nausea roiled her stomach. Raven concentrated on breathing; in and out, in and out. It didn't help. Drawing on every ounce of willpower she possessed, she fought the urge to break out of the carriage and run as far as her legs could take her. The only thing that kept her from doing so was the fear that she probably *would* get lost.

The forest – which had kept its distance from the road up until now – began closing in like a noose. As the sun sank lower on the horizon, a heavy fog crept in, obscuring the road. Looking out the carriage window was like opening her eyes under water. *Her entire life was a blur.*

When they finally reached Fastwater Inn, Raven wasn't the only one who was more than eager to stop for the night. Melodea fairly sighed with relief, quite done in by the tension.

The innkeeper was waiting at the door to greet them. His wife – who introduced herself as Donna – did most of the talking for both of them, giving herself airs at the princesses' arrival. Her graying hair was pulled into a tight bun, and she wore a gown of deep green that was far more costly than her station – or income – merited.

Donna snapped her fingers, sending her husband rushing forward. "Show the men where to stable their animals."

He nodded meekly. "Yes, dear." Gesturing for the carriages to follow, he scuttled behind the building towards the barn, while Donna showed the guests inside.

"Dinner will be brought to your rooms," Donna said. "If you need anything, ask my servant girl, Ashly."

Ashly, who had just appeared from the kitchen, curtsied deeply, not daring to meet anyone's eyes.

Donna scowled at the girl. "See to it that these honored guests are taken care of properly. And mind your manners," she barked. Donna bowed once more to Raven and smiled pleasantly. "If she misbehaves, I will see to it that she is properly disciplined. The girl can be unruly at times, and I would be ashamed if she caused you any trouble."

Raven raised her chin. She kept her voice civil – barely. "That won't be necessary. Thank you."

Donna acquiesced with a tilt of her head before excusing herself.

"Th-this way, please," Ashley stammered. She tripped multiple times as she ascended the stairs, apologizing profusely each time. As soon as she'd shown Raven her room, Ashly bowed and fairly fled back down the stairs.

Raven washed her face and neck while Breeanah began unpacking select wardrobe items. Their conversation – which Raven had become so accustomed to every evening – was oddly lacking, and Breeanah was quiet to the point of being evasive. Raven had opened her mouth to comment when a quiet sob broke the silence.

"Breeanah? What's wrong?" Raven wrapped her arm around the maid's thin shoulders.

Sniffling, Breeanah swiped at her eyes. "It's nothing, I just – remember when ... when I was a servant girl, like Ashly. The matron made me go without meals, even beat me when I misbehaved. I can still hear them, scolding me. *You stupid girl. Can't you do anything right?*" Breeanah reached for the suitcase latch, fingers trembling so badly she could barely grasp it. She jerked her hand back and clenched it against her chest.

"I had no idea ..." Raven sucked in a breath past the lump

constricting her throat.

Breeanah nodded slowly, using the back of her hand to push a strand of hair out of her face. Her green eyes, wide and red-rimmed, flitted between Raven's face and the floor. "It's like seeing a ghost of myself." She smiled, but her lips trembled.

Voice raw, Raven asked, "What happened?"

For a moment, Breeanah struggled, jaw working noiselessly. Finally, she whispered, "I ran."

⁛

The next morning, Raven awoke late from a fitful sleep. She hadn't asked about details from Breeanah's past, and Breeanah hadn't offered any. They'd just fallen into a companionable silence, an unspoken understanding that communicated what words couldn't.

After Breeanah helped secure the numerous undergarments – including an acutely uncomfortable corset – Raven donned her dress. It was a lime green brocade adorned with a long, silver cloth belt with matching trim around the neck and above the flare of the sleeves. The outfit was as beautiful as it was uncomfortable.

"I don't see why I have to wear such fancy dresses for a dusty trip on the road," Raven groused, clenching the arms of her chair as Breeanah brushed her hair. "It's not like I have to make an impression on any passerby villagers. And even if I did, they only see half of my dre– *ouch!*"

"Sorry, M'lady, but your hair is being especially – well, knotty," Breeanah quipped.

Raven offered a wry smile. "Well, if it wants to misbehave, then let it. Otherwise, I'll be late for breakfast, and then what would the countess think?"

When Raven arrived at the table, she was, in fact, the last one. Yet another breach in etiquette for Farah to hold against her … but at this point, who cared? The countess could think what she wanted; another week or two and Farah would be gone, back to marry her Wil*bore*. And Raven … it was best not to think about where she'd be. Or rather, who she'd be marrying. *As long as it isn't Sir Fredrick. I'd sooner elope with a stable hand.*

"Good morning, I trust you slept well?" Melodea's greeting was the epitome of politeness, as usual. Apparently, she'd recovered from her distress at Raven and the countess squabbling ... or she was finally learning to mask it.

Raven cleared her throat. "Fine." An awkward pause. "And you?"

Another pause. "Good, thank you."

Breakfast was brought in, offering a timely distraction.

Kirgan spoke through a mouthful of fish, "We should arrive at Roehn sometime this afternoon."

Raven bobbed her head, and a dull "that's good" was all she could think of to say.

Farah was more enthusiastic. "Indeed!" she exclaimed. She appeared to have forgotten – or was deliberately overlooking – yesterday's argument. "I hear the prince is quite charming."

More out of obligation than interest, Raven forced herself to smile. If the countess was willing to overlook their disagreement, Raven wasn't about to be the one to dredge it back up. "What's his name?"

"Taelon," Farah breathed. "He's a renowned hunter, and a *divine* dancer. In fact, I've heard from many women that he's the epitome of charm itself. You'll like him, Raven, honestly."

Farah prattled on, and if Raven hadn't known better, she would've believed this Taelon was a god, sent down to grace the human race with his presence.

Tristan sat on the far end of the table, actively avoiding Raven's gaze; whether it was because of the current topic or her harsh words the other night, she wasn't sure.

Raven avoided looking at him, too. Tristan's feelings were his own, and they were not her problem. She couldn't *let* them be her problem, otherwise, she'd need to trust him.

And then she'd have another problem entirely.

Princess of Roehn

Raven couldn't contain her smile as they drove away from Fastwater Inn. After listening to Breeanah's story, Raven had arranged for Ashley to work as a maid at Caritas; she would leave as soon as transport could be arranged. The innkeeper – his wife, actually – was promised substantial compensation in return.

Breeanah had thanked Raven profusely – and repeatedly.

Glancing back at the inn, Raven saw the proprietors waving, enthusiastic after their guests' generous payment. *Donna will probably have a new girl to mistreat by week's end.* The smile faded.

Silva, the capital of Roehn, lay only a half-day's travel to the north; it was a thickly forested kingdom with a prosperous timber trade. Raven had met King Albastan only once when she was young, but she remembered him as slightly rotund and good-natured. Her memories proved more than accurate.

Unlike King Taungan, Albastan met them as soon as they stepped out of the carriage, rushing forward to take Raven's shoulders and kiss her lightly on each cheek. "My dear princess, I am so glad you've come! May I offer you a most hearty welcome?"

His infectious enthusiasm left Raven no choice but to like him immediately. "Thank you, King Albastan," Raven said warmly. "My father extends his good wishes to you and your family, and thanks you for your hospitality." Wilgaun had instructed Raven to repeat the rehearsed greeting at every kingdom … and she had entirely forgotten until now. *King Taungan wouldn't have noticed*, she thought acerbically.

"Very kind, very kind," Albastan said. "Well, you must be tired, so I won't babble any longer until you've had a decent nap. Courtney, my dove, please show our guests to their rooms."

Raven watched as a lithe, slender young woman – a little

younger than her, Raven guessed – stepped forward. A mischievous grin hovered on the corner of the girl's lips; thick golden-blonde hair cascaded down to the waist of her elegant cobalt gown. She curtsied, unabashedly scrutinizing every inch of Raven.

"Oh!" Albastan added, almost as an afterthought. "This is my daughter, Courtney, the beauty and brains of the family. I'm afraid my son is off gallivanting through the forest, as usual." He chuckled, removed his crown, and ran a hand through his auburn hair, effectively undoing any ministrations of his stylist. When Albastan put the crown back on, tufts of hair stuck out in every direction.

Raven hid a grin. "A pleasure, Princess Courtney," she said, returning the curtsy.

As Albastan welcomed Melodea, Kirgan, and Farah, Courtney seized Raven's arm, leading her away from the entourage. Pulling her close, Courtney let out a giddy squeal. "I can't begin to tell you how *excited* I am you're here! I've had no suitable company for ages, and you seem *so* unlike all the noble girls I have to put up with. I think we'll be great friends!"

Equal parts flattered and overwhelmed by Courtney's enthusiasm, Raven managed a nod. "I – I hope so ..."

"And the other one must be King Taungan's daughter, Melodea?" Courtney didn't wait for Raven to reply. "She looks positively stuffy. How did you put up with her the entire trip?"

"It's only been a few days –"

"Dreadful. Absolutely dreadful. I think I'll abhor her, but my father wants me to be hospitable to both you and Melodea, so I'll try my best not to ignore her entirely. Goodness, she is *pale*, isn't she?"

Raven gave a hesitant nod of agreement, uncomfortable talking behind Melodea's back. But was it wrong if everything said about her was true?

"She's hardly spoken two words to me, and when she does, it's always prim and proper – like she's at a tea party," Raven confided.

Courtney gasped. "King Taungan has visited a few times, and he's intolerable. So is his wife, when she manages to get out of bed. I'm not surprised in the least their daughter is the same, but still … you poor thing. Can I call you Raven? You can call me Courtney, of course." Once again, she was bright and merry, disarming with her wide smile.

Raven returned the smile. "Sure." She drew herself up, assuming her most pompous air. "I think that would be appropriate, given the circumstances, for us to put aside our station and regard one another as equals."

The two princesses burst out laughing, drawing stares from Farah and Melodea.

Oblivious, Albastan shooed the guests after Courtney. "Try not to talk their ears off, Dove!"

"Oh dear." Courtney stuck out her lower lip in a mock-pout. "I was about to say the same to you."

Albastan laughed jovially. It was clear who Courtney had taken after; aside from their hair color and the size of their waists, they were quite similar. No wonder Raven liked them both.

Courtney took the guests upstairs, chatting freely and rarely letting anyone get a word in edgewise. She showed each guest to their quarters, ending with Raven. "This is the finest spare room in the castle," she boasted. "It overlooks the forest mostly, but from the balcony, you can see the soldier's barracks. I love watching them train, don't you?"

Raven shrugged noncommittally. "I'd rather go riding or practice sword fighting myself, not watch others do it."

"Riding?" Courtney gawked. "I have to introduce you to better pastimes. Riding is so mundane … sitting for hours on end in an awful side-saddle, watching the trees slowly drift by." She waved dramatically. "There are far better things to do, like croquet and billiards and such. You simply must try them."

"Trust me, if you rode the way I do, you wouldn't be bored."

"Oh?"

Glancing behind her to make sure the countess wasn't listening, Raven whispered in a conspiratorial tone, "I run my stallion as fast as he'll go. Astride."

Courtney gaped, delighted. "Astride? How scandalous! My mother would hate it!"

"Countess Farah would too – if she knew," Raven agreed impishly.

"But at least she's not old and stuffy."

Raven snorted. "She acts more like my governess than my companion."

"I could never stand *that*." Courtney clucked disapprovingly. "I've always had things my way; if someone told me otherwise, I'd fairly die of anger."

This princess was rebellious, and a bit dramatic, Raven would give her that. But it was almost refreshing, compared to all the insipid nobles' daughters. And a little rebellion didn't hurt anyone, right?

Maybe she was fishing for sympathy, or maybe she wanted someone to tell her they understood, but Raven found herself divulging her own tediously structured life. "Father assigns me tutors to make sure I know everything to one day become queen. I've never really wanted to rule, but I don't have any siblings, so the burden of the throne falls to me – which I am constantly reminded is a *privilege*." She smirked wryly. "Maybe I'm just afraid I won't measure up to everyone's expectations. Being a queen requires so many obligations."

"Oh, how dreadful. My brother will inherit the throne, so I don't have to worry about it. But even if I were first in line, I wouldn't have to rule – Father won't make *me* do *anything*," Courtney said, raising her chin defiantly. "But I'd rather like to rule – personally, I don't think my brother Taelon is capable. He's always running off, wasting his time hunting and sword fighting. Besides, he has a terrible habit of consorting with peasants. He's far too common, if you ask me."

Raven nodded, but she couldn't help noticing how Courtney had skimmed over Raven's concerns and turned her reply into another chance to talk about herself. Clearly, the young princess didn't understand the weight of the throne … or the burden. If she had, she wouldn't be so flippant about ruling. And even if Raven had sworn to dislike Taelon as a suitor, she couldn't help but agree with his methods. Getting to know the common folk was essential; even Wilgaun had allowed Raven excursions so she could understand the plight of her citizens. Before she could stop herself, she found herself echoing his words.

"My father always told me that knowing your people is essential to being a successful leader. I'm not sure you *can* be too common, in that sense."

"I suppose," Courtney said airily, unconvinced. She started, suddenly aware of the time. "You have to get changed and cleaned up for this evening! Silly me, sitting here blabbering on. Sometimes my tongue really does get away from me," Courtney apologized, though hardly contrite. "I'll send for a maid to bring you hot water at once."

"Oh, please, I can have one of my –"

"No, I am already on my way," Courtney insisted; she flashed Raven a saucy smile and shut the door.

Raven had already decided she liked the princess – she was interesting and knew her own mind. But she also had a temper and could be a bit narcissistic. Plus, if her assessment of Melodea was any indicator, she had no trouble making her dislike of others known. What if Raven and Melodea's roles had been reversed?

Raven brushed the thought – and guilt – away. Courtney only disliked Melodea because she *was* stuffy; it was a flaw on Melodea's part, not Courtney's. And not her own, either.

∞

A decisive knock reverberated through the door. "Raven? I came to fetch you for dinner," Courtney said, peeking her head through the entryway.

"I'm almost ready." Raven studied herself in the mirror, checking for last minute adjustments.

Breeanah excused herself, ducking past Courtney to have her own supper with the servants. With Raven, the maid opened up, but she barely talked around anyone else – maybe because she had trust issues, maybe because she was shy around royalty.

Courtney watched her leave. "What a sad, skinny little thing. Where'd you find her?"

Raven blushed. Breeanah *was* skinny – and gangly. And awkward. Raven had never thought about how that would reflect on her as a princess. She opened her mouth to agree with Courtney.

And then closed it with an audible snap.

Breeanah, despite her physical deficiencies, was a sweet, kind, emotionally injured girl. She deserved any good thing she could get – not Raven's, or Courtney's, criticism!

Raven's temper flared, but her words came out with deadly calmness. "Breeanah has suffered more abuse than any girl should have to go through. You have *no right* to judge her because she's thin, or because she ducks her head when she walks. You don't know her at all."

Courtney took a step backward. "I – I'm sorry," she stammered, and for a moment, she looked sincerely apologetic. But then she put on a winning smile and gave a toss of her head. "Anyway, you look lovely. I think we're going to have a *splendid* evening." Tucking Raven's arm in her own, Courtney dragged her toward the dining hall.

Raven maintained her stony silence.

As they entered the great hall, the crackle of a warm fire greeted Raven. The room was alight with dozens of tapers and lanterns; a brass chandelier was adorned with small glass orbs that reflected the golden candlelight.

King Albastan sat at the head of the table with his wife – Queen Helen – standing to his right. Helen surveyed the room with a cool, calculating gaze; dark hair framed sharp, elegant features, and she wore a tolerant expression that clearly indicated her perceived superiority to all present. The queen met Raven's eyes, smiled, and glided gracefully towards her.

Courtney leaned in and whispered, "I didn't mean it. Don't be mad at me for keeps."

Raven hesitated, then acquiesced with a reluctant smile, watching as Courtney skipped happily to her seat. After all, it wasn't Courtney that Raven was actually mad at. It was herself. She had almost gone right along with the game, picking apart Breeanah's appearance and inferior social skills. *Harmless teasing*, she would have called it. Just like she'd done with Melodea.

In that moment, Raven despised herself.

"Hello my dear. It has been far too long." Helen lightly kissed Raven's cheek. The queen's expression was one of complete benevolence; perhaps Courtney took after her mother more than Raven had initially thought. But Queen Helen was a thousand times worse.

"You remember me, naturally?" Helen continued. "You were very little when I visited your – *charming* kingdom," she added with a patently false smile.

Raven bobbed her head and forced a smile of her own. She hoped it didn't look *too* sincere. "I remember. It's nice to see you again as well."

The last time Queen Helen had visited, she had told her father what a naughty little princess he had raised, and that he really ought to discipline her more. Riding astride and playing with wooden swords was for boys, not girls.

Wilgaun had defended Raven fiercely, arguing that she was far cleverer and more capable than the *spoiled little brat* Helen was raising; he must've meant Courtney. The memory almost surprised Raven. She'd forgotten how her father had stood up for her. No matter how much he scolded her, he always defended her from spiteful noblemen and visiting royals.

Raven bit her lip, remembering her last conversations with

105

her father. They were neither pleasant nor deserving of the care he had always shown her. What happened to those times when she'd looked up to him as her hero?

Helen's words brought her back to the present with a harsh jolt. "And this must be your companion, Countess Burina. A pleasure, I'm sure."

"It's an honor to meet you, Your Majesty. Your kingdom is beautiful, and everywhere I go, I see signs of your people's prosperity." Farah gave a low curtsy.

"Why, thank you." Helen's smile widened; she was utterly taken in by Farah's smooth words. "It has taken hard work and diligence to achieve our state of affluence."

"I'm certain it has."

Albastan tapped his pewter goblet with a spoon, silencing the chatter. "Please be seated. I would like to welcome Princess Raven, Princess Melodea, Ambassador Kirgan, Countess Farah, and their company to Silva! Let's have a toast in their honor." Those present, mostly courtiers and noblemen, cheered. Raven smiled, dipping her head in acknowledgement. To her left, Melodea did the same.

After everything she had spoken behind Melodea's back, Raven found she couldn't bear to look at her.

"Now we're just missing ... Prince Taelon," King Albastan observed, an amused smile lighting on his face. "Probably off chasing dragons or hunting cave trolls."

Queen Helen's gaze narrowed. "*No doubt.*"

"I'm here, Father!"

All eyes turned to the latecomer. The prince swung the doors open and strode quickly across the room. "I apologize for my tardiness - the hunt took longer than expected." Prince Taelon made his way to his seat at the king's right hand. His black hair was long and wavy, parted off to one side and nearly reaching his shoulders. A quiver of arrows was still slung across his strong, lean back, and a hunting knife lay strapped against his thigh. Another man sat next to him, who – from his polished armor and decorated badges – Raven assumed to be the captain of the guard.

"No harm done," the king replied lightly. "Let's eat, and you can regale our honored guests with the tale."

As the feast was served and the guests dug in, Prince Taelon began his tale, green eyes sparkling with adventure. They bore the same mischievous spark as Courtney's, but with a boyishness that belied his sister's coquettish glint.

"My men and I stole through the forest, making our way around the large glacial lake, north of the castle. Nothing moved. The woods were as still as a hushed starry night on the northern tundra. Only the wind whispered through the branches, stalking us like a wild cat." Taelon looked around. His gaze rested on Raven for a moment, and he grinned.

"We prepared to move on when a rustling came from the brush nearby. We thought it was a rabbit or maybe a deer, but what emerged from the woods was far, far bigger. And far angrier." He paused again, allowing the suspense to seep into his audience.

"The rustling grew louder, getting closer. The horses began to grow uneasy. We were about to retreat … and then a huge, smelly, wild boar came tearing out of the underbrush, straight for us!" Taelon slapped the table, causing a few nearby courtiers to jump. Raven quirked a brow, trying to hide her growing smile. It wouldn't do for her to encourage him … but his tale, if true, was rather engaging.

"As the boar charged, he sent us scattering on our mounts. He was livid with bloodlust and rage that we – so puny of hunters – would dare to hunt such a mighty beast! He left us no time to recover before he charged again. Scrambling, we broke apart, surrounding the creature in a semi-circle. When the boar charged again, we were ready. A volley of spears rained down, but only one found its mark. The beast fled, squealing in a frenzied fury, with a lone spear protruding from his side."

"The prince's spear, I might add," the captain of the guard

107

put in mid-chew.

Taelon laughed, unconcerned with the detail. "Yes, Captain, my spear. So, naturally, we took chase! He led a merry one at that, and it was nearly a half-hour before he made it to the far side the lake, where he took his last stand. One of my men almost took a tusk to the leg, but at last we felled the mighty creature." He leaned back, and the noblemen let out a collective sigh of appreciation. "It took all our strength just to lift that beast onto the canvas, but now – even as we speak - we have a fine boar being roasted in our kitchen!"

Taelon stood with a bow as everyone applauded, and Raven couldn't help but be drawn to this cavalier prince. He was still a boy in many ways, but he was good-natured and sincere. And yet ... could she marry him? Love him? She should *want* to love him; she liked his family – except maybe his mother – and he was handsome and adventurous. But the thought of loving him seemed as absurd as loving a brother or a good friend. He simply wasn't *that type.*

Would her father expect her to marry Taelon? He was the only prince among their allies close to Raven in age. But if she married him, and he inherited the throne of Roehn, who would rule Laynia in her father's stead? Maybe, just maybe, that reason alone would keep her father from arranging a marriage between them.

It was a tenuous maybe.

Albastan roared with laughter, slapping his son on the back. "Good job, my boy! Our prince is one of the finest hunters in the land, although he'll never admit it!"

The prince chuckled. "Father, you know perfectly well that the men *let* me take the final blow."

The captain was quick to protest. "Absurd, Majesty. You always beat us to the kill before we have a chance to throw our spears."

"Because you're deliberately slow!" Taelon insisted, gaping with mock indignation.

The captain grinned. "Whatever you have to tell yourself, Highness."

The sharp clearing of Queen Helen's throat broke off the banter. Her words were quiet, but Raven could just make out Helen's reprimand. "That's quite enough of your silliness, Son. You ought to be talking with our guests, not reliving the hunt with your men." Her significant glance in Raven's direction was unmistakable.

Taelon dipped his head in acknowledgement. "Of course, Mother."

Mother. The word brought a host of unbidden feelings to Raven's mind. What was it like? Having a mother who talked with you, scolded you, loved you? Who was always there for you? Queen Helen certainly didn't seem like the most tender mother, but at least she was still there for her children.

What kind of mother would Queen Mariah have been? Raven knew little about her – Father rarely talked about his wife, although Synthia occasionally described her. Always kind, beautiful, and gentle – exactly what a queen ought to be. A difficult measure to live up to. Sometimes Raven imagined she could see her father watching her, comparing her to his perfect wife. No wonder he was always disappointed in his unruly, imperfect daughter.

A light hand touched her arm, and Raven jumped.

Melodea had been studying Raven, that much was apparent. "Are you alright?" she whispered, her large, soft eyes filled with … *compassion?*

Raven could feel Courtney's gaze from across the table, observing the interaction with a curious – or was it disapproving? – expression on her face. Raven quickly looked away, busying herself with her food.

With a curt tilt of her head, Raven replied coolly, "I'm fine."

Melodea withdrew her hand.

Truth Revealed

Later that evening, they gathered around the great hall's roaring fire, where a jester performed a comedic act. Raven barely noticed. Instead, her thoughts drifted back to Mariah. What had happened to her? Synthia adamantly refused to talk about it, and Raven had only dared to ask her father once, long ago. The only response he'd had on the subject was that he would "explain when she was older." An infuriating answer which offered absolutely no reassurances.

It was time she found out for herself.

"King Albastan?"

Albastan turned, smiling benevolently at Raven. "What can I do for you, my dear?"

This was it. This was her chance. But could she go behind her father's back, even to discover the truth about her mother?

No, it wasn't going behind his back. If Wilgaun had wanted to tell her, he would have. He forfeited his chance – and his right – to withhold the story of Mariah's death. Albastan was the only person she'd met who might know what happened but didn't answer to her father. Raven set her jaw. "Tell me what happened to my mother."

He shifted, stalling. "Has your father ... not told you?"

Raven shook her head. "But don't I have a right to know?" She gazed steadily into his eyes, hoping her resolve would be enough to sway him.

It was.

Albastan dipped his head in acknowledgement. "Very well. But I warn you, this is not a happy tale."

Taking a deep breath, Raven steeled herself. "Nevertheless, I *need* to hear it. I'm ready."

Albastan began.

110

And in some ways, Raven wished he never had.

ഔ

Seventeen years earlier, after the assault on Caritas ...

The bodyguard stumbled out of the high tower, feet skidding in his haste down the staircase. Each step took only a fraction of a second; each step took an eternity. Overextending, he missed a stair and crashed onto the hard stone slabs, leaving a dent in his shin and a small trickle of blood. He quickly pulled himself to his feet and kept running.

He *had* to keep running.

ഔ

The king tapped his fingers on the council table, rings forming an erratic rhythm. If any of his commanders noticed, they gave no indication. Tracing the upper section of the topographical map, Wilgaun created an invisible line above Caritas. "Send out scouts to the forests bordering Tharland and here," he pointed, "southwest towards the sea. If we can find out who is behind this attack, perhaps –"

Footsteps approached with alarming speed. Wilgaun whirled around, drawing his sword and levelling it at the neck of the intruder.

The intruder – who happened to be Wilgaun's unfortunate bodyguard – slid to a stop, gasping for air and raising his arms in a pitiable defense.

Wilgaun rolled his eyes, sheathing his sword. He had lost interest in the man the moment he identified him. His gaze returned to the map. "As I was saying –"

For the first time in his life, the guard had the audacity to interrupt Wilgaun. "Sire ... it's Queen Mariah!"

A pit formed in Wilgaun's stomach. It took him a full ten seconds to form the question. "What happened?"

"In the high tower. He said – come alone," the guard panted.

"Who?" Wilgaun demanded, advancing towards the guard.

Flinching, the man raised a hand protectively over his head. "I don't know, I don't know!! H-he called himself ... Nimrooden!"

Nimrooden. The word struck Wilgaun like a physical blow. "*What*?" he roared. "And you left her, my wife – *your queen* – alone with him?"

The guard's mouth formed a wordless cry, eyes squeezed shut, head cowered in subservience.

Afraid of his king.

Wilgaun swallowed, tried to force down the anger rising inside him. He laid his hand on the guard's shoulder. "It – isn't your fault."

The guard raised his head incredulously.

"It's mine." The admission was painful to swallow. A dozen protests rose to Wilgaun's mind – the guard had misheard his order; the castle hadn't been watched closely enough. But it all ultimately came down to him and his decisions. The clarity of his orders, the consequences of his decision to send Mariah to the most remote portion of the castle, where no guards were stationed. *Where* he *found her*.

Turning to Captain Illan, Wilgaun's gaze hardened. "Follow me – *quietly* – with your best men. But do not enter until I say so!"

Illan frowned, nodded reluctantly.

Wilgaun's grip tightened on his sword hilt. "The only blood left to be spilled is Nimrooden's."

෴

"Ah, you are not one to keep your guest waiting. Good."

The soft, lilting intonation gave Wilgaun pause. Sword in hand, he cautiously advanced into the darkened room. Illan and two of his men stood ready at the door; a dozen men were making their way up the staircase at that very moment.

And yet Wilgaun had never felt more out of control in his life.

"Where. Is. My. Wife?" The king's words fell with deathly calm; a stark contrast to the tempest raging inside him.

Nimrooden made no reply. Pacing towards the window, he ran his finger along the sill. The sun broke through the cloud cover, and a multitude of crepuscular rays cast a deathly shroud around his imposing figure. "Do you think I am so foolish as to relinquish my greatest bargaining chip? I have demands."

Nimrooden turned, stepping forward into the light of the lone lantern that hung in the center of the room. His eyes glinted; they were a pale, decaying blue, flecked with yellow. Predator eyes, utterly devoid of any feeling except primal dominance and bloodlust.

Eyes Wilgaun had never expected to see again.

Nimrooden paused, daring Wilgaun to challenge him. When the king didn't reply, Nimrooden resumed pacing. "My ultimatum is this: surrender the kingdom and all its forces. Or watch your family die." At the snap of his fingers, two men emerged from the shadows. Bound and gagged, Mariah was dragged between them and thrown roughly onto the floor. Princess Raven, held by one of the men, wailed and squirmed against her captor's awkward grip.

For the first time in his life, Wilgaun found himself without words. For all his power as a king, he was … *helpless*. Useless. Powerless. Yes, that's what it came down to – he had been stripped of every advantage that royalty granted him; he had been laid bare, forced to choose between his duty and his heart. All because he hadn't killed Nimrooden when he'd had the chance.

Wilgaun stared at Mariah, lips forming her name. But no sound came out. Would Nimrooden really kill her? Wilgaun didn't doubt that this madman would.

He had every reason to take revenge.

Wilgaun's eyes met Mariah's. His wife or his kingdom? That's what Nimrooden's ultimatum boiled down to. Give up his people, his crown, abandon every oath he'd sworn as king. Or watch as his wife and daughter were murdered before his very eyes.

Wilgaun stared at his wife, pleading. *Decide. You have to decide for me. Ask me to give up my kingdom.*

But before she answered, Wilgaun already knew her decision.

&

Mariah knew her decision before Wilgaun comprehended the ultimatum. There was no choice, no question … Nimrooden's word could not be trusted.

She of all people should know.

Her eyes flitted to her husband's. Ask. That's what he wanted … an assurance that losing his kingdom was worth the cost. He wanted Mariah to excuse his surrender.

And her answer was no.

Nimrooden ripped away the queen's gag, and lint flooded her parched throat; she coughed dryly. Biting her lip, Mariah gazed steadily at her husband and nodded.

An assent to her execution.

Her captors moved away at Nimrooden's approach. Leaning close, his breath hissed into her ear; her final warning. "Any last words, *my lady*?"

Mariah glared, spitting indecorously at his feet. She'd been waiting to do that for a long time.

Turning back to Wilgaun, her mouth slowly curled into a smile. "It's alright," she whispered.

A tear ran down Wilgaun's face. Inhaling a shaky breath, his lips moved noiselessly, begging Mariah to yield.

So he did love her after all.

His tears were the final push, the strength needed to turn her resolve into action. Mariah glanced up at her precious daughter. Raven's face was red and scrunched from crying, but she had fallen into an uneasy silence, and simply stared at her mother.

"I love you, my precious daughter," Mariah murmured.

Struggling for balance, the queen stood. Awaiting her death.

&

Wilgaun cleared his throat. He tried to speak – tried to

114

proclaim his decision. Words that would end the lives of those most precious to him.

They wouldn't come.

Nimrooden smirked, content to watch the king destroy himself. Wilgaun could feel the hatred, the venomous contempt. No matter what choice he made, Nimrooden would still come out on top. It was check mate in the truest sense of the words. Only it wasn't the king who would die in this diabolical game – it was his wife and child.

He couldn't be responsible for their deaths.

Bowing his head, Wilgaun spoke the words that would betray his country … and his wife's trust. "I accept your terms of surrend–"

Mariah whirled around, slamming her bound hands into the face of the nearest captor. Before the other could react, she had snatched Raven from his grasp and begun running towards Wilgaun.

And Nimrooden's sword plunged through her heart.

"Mariah!" The scream erupted from Wilgaun's throat. He rushed blindly towards her, caught her as she fell and eased her to the ground. Raven slipped from her mother's arms, rolling gently to the ground. Wilgaun was vaguely aware of men rushing into the room, watched as Illan and ten other soldiers cut Nimrooden's men down where they stood. Heard Raven's cries as Illan picked her up, rocking the babe.

But Wilgaun's gaze was transfixed on Nimrooden.

A dark rage flashed across Nimrooden's face as his eyes flicked from the guards, to Wilgaun, and then to Mariah's fallen form. He slowly backed away, stopping only when his back struck the far wall. "*You will regret this.*"

Lunging, Nimrooden crashed through the window. Amidst shards of glass and droplets of blood, he plummeted into the moat below, disappearing beneath its murky waters. Arrows nocked, the guards waited for their target to resurface, but he never did.

And the king clutched Mariah's broken body and wept.

"I'm sorry!" he gasped. Tears ran down his short beard, tapping lightly against his breast plate and onto Mariah's crimson-stained gown. "Sorry that I was never there for you ... sorry I could never be the husband you needed me to be." He groaned, rocking back and forth and stroking her soft black hair. "This is all my fault!"

Mariah's warm hand touched his face, and a smile lit upon her beautiful, blood-flecked lips. "Shh. It's alright. Just take – care – of her. Love her – like you couldn't ... love me." She began to cough, shivering uncontrollably. Wilgaun ripped off his armor, cradling his wife against the warmth of his chest.

"I can't – I can't do it without –"

Mariah grasped the back of his neck. "You have to!"

An eternity later, Wilgaun nodded.

Exhaling slowly, Mariah lay her head back against Wilgaun. "Good," she murmured. "Please ... let me hold her?"

Illan cautiously strode forward, kneeling and gently placing Raven in the arms of her mother. Then, without a spoken word, the captain and his men quietly left the room.

Left Wilgaun to say goodbye to his wife.

Laying her cheek against Raven's downy head, Mariah's eyes fluttered shut. Gradually, Raven's whimpers ceased. Gradually, Wilgaun's tears slowed.

And gradually, the queen's chest stilled.

Wilgaun stroked her ashen cheek, hand shaking. Slowly, his eyes turned upwards; bitterness seeped like poison into his heart. "How can you do this to me?" he shouted to the heavens. "You said you would be with me, and now you have taken *everything*! Why?!"

A quiet cry was all that answered the king – the only part of Mariah he had left.

Her daughter.

Wilgaun lifted the babe, cradling her softly. Her pure, innocent gaze condemned him. He had failed them both – not just his wife, but his child as well.

But the High Regium had failed them all.

Kissing his daughter's forehead, he slowly rose, glaring at the roof as if he could see through it straight to the kingdom of heaven. "You were never with me. *Never*." He walked from the room, leaving his fallen queen behind.

And his God, who his queen had trusted unto death.

∞

Raven stared at Albastan, her face void of emotion. Instead, the emotions swirled in her eyes, a torrent of thoughts screaming to be released. An aching love for her mother. Rage at Nimrooden. And a new-found compassion for her father. The moment she grasped one coherent thought, a different took its place, leaving her lost – a boat without an anchor, a tree without roots.

A child without its mother.

Albastan touched her shoulder, said something to console her. But Raven didn't hear any of it. Her father loved her. He loved her so much, he would have given up his kingdom so that she and her mother could live.

And for now, that was enough.

BETRAYAL

Sleep toyed with Raven like a cat with its prey, stalking her through the tendrils of mist that swirled in her mind. One minute she wanted to cry, the next to run into her father's arms and have him make everything right. But mostly, she wanted to see Nimrooden's face when she ran her sword through his gut.

Except for crying, none of those scenarios were likely to happen any time soon, so Raven eventually gave up trying to sleep and threw on her cloak. She slipped by the sleepy guards posted outside her door, whispered she'd be back soon.

Her bare feet padded softly against the flagstone. Cold seeped up her legs. As she stepped into the cool night air, the fog swirling in her head dissipated. A thousand stars blinked down on her from the heavens, dancing around the waxing moon. Raven exhaled quietly, finally able to breathe.

And then she heard voices.

Gripping her cloak tighter around her, Raven crept through the shadows towards the sound. No one should have been out at this hour. Aside from the occasional guard, the entire castle slept. And why would anyone meet in the courtyard? It was cold, dark, and secluded. *Unless* ... Raven paused, blushing. Unless two lovers were meeting in secret. That *would* be embarrassing to stumble upon.

A raised voice halted *that* train of thought, and she continued creeping forward. The voice sounded oddly familiar, almost like ... *Sir Kisby*? Raven ducked behind an ivy-laden arbor and peered through the trellis. Trying to ignore the pounding of her heart as it fought to escape her chest.

Under the gazebo, a small group huddled around a low-burning candle. They wore hooded cloaks, but even with their disguises, Raven identified Kisby and the countess. The third she didn't recognize.

"Are we going to visit every wretched kingdom in Alarkin? I say we act now!" Kisby slammed his fist on the table, glaring down the other two figures.

Farah started to answer, but the third person raised his hand, halting her. "Patience. We must wait until Gauln gives the order." Raven recognized the voice – Ambassador Kirgan. So all three of them *were* in on ... whatever this was.

Whatever Tristan had tried to warn her about.

"All due respect, sir, but I'm done playing this charade," Kisby said. His words sounded taut, like they were spoken through clenched teeth. "After we leave Silva, we should wait outside of Tharland for word from Gauln. At that point, she'll obviously suspect, so we'll just tie her up. No more diplomacy, no more kissing up to pompous royals. And no one will be the wiser."

"Why, Kisby – are you nervous?" Kirgan asked, amused. "What could possibly happen? Our naïve little princess hasn't a clue; Farah has kept her distracted with petty worries about suitors and kingdoms. And all the guards are on our side!" He slapped Kisby on the back, earning a grunt. "Are you worried about the servants? I'm sure they would lead a dangerous revolt, armed with fans and kitchen utensils."

Nausea churned in Raven's stomach. *All* the guards? But that meant ...

"That's not entirely true." Kisby shifted uncomfortably. "That boy – Tristan – was never supposed to come, but General Altin insisted he be brought for additional training and hands-on experience. I presumed he would be killed in the attack at Burglar Valley, but ..." He shrugged. "As you can see, he's very much alive. And not bad with a blade, either."

Presumed he would be killed? Meaning Kisby knew about, if not orchestrated, the attack? *He sentenced all those men to death for a façade.* Or was she the intended target?

No – the entire attack was to kill Tristan. To silence him.

Kisby had wanted to make sure there was no chance of being discovered, so he'd arranged for an inconspicuous way to dispose of Tristan. Unfortunately for Kisby, his plan had backfired, planting the seed of suspicion in Tristan that never would have existed had it not been for the attack.

Raven groaned inaudibly. Tristan had almost died because of his innocence, his loyalty to Wilgaun, then risked his life to warn her. And what had she done? She'd almost thrown him to the wolves! What would have happened if she'd told Kisby about Tristan's suspicions?

Kirgan gripped the table, leaning inches from Kisby's face. "You compromised this mission based on a *presumption?* He could expose you! He knows you lied to Taungan's face – not to mention Princess Raven. Exactly how did you expect to answer those charges?"

"Enough." Kisby waved him away. "I knew he wouldn't have the nerve to contradict me. And even if he did, none of my men would back his story. He'd be decried as an instigator, at best. At worst, unsound of mind. And we know what happens to lunatics ..." He let the implication settle in.

If Raven had told Kisby, Tristan would've been dead before she could blink. She'd nearly signed his death sentence! *Kisby isn't the only traitor. I almost became one myself.*

"Still, this changes things," Kirgan said. "We need to contact Gauln immediately and ask him to –"

"You *gentlemen* could stand there fretting, or I could tell you our next move," Farah interrupted. A smile crept across her lips, barely visible beneath the folds of her hood.

Raven should have been mad. Should have been furious. But she was beyond both. It was so obvious! Farah *conveniently* introducing herself to Wilgaun right as he was searching for Raven's companion. No doubt Kirgan was behind Farah's sudden appearance, along with Kisby's help. Altogether, the injustice of this insurgence was enough to make Raven's blood boil.

But Raven felt nothing, no rage, no sense of betrayal. Only a mind-numbing ache that spread over her entire body.

Kisby snorted. "Why didn't you say so in the first place?"

"Maybe I find pleasure in watching you bicker like children."

"Farah, focus. What is the message?" Kirgan said shortly.

Still smirking, Farah conceded with a patronizing nod. "We act now. King Nimrooden and his men are camped on the eastern fringe of Tharland. He ordered us to join him." Her smile widened. "With the princess in irons."

Raven let out a quiet gasp as a single word broke through her numbness. She stifled the noise with her hand. *Nimrooden? He's still alive?* And he was hunting *her*.

Kisby glanced in her direction. Had he heard her gasp? Taking a slow step forward, he stared over the waist-high lattice, peering into the inky darkness above her head. Raven didn't dare to breathe.

Kirgan chuckled. "Hearing ghosts, Kisby?"

"Nothing of the sort." Kisby watched a moment longer before turning back to the others. "Just the wind."

Raven sucked in a lungful of air.

"Very well. We depart Silva in two days," Kirgan said. "Once we're outside the walls, we'll kill that welp of a guard, along with the servants. Then we transport the princess – in irons," he nodded to Farah, "and join Gauln in Tharland."

"The army marches on Laynia within the fortnight," Farah concluded. "Wilgaun won't refuse a second time – when he sees our army and his daughter in chains, he'll surrender." She gave a throaty laugh. "And we'll butcher his men like pigs at the slaughter."

The word *slaughter* rang in Raven's ears, drowning out the sound of retreating footsteps.

Kisby was the last to leave, stepping off the pavilion dangerously close to Raven. She curled tighter into a ball and hid her face and hands from the torchlight, eyes squeezed shut. Only after the last of his footsteps had faded away did Raven dare to let her heart resume beating.

"Tristan," she whispered, "what have I done?"

ᔑᓂ

"Princess, there you are! You took so long – I grew worried."

One of Raven's guards nearly collided into her halfway down the hallway. His gaze darted everywhere, almost like he was searching to make sure they weren't being watched. *More like making sure no one has discovered how negligent he's been during the Traitor's Meeting.* Raven could feel her cheeks flushing in an attempt to keep her anger from showing.

"I'm fine. I … just went to the privy." She continued toward her room – a good excuse to hide the grimace spreading across her face. The privy, really? For fifteen minutes? As far as excuses went, that was as lame as they came.

"Oh, my apologies." His face was even brighter red than Raven's. "You didn't see anyone?"

"Should I have?" Raven barely forced the words out. If this man had any sense at all, he'd realize she was play-acting – and doing a pretty poor job at it, for that matter.

The guard sighed quietly. "No, of course not."

Not that he was doing a great job acting himself.

Reaching her room, Raven about-faced, sending the guard scuttling backwards. "Thank you for checking on me. Goodnight!"

Before he could answer, she slammed the door shut, then leaned against it and slowly sank to the floor. Outside, her guards talked in muted voices; she couldn't make out words, but she had no doubt they were talking about her.

Now what? Nimrooden had resurfaced after seventeen years, with plans to capture her and overthrow Wilgaun. Escape was impossible. Her guards wouldn't let her out a second time tonight, and once Kisby informed them of the new plan, they'd be watching her more closely. And even if she *could* escape, where would she possibly go? Ride all the way back to Laynia … by herself?

122

Raven shot to her feet, started pacing across the room. If she had to, yes! Her father had no idea what was coming. Kirgan said an army was on its way – without warning, Laynia would be overtaken. She wasn't about to stay and become Gauln's leverage to overthrow her father's kingdom.

But the real question was *how*. How to escape her room and into the barn, where Freedom was stabled, and how to get out of Silva unnoticed.

And most importantly, how to alert Tristan … before he was killed.

ESCAPE OR ...

Raven awoke with a start. Had she fallen asleep? It was just past dawn – too early to expect visitors, or to leave. She growled in frustration. Last night's planning hadn't gotten her very far; if she left her room, she'd be stopped at the gate, or overtaken on the road, or ...

The negative outcomes were endless.

The doorknob rattled, sending Raven scuttling behind a drape, knife in hand. Technically, it was a letter opener, but it was the only weapon within reach. Had her guard been suspicious and reported her? Was Kisby going to take her prisoner early, rather than risk her escaping? Or had Nimrooden ordered her killed instead? Her grip tightened around the handle.

The door finally opened, and a figured stepped into the room, armed with firewood and protected by a thin, rat-hemmed skirt.

Raven let out an audible exhale of relief, stepping from her hiding spot. "Breeanah!"

Breeanah jumped, dropping the load of firewood. "Oh, Princess!" She launched into her customary apology. "I'm so sorry, I didn't know you were awake, and you startled me, and I dropped the wood –" She stopped abruptly. "Why do you have a letter opener?"

Raven grinned sheepishly, setting the blade back on her desk. "Um, long story." She glanced out the hallway, checking both ways, before shutting the door and beckoning Breeanah closer. Raven's voice dropped to a whisper. "Tristan was right all along. Kisby, Farah, Kirgan – they betrayed me, all of them. They plan to take me prisoner to their leader, Nimrooden." Raven squeezed her eyes shut, determined not to cry.

Crying accomplished nothing, and she wouldn't show

weakness, even to Breeanah. But a lump still managed to lodge itself in her throat.

Breeanah gaped. "I – we – what will you do?" she stuttered.

Gaze narrowing, Raven pursed her lips. "I have a plan."

∞

The maid bowed her head as she passed the guards, hair hidden under her wimple, eyes lowered. True to her station, dirt smudged her face, and her clothes needed washing. But she walked a little too boldly and with a little too upright of posture. However, the guards only gave her a perfunctory glance before losing interest. No one paid attention to a servant – which worked to her advantage.

As soon as she was out of sight, Raven grinned, though she didn't dare to remove her disguise just yet. *So far, so good.* But would he give her another chance?

Raven wandered around the yard until she found the entrance to the soldier's sleeping quarters. They were in a relatively similar location to those on her castle grounds, so finding them was the easy part. Getting Tristan alone, and convincing him to help, would be the hard part.

She hesitated in front of the doors. Should she knock? Send a male servant in to fetch him? No, she didn't want to wait around for a servant to pass by. Raven raised her hand to knock – and the door swung outward. She jumped to the side to avoid being hit.

To her shock, Tristan strode out, continuing towards the castle without so much as glancing her way. Raven gathered her wits enough to follow him but hesitated to call out. Better not to attract undue attention. She closed the distance and reached out to tap him on the shoulder.

Before her fingers landed, Tristan whirled around and leveled his sword at her throat. "Uh – excuse me, miss. I sensed I was being followed …" Tristan's studied her, sheathing his sword. "Why *were* you following me, anyway?"

Raven beckoned, leading him into the shadows. Glancing

125

both ways, she removed her wimple, and her dark hair cascaded downwards.

"Princess!" Tristan dropped to one knee. "I didn't recognize you. Forgive me for drawing my sword." A flicker of amusement crossed his face, but he quickly hid it.

"Get up ... and don't call me that!" Raven hissed, tugging at his sleeve. Her eyes darted around to see if anyone had noticed.

Confused, Tristan stood. "Why are you – "

"Hush – not here! Follow me." Raven pulled him behind a wain piled high with straw, pressing him up against the side boards. "Listen and listen close!"

Quickly, she recapped what she'd overheard in the courtyard the night before. "So, if I don't escape, I'll be taken to their leader, Gauln – whoever he is," she finished. Her mouth went dry. "All I know is he works for Nimrooden – an enemy from my father's past. His plan is to invade Laynia and use me as leverage against my father, forcing him to surrender."

Tristan nodded slowly, taking it all in. "I've heard stories of Nimrooden. Few enough talk about him, but word gets around." His gaze wandered off. "And to think ... Kisby was working for the man behind the attack in Burglar Valley the whole time ..."

"I'm sorry I didn't believe you, Tristan, and –" She swallowed down her pride. "I'm sorry for taking out my fear on you. I never should have talked to you the way I did. And I understand if you don't want to help me."

Raven lowered her gaze, suddenly aware of her dirty clothes and smudged face. She had no power as princess now – Tristan could easily hand her over to Kisby, or ignore her, and she'd be helpless to stop him. By turning to him, she was placing her fate in his hands. Surrendering her destiny, so to speak. Leaving her vulnerable – helpless. *Had she made a mistake in coming to Tristan for help?*

Raven had just made up her mind to walk away and take her chances alone when Tristan's fingers touched her jaw, gently lifting her head to face him. He grinned. "What's your plan, Princess?" Her title was spoken no louder than a whisper in that teasing lilt only Tristan used.

Relief coursed through her and she returned the smile. "My chambermaid is tending to me 'sick in bed.' She'll direct the other servants to hide as soon as you and I leave – I doubt Kirgan would bother with them once he discovers I'm missing. He'll be too busy trying to find me." She nodded, more to convince herself, and added, "You and I need to be gone before Kirgan figures out I'm not in my room – by nightfall, at latest. We'll ride back to Laynia and warn my father to prepare for war."

War. Had it really come to that?

"That doesn't give us much time. We'll ride through Tharland to cut a few days off our journey." He raised an eyebrow. "What about Princess Melodea?"

Raven frowned. "I hadn't thought about it. Maybe she can stay here with the servants."

"Unless you think King Taungan would be overjoyed that you abandoned his daughter, I wouldn't advise it. Besides, who knows what Kirgan would do if she stays? As it is, I'm worried about your maid. She has put herself in a very precarious position by covering for you."

"We can't very well go traipsing around the countryside with an entire *entourage*, now can we?" Raven felt guilty enough about Breeanah without Tristan voicing her fears. "But you're right," she conceded, "Melodea has to come with us – at least to the nearest village. She can make her way home from there."

"Agreed. We'll gather what provisions we need, then depart. Do you know where to get some –"

Raven slung a bag off her shoulder, revealing provisions and water canteens. Lifting her hem a fraction, she exposed the sword hidden beneath her skirt. She couldn't help picturing Farah's horrified expression if she'd seen Raven. *Raising your skirt above your ankles – and in the presence of a man? How absolutely vulgar!* the countess would say. Then again, Farah hardly had

127

grounds to be criticizing Raven's behavior anymore.

Chuckling, Tristan took the bag and tied it to his belt. "Great. With you and Princess Melodea dressed as servants, I can persuade the guards to let us out. Try and get a hold of a basket of dirty laundry to carry between you. From there we'll –"

"Wait - there's something I didn't tell you." She touched his arm. "You're the only guard not in on Kisby's betrayal. As soon as we left Silva … they planned on killing you. They'll never let you out; they won't risk your escape."

Tristan remained expressionless, but alarm flashed through his eyes. "I'll find another way, trust me." His jaw set. "I will."

ONLY HOPE

Breeanah absently twirled her hair, staring at the elegant furnishings: rich drapes, thick carpets, and a plush bedspread. *The price for these could feed a family for months.* Such opulence was something she'd lived with for most of her life – always to see, never touch, except to clean. In the past, she'd worked for many wealthy households – none to compare to King Wilgaun's castle, or this one for that matter, but all excessively lavish.

Not that luxury in itself was wrong, but she'd seen the way rich people regarded their servants; most didn't deign to give them a scrap from their table. Princess Raven seemed to be an exception. Actually, since coming to Laynia, Breeanah had been treated better than she could remember since … well, ever. *If only I could say the same for the other places I've served.*

She had just started to relax, sinking a little too comfortably into one of the plush sofas, when a knock on the door sent her bolt upright.

"Princess Raven, are you alright? You weren't at breakfast."

Ambassador Kirgan – and he's asking for Raven! Breeanah took a deep, calming breath, rehearsing her speech as she crossed the room. Cracking the door open, she curtsied deeply to the ambassador. "M'lady is not feeling well, and I'm afraid is not fit to see anyone at the moment." *Which was more or less true.* She hated having to lie, but if she told a partial truth to save a life …

Kirgan frowned, trying to peer around Breeanah. "I'm sorry to hear that. But I really must speak with her – a change in plans," he said, flashing a reassuring smile. "May I come in?"

"As I said, she's not fit to see anyone. She's *indisposed*. I'll tell her you called, and you may check on her later, if you wish." Before Kirgan could answer, Breeanah quickly shut the door in his face.

Did I really just give an order to the ambassador of Laynia? She

129

laughed breathlessly, which turned into a nervous hiccough. Now was not the time to be celebrating small victories; the princess had to be warned, and soon. If Breeanah put the ambassador off for too long, he'd grow suspicious, which could compromise the entire escape plan.

Once she was sure Kirgan had left, Breeanah grabbed her worn satchel, threw it over her shoulder, and began snatching a few valuables. Princess Raven had no need of them; she had a dozen replacements for each of these necklaces and jeweled handbags.

But where Breeanah was going, she would need every spare valuable she could lay her hands on.

She had just turned to flee when a sparkle of light caught her eye, and she paused. It had black eyes and its whole body was crusted in pale green gem fragments, no bigger than grains of sand. The wings and tail were white, and larger white gems adorned the back and traced the wings.

Breeanah eyed it for a moment and crammed it into the sack as well. Seconds later, she rushed out of the room, mumbling an explanation to the guards about fetching Raven some soothing broth. That gave her the perfect excuse to race to the servant's staircase, into the kitchen, and to the breakfast table, where all the servants were just sitting down to eat after serving the royal family. She scanned the gathering until her eyes lit on a tall, dark haired manservant.

"Drin!" Breeanah hissed, beckoning.

Drin turned to face her, eyes lighting up. He left his half-eaten mound of pancakes and followed her out of the kitchen into the hallway. Not for the first time, Breeanah noticed how small and thin she was compared to the large, well-muscled man. *He could snap me in half like a twig if he wanted to, and here I am about to order him around.* Her cheeks colored slightly, and she hesitated, unsure of what to say.

Still smiling, Drin raised his eyebrows expectantly. "Did you want something?"

She returned a half-smile. "Yes. No. Sort of." She brushed a piece of hair out of her eyes; normally she wore it pulled back in her wimple, but since the princess had borrowed most of her clothing, Breeanah's hair fell loose about her shoulders and onto her gown. The dress was far above her station, despite being the plainest in Princess Raven's wardrobe. Hardly conducive to clandestine meetings and secret comings and goings.

Breeanah shoved her hand into her pocket, withdrawing a crumpled piece of paper. She handed it to Drin. "I need you to deliver this to the princess. After that, you need to get all the other servants to safety as soon as possible."

"What - why?"

"It happened."

Drin froze. "You mean –"

Breeanah jerked her head. "Princess Raven will make her own escape, but I have to take care of some things first. You have to make sure all the other servants are out of sight until Kirgan is gone."

"This isn't how we planned it. Are you sure I can't go with you?" Drin asked quietly.

Breeanah gazed into his warm brown eyes, drawing from his strength. "I have to do this alone. Goodbye for now, Drin – may the High Regium watch over you." She quickly kissed his cheek and vanished back into the shadows.

"And you as well," Drin whispered.

☙

Raven, Tristan, and Melodea crept down the back hallways of the castle, making their way towards the rear exit through the kitchen. Even after Melodea agreed to come with them, Raven still wasn't sure if she believed their story; in fact, she spoke so little, Raven didn't know much about her, period.

Melodea had agreed to arrange passage for herself to Mieldren at the closest possible town, which was a relief. *The less time I have to spend around her, the better,* Raven thought. Having the 'perfect princess' around all the time was just another reminder what an absolute mess Raven had gotten herself into. Not to mention the nasty words she'd spoken behind Melodea's back. They hung over her head constantly – and she couldn't afford distractions. Not with so much at stake.

"Ouch!" Raven's face collided with Tristan's back, and she stumbled backward, almost running into Melodea. "What are you –"

"Shh!" Tristan hissed. "The door is being guarded by some of our – *Kisby's* men." He motioned the princesses to go back, then followed them around the corner. "We'll have to find another way out."

Raven scowled. "That makes no sense. Why would our men be here, unless ..." She squeezed her eyes shut. "Unless they knew we were coming. Stupid, *stupid* princess!"

Melodea looked up, almost affronted. "I'm sorry?"

Waving her away, Raven addressed Tristan. "The guards must have reported my absence last night, and someone grew suspicious. Now they're guarding the exits as a precaution."

A group of servants passed; Raven led the others into a supply closet, bolting the door behind her. She'd replaced the wimple, but even without her black hair, some of her servants might recognize her. Unlike the guards, they hadn't been up all night. If any of the servants reported Raven, the guards would be after her in seconds.

Once they'd passed, Raven started pacing. "I hate all this hiding!" she growled. "I'd rather fight my way out, bloody the whole lot of traitors."

Tristan dared a laugh. "*You'd* rather fight? How do you think *I* feel?"

A quiet thumping rattled the door. Tristan's hand shot to his sword as Raven squinted through the keyhole. She let out a quiet breath of relief, unbolting the door.

"Drin, what are you doing here?" Raven asked. Behind her, Tristan grunted his displeasure at the surprise.

The servant ducked through the doorway. "I followed you

from the kitchen – Breeanah sent me with a message."

Raven snatched the note, quickly uncrumpled it, and read:

Princess Raven,
Ambassador Kirgan is asking for you. I'm doing my best
to stall him, but it's only a matter of time before he finds
out you're missing. I may not see you again … I have an
important task that can't be delayed any longer. Whatever
happens, you must get to Laynia and warn them!
Good luck,
~Breeanah

For a moment, Raven stood in silence. Suddenly, everything about this situation was becoming real – they were dodging guards, hiding in the shadows, and … saying goodbye to friends. Maybe forever.

Drin cleared his throat. "It's time I take my leave." Raven murmured a quiet word of thanks and he bowed, ducking back through the doorway and out of sight.

Once he'd gone, Raven turned to the others. "Alright," she exhaled. "It's time to go."

"Go where?" Tristan pointed in the direction of the kitchen. "We're locked in, with guards watching every exit. Unless one of you has a secret way out you haven't mentioned …"

"We could ask Princess Courtney," Melodea blurted. Raven and Tristan turned as one, and Melodea lowered her head shyly. "If you think that would be a good idea."

"I don't know if we should involve –" Raven started.

"We have no choice," Tristan interrupted.

"Can we trust her? At this point …"

"You seemed friendly enough with her when you first met," Melodea put in. Her words weren't accusing, but it was enough to make Raven's jaw shut with an audible *clack*.

She knew she was only being reluctant out of stubbornness, not wanting to admit Melodea was right. Certainly, involving

Courtney had its own risks, but at this point they had little choice. So why was she being so full of herself?

Raven reluctantly nodded her assent. From the corner of her eye, she could see Tristan watching her curiously, and she quickly turned away.

Before he could see the shame written across her face.

ഇ

When they drew close to Courtney's room, Tristan waited with Melodea, out of sight, while Raven continued on. Still disguised as a maid, the guards offered Raven no resistance, and she slipped inside.

Courtney raised her eyebrows. "I didn't ask for a serva– oh, Raven!" She rushed forward, taking Raven's hands and frowning. "What in *Alarkin* are you wearing? And why didn't you just send for –"

"Please, I don't have time to explain." Raven drew in a shaky breath, emotions raw. "I wouldn't have come here unannounced, but I need your help. *Desperately*."

Courtney sobered instantly, leading Raven to the settee. "Of course. What's wrong?"

"My father's ambassador – along with Farah and almost all my guards ... have betrayed me." There, she'd said it. A weight lifted off Raven's chest, and she spoke freely. "They've allied with an enemy of my father in an attempt to kidnap me and overthrow Laynia."

Courtney gaped, pretty pink lips working noiselessly. Finally, she managed to ask, "What will you do?"

"I need to escape, but they're watching all the entryways, making sure I don't leave before they can capture me and bring me before their leader. That's where you come in."

"Me?" Courtney squeaked.

"Yes. I need to escape the castle, along with Princess Melodea and one of my trusted guards. But with the entrances blocked ..." She let the scenario dangle for a moment. "I was hoping you knew of another way out. Some way we could get

134

past the guards. My servants will stay here, under your protection, until I can send for them; I doubt Kirgan has any use for anyone he can't use as leverage."

Courtney slowly shook her head back and forth. "Bu – but ... why? I mean, why would you need my help? You could just alert my father, and he'd arrest all of them!"

"I can't do that," Raven sighed, "or tell you why. But I have to return to my kingdom as soon as possible. If I don't, I *promise* you ... people *will* die."

"You want me to help you and you can't tell me *why*?" Courtney stood up abruptly, eyes flashing. "If you want my help, Raven Rivanstar, you can't ask me to risk my life – and possibly my kingdom's safety – without at *least* giving me some answers!"

Raven conceded with a nod, the barest smile playing at the corner of her mouth. Maybe there was more to Princess Courtney's leadership skills than she'd originally thought. "Alright. Fair enough."

༄

Waiting in the shadows, Tristan rocked back and forth on his toes, glancing down the hallway every five seconds. Melodea had barely uttered two words. *This is taking too long; she should be back by now.* He started pacing, stopped, then started again.

"Tristan, you should check on them to make sure –" Melodea started.

Raven walked around the corner, followed by Courtney, both cloaked and laden with extra supplies, as well as a torch.

Hiding his irritation – which he knew was only a result of his unease – Tristan forced a grin. "Ah, there you are. I was beginning to think you'd been carried away by a dragon. They say that dragons are attracted to princesses –"

"We can sit around talking about dragons, or I could show you the way out before you're all killed," Courtney interrupted.

Tristan raised his eyebrows at Raven, but she grinned and walked wordlessly after the other princess. Tristan shook his head, gestured for Melodea to go next, and then followed. *Great. I'm surrounded by bossy princesses.*

After navigating through a maze of back staircases, dark corridors, and unoccupied rooms, they came to a large oak door. Courtney pulled out a key from her bodice and inserted it into the lock. It turned with a deep *clunk*, and the door creaked open.

"This is the old part of the castle, built long before I was ever born," Courtney said, voice muted. "Besides storage or the occasional tour for visitors, it's fallen out of use and into a state of disrepair. *Don't* touch anything."

Tristan raised his hands in mock defense. "I wouldn't dream of it."

Courtney scowled but didn't reply. "I still don't understand why you and Raven won't let my father arrest your traitorous usurpers and be done with it. No need to sneak through dusty old castle wings or creepy tunnels."

Next to Tristan, Melodea missed a step.

"*Because*," Raven explained, tone deliberately even, "if Nimrooden found out your kingdom was involved, he may attack yours as well as mine." Courtney *hmphed*, leading Tristan to guess that this wasn't the first time Raven had discussed the option.

"With Princess Raven disappearing into thin air, Kirgan will have no idea you helped her," Tristan added. "He'll leave your kingdom and rejoin the army in Tharland, then hopefully start combing the land for us to the south, where we *won't* be."

He and Raven had extensively discussed involving Roehn; both had agreed they couldn't risk Nimrooden's wrath turning against King Albastan. Besides, waiting for all the traitors to be rounded up could mean a delay in sending word to Laynia, and Tristan didn't trust anyone else to deliver such an important message. It had to be them; Raven's word would be undisputed, and he could keep her safe. Hopefully.

Courtney stopped in front of a large tapestry and turned to address the others. "Alright, stay close, there are a lot of dead ends. And it's going to get pretty cramped, so I hope no one's claustrophobic or else – well, you'll just have to deal with it," she said with a smirk. With a sweep of her arm, she pulled aside the tapestry, revealing … a wall.

"So, where *is* this passageway? Hidden by some enchantment?" Tristan quipped.

Courtney turned to him with a scathing glare that he could only guess to be *the look* – something his father once told him about. Apparently, it was the expression all women use, and he'd know it when he saw it. And had better repent of whatever foolishness had earned him the woman's wrath. *Now I know why*, he thought with a quiet chuckle. He took the torch Courtney proffered and held it while she examined the wall.

Tentatively brushing her fingers across the bricks, Courtney felt along until she found the marker she'd been searching for. She removed a small knife from her hair, cleverly fitted into her jeweled barrette, and inserted it above the stone. A small *clink* sounded, and the wall to their right shifted. Together, they pushed it to the side, revealing a black, gaping maw.

THE LABYRINTH

Damp, musty air wafted out of the passageway. Tristan's torch flickered, casting twisted, eerie shadows along the stones and cobwebs. The four stood motionless, gazes locked on the tunnel, feet glued to the floor. A draft snaked up Tristan's spine; he shuddered as a chill raced through him.

Raven was the first to move, turning towards Courtney. "You know the way, right?" At Courtney's nod, Raven jerked her chin toward the labyrinth with a halting laugh. "Then let's go, before I lose my nerve."

Courtney snorted. "The only monsters in here are dead." She stuffed the knife back in her hairpiece and nudged Tristan. "Take the extra torches from the wall. I don't want anyone falling down some old shaft or something."

Tristan lit three more torches, handing them to each of the princesses in turn. Raven was the last to receive hers. As the torch hovered between them, the flame illuminated her face and danced in her wide eyes, leaving him breathless. Did she know how beautiful she was?

Probably. She was a princess; every day of her life was filled with courting nobles and strutting princes. The better question was, how many times had someone – a young man, if he was being honest – told her as much? And how many times had her heart been stolen by a dashing suitor? *Not that it matters. It's none of my business; the heart of a princess is her own affair.* Still, Tristan couldn't help but wonder.

Cobwebs fluttered in the semi-darkness, often startling one of the princesses by brushing against their cheeks or hands. Tristan stoically volunteered to walk in front to take the brunt of the abuse, burning or knocking down the majority of the webs. The grunt work, soldiers called it. Good thing he was used to it by now.

"What did they use this for?" Raven asked, voice echoing in the unnatural stillness. She let out a quiet *ew* and kicked away a decomposed mouse skeleton. Tristan coughed to cover a laugh, and he felt her elbow dig into his ribs.

"Money-hungry traitors within the castle used it for illegal smuggling," Courtney said. "After the smugglers were caught, my ancestors turned it into an escape route." She shrugged. "I never thought we'd actually have to use it."

"What did they smuggle?"

Tristan stopped mid step, and Courtney paused next to him. "Slaves," she whispered.

Raven gasped, and Melodea's hand shot to her mouth, stifling a scream. A decaying corpse – little more than a skeleton – curled in fetal position in the middle of the path. The jaw hung open in a silent cry of terror, its skeletal hand raised above its head in a plea for mercy.

A rusty sword wedged tightly between two ribs, piercing its chest.

Tristan sighed, closing his eyes briefly. "Such evil, casting equality – and often humanity – behind. 'The weak die, the strong survive,' so they claim. And use it to justify the atrocities of putting human beings in chains."

They settled into an uneasy silence, each lost in their own thoughts. A few more skeletons – in various stages of decomposition but all long since void of flesh – marked a grisly path through the labyrinth.

"Why hasn't anyone buried these poor people?" Raven asked, blanching as they passed another.

"My father says they'll keep intruders away, should they happen upon the tunnels," Courtney said. "I don't see the point; no one could find the way in – or out – anyway. I wonder if that's what happened to some of these people … wandering until they died of starvation or thirst." She shivered, glancing around the cavern. "We're almost to the surface."

The further along Raven went, the more the air began to clear. Daylight filtered through cracks high above them in the vaulted stone ceiling. They came to an old, rotted door, unlocked, but the latch stuck with age; Tristan gave it a swift kick, dislocating it from its hinges. Blinking against the light, Raven emerged into a small cave. Vines covered the walls, and mineral water dripped from short stalactites. A small body of stagnant water pooled in the center of the cave, reflecting rippling beams of sunlight along the walls.

Courtney paused in the doorway. "Raven, we discussed where to go from here. This is where I say goodbye."

A heaviness settled over Raven; she slowly turned, regarding the brave princess. An unlikely friend – and hero, in a way. "Thank you … for everything," she said embracing Courtney. Melodea hung back, only offering a brief curtsey.

"Good luck!" Courtney said brightly, tone belying the gravity of the moment.

Tristan gestured towards the labyrinth. "You're going back through there – *alone*?"

"Like I said – the only things to fear in there are dead."

"You're pretty brave – for a princess," Tristan teased, but followed it with a sincere nod of respect. "We are indebted."

Courtney grinned. "Thanks … I think." With a final wave, she slipped back into the pitch black of the labyrinth, her torchlight disappearing as she rounded a corner.

"May the Highest Regium watch over you," Tristan murmured, turning away.

The Highest Regium. Raven couldn't remember hearing the name before, but it sounded oddly familiar – like a lost dream. A shiver, not unpleasant, worked its way to her toes. She followed Tristan, resisting the urge to tug on his sleeve like a small child. "Who is that?"

"Who?"

"You said 'the Highest Regium' … who is that?"

He did a double take. "You haven't heard of –"

A piercing neigh interrupted him midsentence, and Raven shot forward like an arrow from a bowstring.

"Freedom!" Raven gave a girly squeal and threw her arms around the stallion. She hung, suspended, bent over backwards with her entire core pressed against his neck and face covered with his long, thick mane. She inhaled deeply of horse, not really caring what anyone thought of her. "I've missed you, my boy," she whispered. In reply, Freedom indecorously snuffled her for treats.

"Hey, Destiny – I didn't expect to see you here." Tristan stroked his destrier's face, tilting his head at Raven with an unspoken question.

"Courtney and I arranged for her guards to bring them here. My gua–" She winced, then continued, "*Nimrooden's* men didn't think to question why. Probably didn't even notice whose horses they were."

Raven nodded to the third horse – a flaxen-maned palomino, the most docile mare in King Albastan's stables. Although she wasn't sure of Melodea's equestrian skills, she didn't want to take any chances.

"This is Sunflower," she said, beckoning Melodea over. "I hope you don't mind riding astride; it was the only way the guards could take her out without seeming suspicious."

Melodea dipped her head but her eyes widened slightly. "I think I can manage." Fitting her boot in the stirrup, she grabbed the cantle and pommel, using it to swing herself up. Despite her thin frame, the weight pulled the saddle down to the side, and she had to compensate by shifting the saddle once seated.

Raven fought the urge to roll her eyes, deftly mounted Freedom, and sidled him next to Sunflower. "You good?"

Blushing, Melodea nodded and brushed a hand across her mare's neck. "I haven't really had to get on without …"

Raven raised an eyebrow. "Without servants and a mounting block?"

"Yes, I suppose."

Tristan rode over and brought Destiny in between the two princesses. "We'll have to push the horses as fast as they can maintain for a few days. With you missing, Princess Raven, Nimrooden's army might leave sooner than planned." His hands tightened on the reins. "Let's pray we make it in time."

§

The sun rose and sank across the horizon as they picked their way across Roehn, alternating their horses' gaits between a trot and a brisk walk. Sunflower was a few hands shorter than either of the stallions, and certainly less muscular, but she held her own on the long journey.

Following flat, well-maintained roads – as well as having access to fresh water sources – aided their progress, and by the end of the day, they'd made it halfway to the border of Tharland.

"There's a small village up ahead, and an inn – one of the few we'll have the pleasure of staying at," Tristan said, jerking his chin in the general direction. "The only one, actually. In the morning, you can arrange for transport back to your kingdom, Princess Melodea." Melodea bobbed her head absently, staring at the open expanse of road stretching out before them.

They arrived a few minutes later at the Thorn and Thistle, a modest establishment located on the outskirts of town, bordering the edge of a forest. They couldn't afford to be seen in town; town meant soldiers, and soldiers meant spies.

The princesses followed Tristan around back, where they dismounted stiffly and handed their horses off to a stable hand. From there, they made their way inside the two-story establishment. Warm firelight, laughter, and clattering dishes created an inviting atmosphere.

But not for Raven.

She shrank behind Tristan, overwhelmed by the sensory overload and raucous crowd. In the past, the inns she'd stayed at were nearly deserted, left empty for the visiting royalty. This place, however, was jam-packed full of common folk, some whose reputations were questionable at best. Alcoholic drinks flowed freely, and 'friendly' gambling was a common past-time for many of the menfolk. Barmaids, scantily clad, wove in between patrons with wooden salvers laden with tankards, hunks of meat and crusty bread, and steaming soups.

Overall, an intimidating tidal wave of common life – so unlike the polished, carefully planned exposures to "everyday life" Raven had glimpsed in her previous outings. She wondered if Melodea was experiencing similar feelings, but a quick glance in the princess's direction revealed nothing.

"What can I get for ya?" A lively barmaid sidled up next to Tristan, balancing a tray of tankards – filled to the brim – in one hand. When he moved away, the tray swayed precariously. Raven was tempted to reach out to steady it, but something about the way the young woman was looking at Tristan made Raven want to see her drop it. It was a petty thought, but she couldn't help it. The tray never fell, however. Moving with ease, the maid compensated the shift with a tilt of her wrist.

"Two rooms, please … and whatever you have for supper." Tristan dropped a few coins in her hand, enough for the rooms, and the barmaid bobbed her head.

"Ya sure ya'll be wanting *two* rooms?" She winked audaciously at Raven, as if sharing a delicious secret.

Tristan's face turned beet red. "As I said."

"If yer sure, Luv." The maid gave Raven a shrug of her shoulders, as if saying, 'I tried.' "Betsy'll get ya yer key." She hollered toward the bar. "Ay, Betsy!"

A young woman, doe-eyed with a mop of curly red hair, popped over the counter.

"Git these here folks *two* rooms, and make it snappy!"

Betsy nodded, limping off in a decidedly un-snappy pursuit of the keys, returning to the three guests a few minutes later. "Right this way," she directed, leading them up the staircase as fast as her disfigured foot would allow. She pointed out their rooms, handed them keys, and offered an awkward curtsy.

"After you settle in, come downstairs an' give a holler, an' someone'll fetch yer dinner."

Her eyes lingered on Tristan a few seconds longer than necessary, and – for the second time that evening – Raven felt an unfamiliar twang of jealousy rise up. Unconsciously, she found herself glaring at the girl, who took an inadvertent step backward. Raven smirked at her discomfort. If that barmaid knew who she *really* was, she'd see how unworthy her attentions were.

What foolishness! This girl was nothing but a disfigured strumpet who served drinks and wore plunging bodices and hiked-up skirts to get attention! Why did Raven care what she did? And Tristan was only a guard; Raven wasn't even sure if she could call him a friend. Why shouldn't his head be turned by a pretty face?

The entire notion of jealousy was absurd!

Guilt replaced the jealousy, and she lowered her confident gaze. Forget status – she wasn't sure she *deserved* Tristan's friendship. After all he'd done, and the way she'd doubted him at every turn …

No, it was Raven who wasn't worthy.

Raven curtsied at Betsy – hardly required from a customer, and certainly not from a princess, but a penitent gesture Raven thought necessary. "Thank you. We'll be right down – it smells delicious."

A grin lit up Betsy's face, and for a moment, Raven was reminded of Breeanah. "Thank ya, mum. Yer right kind t' say so." Carefully, she made her way downstairs, humming an off-tune but cheery ditty about a willow princess and her lover.

Raven couldn't help but smile.

They unloaded their sparse luggage into their rooms – Tristan in one, Raven and Melodea sharing the other – and headed downstairs, carefully weaving through the rowdy crowd. A few men offered the occasional lewd comment as the princesses passed by; others openly leered. Both were equally insulting.

Here, however, Raven was no longer a princess, so she absorbed the lowbred, crude behavior without response or acknowledgement. But inside, she seethed. A punch in their fat, swollen jowls would do them some good … or at least, it'd do *her* some good. It was all she could do to restrain herself as they took their seats. And if Tristan's clenched jaw was any indication, he was experiencing similar feelings.

The full face of the moon stared back at Raven through the lead glass window, the orb lost in a sea of inky black sky. Alone. *Exactly like I'll be tomorrow, racing across the wilderness of Tharland. Alone – except for Tristan.* Her gaze wandered to Tristan's face. He was scanning the crowd, shoulders loose but eyes darting like a hawk's. What was he thinking about? What did he think of *her*? Did he see her as a spoiled princess, needing his help? Or as a young woman, lost and betrayed by everyone she believed she could trust?

Almost everyone.

Without warning, his gaze shifted, and his eyes met hers. For a moment, neither looked away.

§⌒

Tristan was the first to break eye-contact, returning his attention to the crowd. Since entering the Thorn and Thistle, a sense of unrest had been hanging heavily over him. *And the last thing I need is to be distracted by someone who I could never hope to equal.* Rank was a puzzling conundrum, an oxymoron within his beliefs. First and foremost, he saw everyone as equals under the High Regium. There was no such thing as greaters and lessers, royalty and commoners. But as a guard of Laynia, it was his duty to serve those of higher rank than himself.

So when it came to the princess, how could he reconcile these conflicting beliefs?

He pushed aside his muddled thoughts and refocused on the bustling interior. It was jam-packed with people of every sort; rich, poor, locals, foreigners. *Sober … not-so-sober.* He chuckled quietly to himself. Still, drunkards were the least of his worries.

He didn't want to alarm the princesses, but something was definitely off. *Or someone.*

His eyes came to rest on a back corner table. Four men were crammed in the booth, all hooded and concealed in dark colors. Hardly inconspicuous, but in this place, he doubted they had any reason to hide their less than savory natures.

"Here you are, Luvs."

Tristan nearly bolted out of his seat, barely managing to contain himself as a quick glance revealed the barmaid had arrived with their food. He forced a smile and accepted the steaming dish.

Relax, or you'll end up dead. How many times had Kisby drilled that lesson into his head during sword training, smattered with merciless swipes at every exposed inch of flesh? All his fellow cadets agreed that Kisby was a hands-on teacher, more apt to knock sense into his students literally than figuratively. First and foremost, though, Tristan had been taught to accept every situation as it came, learning to be aware of and then adapt to his surroundings.

The group of cloaked men glanced in their direction. It had to be assumed that all were heavily armed; and, more importantly, they outnumbered Tristan four to one.

In spite of Tristan's best efforts to relax, his palms began to sweat. How could he expect to fight four men *and* defend the princesses? He closed his eyes and breathed a prayer. Right now, it was all he could do.

&

Raven was acutely aware of Tristan's posture; eyes shut, hand clenched on his sword hilt – an action he had a tendency toward whenever he was uncomfortable. She refused to accuse him of being afraid. Because if he was afraid, she had more than every reason to be. And she wasn't as brave as Tristan.

"Is everything alright?" she whispered, touching his arm.

He started, head swiveling to face her. "What? Oh, yeah, it's fine." After a moment's pause, he leaned forward, casually reaching across the table for the salt. His voice came in a muted, strained timbre. "Behind us you'll see four men, all armed and not eating or drinking anything. It may just be a bad feeling, but ..." He licked his lips, fingers rapping against the hilt of his sword. "Best keep an eye on them."

They ate in silence, all sending furtive glances around the room. As if it wasn't enough that they were watching out for Kisby's men – now, there were bandits to contend with? Raven really couldn't get a break, could she? First, her life was boring to the point of monotony. Then everything was plunged into chaos with no hope of returning to normal anytime soon.

Once they finished eating, she and Melodea were beyond eager to follow Tristan upstairs. As Raven entered the large, dark bedroom, panic crept into the corners of her mind. There were no guards at the door. No garrison to come storming into the room at her beck and call. No one to guard the perimeter.

No one to protect her.

This was the life of a commoner, she realized. To rely solely on yourself; nothing in between you and the rest of the world. No king to save you, no soldier to lay down his life for yours. To be powerless in the face of life's perils.

She shuddered, easing the door shut behind her. Maybe the life of a peasant wasn't so grand after all.

After dousing the oil lantern, Raven dove under the covers. A damp, smoky fire flickered behind the grate, barely emitting any heat. To add insult to injury, a steady flow of cold air seeped through the floorboards and between the cracks in the heavily plastered walls.

Despite the cramped space, she was glad Melodea lay beside her. Though unspoken, they shared more than heat; they shared courage. Just knowing someone was next to her, and she wasn't alone, was the only thing that kept the tears at bay.

Not that she deserved any comfort from Melodea.

Raven curled herself into a ball and nestled deeper under the cocoon of blankets. "Goodnight," she murmured. A muffled *goodnight* came from the other side of the bed, barely more than a soft breath. *Is Melodea crying?* Raven peeked out at the princess's inert form, but Melodea kept her face buried in her pillow. They slipped into silence, but neither could sleep for a long time.

NIGHT RAID

Tristan tossed restlessly, coming close to tumbling off the narrow bed. His covers constricted around him like an anaconda; slowly, surely, suffocating him, dragging him to its lair where it would devour him …

He sat up with a start, enveloped in complete darkness. It took a moment to reorient himself to his unfamiliar surroundings; he laid back with a groan, not bothering to try and fall back asleep. He'd been edgy all night, constantly waking himself up and taking eons to fall back asleep. It was getting annoying, and he wondered if it might be better to just stay awake and check on the princesses.

He started to flip the quilt back when a noise stopped him in his tracks. It was so subtle, he'd almost missed it.

The noise of a window being unlatched.

Tristan's fingers groped in the darkness until he found the hilt of the knife hidden beneath his pillow. His sword sat at the foot of the bed, illuminated by a glimmer of moonlight, but he didn't dare reach for it. Instead, he slipped out of bed and melded into the shadows along the wall. Weapon raised, adrenaline surged through every vein in his body.

A glint of steel. A creak of floorboards. A slow release of breath.

The silhouette crept stealthily, neared the bedside. The form raised a dagger, swiftly plunging it downward into the mattress – right where Tristan should have been … had he been able to sleep. Lunging forward, Tristan drove his knife into the shadow's back; the intruder crumpled with a groan, dagger skittering across the floor.

A quick check revealed no pulse. Tristan closed his eyes. "It didn't have to be this way," he whispered. Such needless death.

149

And for what? A bag of coins?

Tristan scooped up the dagger, examining it briefly. The hilt was wrapped with leather – which served well to grasp – and the blade protruded black and semi-jagged. *Designed for messy kills.* It had only a half cross guard, and the pommel was adorned with a single gold skull inlaid with a red ruby. The face leered back at him, jeweled eye glittering, taunting him.

The dagger was fancier than Tristan would expect of common thieves. If he hadn't known better, he'd say it was more the type carried by members of a gang ... or a bounty hunter –

Bounty hunters. Hired by Kisby to spare him the embarrassment of losing his prisoner ... and to reclaim his lost prize. Panic replaced coherent thought; it raced through Tristan like wildfire. All he knew was he had to get to Raven – *now*!

Even that might be too late.

Sword in hand, Tristan raced into the hallway, frantically testing the doorknob. Locked. No voices came from within, but he could hear muffled boot falls and a quiet grunt. If he tried to break the door down, they'd be gone before he got inside. Getting an extra key would take too long.

He rushed back into his room, easing the window open. Thankfully, the moon had slipped behind a cloud. Four horses waited below, but in the darkness, he couldn't tell if there were riders nearby. At this point, it didn't matter; he only had one option. Nearly ten feet separated him from the adjoining window, but a small span of wood trim ran between them, and the roof overhang looked sturdy enough.

Tristan pursed his lips, slung his sword over his shoulder, and grabbed the overhang. With deliberate care, he began edging towards the princesses' open window, hand over hand, toes barely resting on the thin board.

When he reached the window, he stopped, listening. Someone groaned. A rope squeaked into a tight knot.

"Hey, look out!"

The call from behind sent Tristan ducking for cover. But it

was too late – whoever was down there had seen him and was trying to alert his comrades. Hoofbeats retreated into the forest. Tristan waited, undecided, before ducking into the window. At least one of the princesses was still inside the room, held prisoner, and whoever had taken off on horseback was long gone. He prayed Raven wasn't with them.

Metallic scrapes indicated that two swords had been drawn. Tristan eased into a fighting stance, freeing his own blade, waiting for his eyes to adjust.

The blackness around faded. As he'd surmised, two men – both armed and masked – faced him. Behind them, Raven struggled furiously against the cords that wound around her wrists. A wad of cloth had been shoved into her mouth, gagging her. For a moment, no one moved.

Then the first man lunged toward Tristan with a quick diagonal slice. Tristan batted it to the side and dragged his sword against the man's bulging gut. The bounty hunter cried out and fell to the ground, writhing, clawing at his stomach.

"You should have attacked together," Tristan muttered. He often found himself correcting his opponent's fighting style mid-attack. It was a bad habit his commanders had assigned him push-ups for on more than one occasion. *Never give your enemy an undo advantage,* they said.

Apparently, the other hunter took his advice to heart, and was more cautious, pacing and re-assessing after his comrade's failure. He had just raised his sword to strike when something crashed against his head. His eyes rolled back in his head and he collapsed, unconscious.

Raven stood behind him, bound hands clutching the remnants of a clay pitcher. Her eyes were wide, body trembling, but she calmly held out her hands while Tristan cut away the ropes.

"Thanks for your help, Princess," Tristan teased. His fingers, almost moving of their own accord, brushed a strand of hair out her face.

She pulled back as if burned.

Tristan's hand dropped away. What had he done to make her react like that? It wasn't like he'd tried to kis– never mind. It didn't matter now. "Are you alright?" he asked stiffly.

She looked away, appearing to fight back tears. Not wanting to show weakness in front of him, because … she didn't trust him? Or didn't want him to think less of her?

"Yes – I'm fine," she said haltingly. "But they took Melodea!"

჻

Melodea groaned, head throbbing rhythmically, not unlike the hoofbeats pounding beneath her, carrying her away to – *wait, hoofbeats?* She forced her eyes open, but all she could see was the ground rushing beneath her, feel the horse's withers as they dug into her stomach. She grasped uselessly with her bound hands, trying to find purchase, but only managed to make her head hurt worse.

It all hit her at once – she had been dragged out of bed by masked men, then gagged and bound. Raven had struggled with one of the men, while the other grabbed Melodea and threw her out the window like she was no more than a child. After that, she could remember nothing – not the landing, nor being slung over the horse and galloping away. All she remembered was falling, too terrified to scream, through the black air.

Melodea struggled, trying to catch a glimpse of Raven, but all she could see was the blurred motion of the horse's legs as they sped across the forest floor. Her gag had worked its way loose, and now hung flapping against her chin. Frayed bits of rope and dust parched her mouth and sucked away every drop of moisture; she swallowed, trying to make her thick tongue form some semblance of speech.

"Where are you taking me?" she rasped.

Her captor, unconcerned that she was awake, didn't react other than a curt reply. "To King Nimrooden."

His tenor, almost boyish voice, startled Melodea – he couldn't have been over twenty. *And already he's branded himself as a criminal.*

They paused long enough for the bounty hunter to set her in front of him in the saddle – far more comfortable than the withers, but unnerving, sitting practically on top of a strange man. His arms rested on either side of her, holding the reins. And although she would never admit it, her rear was excruciatingly sore from that day's ride. She had never ridden longer than an hour at a time – and *never* astride! Now, the prospect of riding yet again for an interminable amount of time ... would the nightmare never end?

Melodea faded in and out of a fitful sleep as the night wore on, jolting awake whenever she felt herself slumping against the firm chest behind her. It was outrageously shameful, but what could she do?

The sun clawed its way into the eastern sky, early rays barely reaching through the forest. Just past dawn, her captor stopped the horse in a small clearing and pulled Melodea from the saddle.

"I wouldn't advise trying to escape." He unbound her hands, and she wrung them together, wincing at the ugly abrasions lanced across her wrists. "If you try anything funny, I'll tie you again – even tighter," he added. The menacing words came across more like he was trying to convince himself, but he crossed his arms in an attempt to seem more intimidating. Still, it was probably best not to cross him – he may be young, but if he was trying to prove his mettle, who knew what he'd do to her?

Melodea nodded, settling back against a tree. "What's your name?" she mumbled. Already her eyelids were beginning to droop; she wrapped her arms around her legs, shivering as the cold ground sucked away her body heat.

"Why do you want to know?"

Melodea had no reason to give, so she lifted a delicate shoulder in response. Even that simple, unladylike gesture would no doubt have her tutors rolling over in their graves. *Raven must be rubbing off on me.* She wasn't entirely sure whether or not that was a good thing. With the current circumstances, though, she'd certainly rather be the resourceful, confident Raven. Anyone better than the useless, born-with-a-silver-spoon-in-her-mouth princess that she was.

There was an uncomfortable pause as her captor fiddled with the saddle. Once the girth was loosened, he pulled it off, along with the bridle and saddlebag, and secured the horse on a picket line to graze. "They call me Quillan," he finally said. He plopped down across from her, staring brazenly from behind his mask. If any commoner had dared study Melodea in such a manner, her father would see him in the stocks.

"I'm Melodea." She colored slightly, glancing away. "But I suppose you already know that, don't you?"

Quillan raised an eyebrow. "You know, I just kidnapped you. We're not exactly at a tea party, so feel free to dispense with the pleasantries."

"My mother taught me to be polite, even in less than hospitable circumstances," she said tersely. Self-conscious, she straightened her posture, folding her hands in her lap. Better not to seem like a cold, desperate prisoner – even though she was.

Quillan laughed – a light-hearted, pleasant laugh, not the vulgar guffawing she would expect from a criminal. "As you please, Highness. Here, hungry?" Without waiting for her to answer, he tossed a small parcel of food. It landed in her lap with a solid *thud*.

She unfolded the cloth, revealing a hunk of bread, some cheese, and a slightly bruised apple. It was, indisputably, the worst meal she had ever been served. "Thank you."

"I only have one canteen," Quillan said, holding it up by the strap. "We'll have to share."

They ate in silence – a foreign, uncomfortable experience. Melodea was used to her little sisters' chatter, or her father's droning business talk. Even the countess had provided conversation on their trip. Now, having nothing else to do, she discreetly studied her captor.

Quillan had pulled his mask down and was unceremoniously digging into his meal, using his fingers to cram bits into his mouth like he hadn't eaten in days. Maybe he hadn't. His dirty-blond hair fell in messy spikes in all directions, hanging over large, brown eyes and a boyish face. He was common enough, though not unattractive. If it weren't for his eyes, she would say he was much like any young man from the northern regions of Alarkin. But there was a weight to his gaze, the look of one who had seen too much pain. Perhaps even caused some.

The look of a criminal.

Melodea quickly looked away.

Once they'd finished eating, Quillan laid back against his saddle and lowered his hood over his eyes. "Don't think about running anywhere, Princess ... I have eyes in the back of my head, even when I sleep." He eyed her from under his hood. After a moment, he tossed her a coarse wool blanket. "Take it. You look cold."

"Thank you. Again. You've treated me well – for a kidnapper." Melodea smiled faintly.

Quillan brushed her comment aside. "I have to keep you alive, otherwise, I don't get paid."

"Oh. Of course." There was little danger of her freezing or starving to death after only a few hours of captivity, but if he needed an excuse to treat her kindly, she'd accept it and pretend she didn't know otherwise. She wrapped the blanket around herself and let out a quiet sigh.

A few minutes later, Quillan's breathing became steady. Melodea peered over the edge of her blanket, watching for movement. *Should I try it? But if he catches me, then I'll be watched even closer. It would be better to wait for him to let down his guard.* Her plan made, she curled up tighter. She didn't dare hope to fall asleep, but at least she could rest her eyes.

The next thing she knew, Quillan was shaking her awake and

they were riding again. This time she rode behind him, awkwardly holding his middle and praying she didn't go sprawling off the back of the horse.

"So how long have you been working as a bounty hunter?" Melodea asked, clenching her teeth together as the horse took a particularly jarring step.

Quillan chuckled. "You certainly are curious, aren't you? Well, I wasn't always in this line of work. But once my mother died, I had to make a living for myself, and I became the Thief in the Night – stealer of people, purses, and pride." He gestured grandly. "Satisfied?"

"And your father?"

"Dead, too. A few years ago. Actually, he's the one who got me into this line of work. Took a misstep though, got himself hanged." He shrugged. "It happens."

Melodea couldn't help recoiling. "You sound as though it doesn't bother you."

"My father's death?"

"No, your work. You speak as though you enjoy ruining other's lives." She peered over his shoulder, trying to read his face, but it was carefully masked with indifference.

"You get used to it." Quillan shrugged, watching the forest. "I usually only target the rich, the well off. Their taxes are the reason people like my mother end up wasting away in shabby hovels, and people like my father take to stealing just to scrape out enough to pay for the doctor. I'm a regular Robin Hood, if you think about it."

She bit back the retort, that Robin Hood helped others, and not only himself, against unjust taxes and cruel kings. But she somehow doubted Quillan cared about technicalities. "Maybe. I don't know who was responsible for the hardships your family went through, but is it really better to take someone else's livelihood and leave them in the same situation as your mother? With nothing?"

He laughed again, a little too loudly. "Those rich fools I steal from will never be destitute. There's always someone they can tax, or some favor they can call in. What do I care if they go without their rose-petal baths?"

"So you think I'm a rich fool, and it's acceptable I suffer for those who've wronged you in the past?"

Something in her tone struck a chord with Quillan – maybe because she actually sounded wounded. Maybe because he knew she'd backed him into a corner. Whatever it was, his smile faded, and his tone turned sober.

"It's nothing personal. When I steal, I do it because I have to – to survive. Sure, sometimes I loathe myself. Wonder how I can go on living the way I do. But," he added with a firm nod, "this is the life I've made for myself. No turning back."

"But do you *like* what you've made for yourself?" Melodea pressed. "If not, why don't you *change*?"

Quillan didn't immediately reply, focusing instead on guiding his horse around a marshy pit. Skunk cabbages grew in large patches all around it and, true to their name, emitted a sickly odor akin to rotten flesh. Not that Melodea had ever smelled rotting flesh before, but she imagined it was similar.

They had traveled in silence for a few minutes when Quillan finally said, "Most people either pity me or despise me, but they all agree on what a horrible person I am. Maybe they're right. But you … you're different. How can you know what I am and still believe I can change?"

The desperate, almost pleading in his voice pierced Melodea. How many lost, confused boys turned to lives of crime, hoping to find riches and vengeance – even belonging – to fill the gaping hole in their hearts? A hole no riches or vengeance could possibly fill?

For the first time since her capture, she was no longer afraid.

Slipping her hand inside his, she gave it a gentle squeeze before releasing her hold. "We *all* make mistakes. We *all* fall short of perfection. But we don't have to be perfect – the High Regium forgives us for *all* our shortcomings."

Quillan, lost in thought, flexed his empty hand.

&

"She's gone?"

Raven couldn't force herself to lift her eyes from the floor. Tristan's words, so desperate and … disappointed. He thought it was all her fault. That's why she pulled away from his touch – she knew he had only been caught up in the moment. Once he realized that she'd failed Melodea …

Tristan ran a hand across his face. "I have to go after her. Those men were bounty hunters, no doubt working for Nimrooden. If his camp is in the forests of Tharland, Melodea could be there by nightfall."

"I'm so sorry, Tristan –" Raven's voice broke. She continued, barely more than a whisper. "I should have protected her."

"That's not your job. It's mine. I should have protected *both* of you." He quickly cleaned the blood off his sword and rammed it into his sheath, avoiding her gaze. "You'll have to go on without me while I find Melodea. King Wilgaun can't afford the delay –"

"I didn't want this to happen!"

Tristan turned at her sudden outburst. "What?"

She alternately clenched and unclenched her fist, wishing she hadn't spoken, but knowing it was too late to take back her words. "I didn't want Melodea to be captured. You have to believe me."

Tristan studied her, obviously confused, but also suspicious. "Why would I think that?" he asked slowly.

The tears she'd been holding in check trickled down her cheeks. She swiped them away, but there was no way Tristan could have missed them. "Because I was jealous of Melodea. Because I couldn't stand having her around, constantly reminding me of what I'm not."

Tristan started to say something, but she rushed on, before she lost her nerve. "But no matter how I felt about having her around, I wouldn't let her get captured – or let her come to harm out of spite or –"

"Raven, I – I would never think that!" All traces of anger were gone, replaced by a deep and sincere expression of sympathy. He reached out, as if to comfort her, but quickly pulled away.

He'd called her Raven. Hearing her name, spoken so softly … like he actually saw her as more than just a princess.

"Really? I thought – back in Silva …" Raven peered up at him, damp lashes veiling her eyes. Tear-stained and unkempt from sleep, she felt filthy from the rough handling of her captors. She must look an absolute fright.

Tristan leaned closer. If he thought she looked anything less than her usual composed self, he didn't show it. "Yes?"

"I thought you knew I envied her, and that you must think so badly of me. Especially after I –" She squeezed her eyes shut but forced herself to continue. "Especially after how I treated you. After you tried to warn me, but time and time again, I treated you like dirt. I pushed you away, afraid you'd see that underneath the polished surface, I'm really a selfish, petty princess."

Suddenly, his arms were around her, holding her close against him. "You are *no* such thing!" A deep, comforting timbre vibrated through his chest when he spoke; she could feel every word as much as she could hear them. "And I *will* get Melodea back, I promise."

The moment ended, and they broke away, each slightly self-conscious, hiding behind shy smiles.

Tristan started, clearing his throat. "I'll saddle the horses."

"I'll pack our things."

After quickly changing and stuffing her few belongings – along with some extra provisions – into her saddlebag, Raven rushed into the stables, where Tristan had finished cinching Freedom's saddle.

Tristan nodded grimly. "They're ready."

They led their horses – including Sunflower – from the stable, mounts pawing and snorting in the crisp pre-dawn air. The sun was only a faint promise on the eastern horizon, and the stars still gleamed faintly in the heavens. A new sunrise. Which meant one less day to warn Laynia.

A stable boy jumped up as they walked by, rubbing sleep from his eyes. "May I –"

"Nope, we're already done." Tristan grinned briefly at Raven.

Outside, Tristan gave Raven a leg up before he mounted, leading Sunflower in tow. They followed the bounty hunter's tracks for a few hours until they reached the border of Tharland. From there, the hoofprints veered to the north and away from Laynia.

"Here is where I leave you," Tristan said.

Raven wheeled Freedom around to face him. "No – we continue together!"

Tristan groaned. "I thought we agreed that I would find Melodea and you would ride ahead –"

"No, that's what you said. I never agreed." Raven crossed her arms, daring him to contradict her.

"This is the only way!" Tristan took a deep breath, calming himself. "Laynia needs to be warned. If I'm captured, or delayed, you need to take the message to your father. And you can't do that if you're with me." His voice dropped to a whisper. "This is the only way."

An eternity later, Raven gave a nod of assent.

"Good." He unfolded a map, tracing his finger toward Caritas. "Continue west through Tharland. You should come to a river; follow it upstream to a waterfall. Be careful and stay out of sight. If all goes well, I'll meet you at Mossy Falls tomorrow, and we'll continue to Laynia together."

"And if you don't?" When Tristan said nothing, Raven continued. "I can't do this without you, Tristan. If it weren't for you, I'd be with Melodea, standing before Nimrooden. Maybe dead. If you don't … make it back –"

"Hey, don't talk like that," he scolded gently. "I will, and I'll bring Melodea with me. Either I'll meet you at Mossy Falls, or back in Caritas. But we *will* see each other again – soon." He touched her face, and this time, she didn't pull away. "Until tomorrow, Princess." He dug his heels into Destiny's side and disappeared into the forest, lost in the twisting shadows and grasping trees.

Raven watched until he was out of sight. Slowly, lethargically, she kicked Freedom into motion, and they set off into Tharland. Alone.

A DEAL WITH THE DEVIL

Tristan rode Destiny at a brisk canter, only slowing once the tracks led off the main road and into the forested underbrush. There, he slowed to a walk, allowing his mount to catch his breath. If they needed to make a hasty escape, Destiny would need his strength. Behind him, Sunflower snorted, delicate nostrils flared and sides heaving. Bred more for bursts of speed than endurance, she wouldn't be able to maintain the pace either. Tristan patted her neck, whispering apologies. Still, they kept moving, rarely dropping slower than a trot and only taking brief rests at the occasional stream.

The bounty hunter who'd taken Melodea wasn't concerned with stealth – without the security of his companions, he seemed more bent on speed, riding fast to the northwest and making his way toward Tharland. Still, the hunter's horse had to carry two riders, so Tristan was slowly gaining on him. But between the bounty hunter's head start, and the time it took to read the tracks, there was little chance Tristan would catch up before nightfall. He should have told Raven to go on. There was no way he'd be able to make it to Mossy Falls by morning, not with how far north he'd ridden … if he made it back at all.

It was a big if.

Tristan knew he had undermined the danger. Once he crossed into Tharland, he'd be in wild lands, ruled by bandits and cutthroats; real criminals, not the weaselly drunkards that fled to Burglar Valley. And if Nimrooden had conscripted the men from Tharland …

The hoofprints led on for miles. Around evening, heavy rainclouds blew in from the north, darkening the sky. The torrent of rain that followed made the path treacherous. Destiny's hoof caught on a root and he stumbled, barely

162

recovering his feet. His muscles trembled with exhaustion, and horses and rider were soaked through from water and sweat. The rain stopped as sudden as it had started, but the foliage was dripping with moisture.

"Whoa, boy," Tristan soothed, pulling Destiny to a halt. He rubbed the stallion's powerful neck until the horse relaxed and lowered his head. "Let's take a break, huh?"

Tristan dismounted, allowing the horses to rest and pull at a few mouthfuls of grass. His eyes wandered south where, somewhere, a princess was riding all alone, in the storm, waiting for him to return. *His* princess. He played the words over, not daring to say them out loud. Was that what Raven had become? His princess? The thought was beyond daring to hope for, but still …

Still. Everything had gone still. Tristan's hand worked its way to his sword hilt, and he listened, scanning the woods. All the creatures had gone silent; even the wind itself seemed to have ceased. Only the rhythmic *drip* could be heard as raindrops rolled off branches and into little puddles on the forest floor. And then a snap sounded behind him.

Tristan whirled around … and found an arrow tip pointing at his face.

∞

Quillan watched the self-proclaimed king stride from his war tent. There was no mistaking his confident, arrogant stride, expensive tunic, and jeweled sword hilt, though Quillan had no doubt that the weapon was as lethal as it was beautiful. This king wouldn't suffer paltry weapons – he placed too much value on his ability to take a life.

Or many, as was often the case.

However impressive, it wasn't any of these qualities that truly gave away the king's identity. Quillan saw past the outward affectations of power – which the king had carefully crafted to enhance his reputation – to the man that lay beneath. This man held a deep hatred and power lust that would cow the

163

fiercest of warriors. But only the pale, lifeless blue eyes, flecked with gold, revealed the depths of this king's depravity.

They disturbed Quillan like no eyes he had ever seen.

If eyes were the windows to the soul, then Nimrooden was no mere king. Or man, for that matter. He was something beyond that. Beyond mortal. An evil deity? A grim reaper? Who could say?

Either way, Quillan knew that King Nimrooden was the last person – or being– anyone should ever cross.

And here Quillan was, about to make a deal with him.

A deal with the devil.

The general – Sir Kisby had said his name was Gauln – accompanied King Nimrooden, along with five bodyguards and a member of the border patrol, who Quillan had conscripted to relay a message.

"Where is my bounty hunter?" Gauln snapped, advancing towards the border patrol.

The patrol, white as a sheet, backed away. "He s-said he would meet us here, sir," the man stammered, not daring to meet the general's gaze.

Gauln scratched his head. "Well, I'm not sure about you, but I see no bounty hunter here. Do you, Your Majesty?"

His majesty didn't reply.

"I didn't think so," Gauln continued, undaunted by Nimrooden's silence. Quillan deemed the general to be either a great fool … or someone who had made himself indispensable. Considering he was still alive, it was probably the latter.

Gauln sneered, drawing his knife. "But since our *reliable* source says he is, it must be true."

The patrol looked like he was about to wet himself with terror. "Please, General Gauln, the man *said* he would meet us here! Don't blame me – I'm just the messenger!"

Gauln chuckled. "But who else am I to –"

Quillan dropped from his tree perch mere feet from the group. "Perhaps your messenger has better eyes than you,

General," he said. Gauln stared blankly, and Quillan flashed him a grin. "Oh, how rude of me -- let me introduce myself. I am Quillan, Thief in the Night." He flourished his introduction with a mocking bow.

"Ah, are you? Forgive me, I mistook you for a jester," Gauln returned. He'd recovered himself enough to resume his arrogant smirk.

"I think we already established the state of your eyesight," Quillan quipped. "So, where is my pay?" He looked around, feigning surprise. "I don't see chests full of treasure."

Nimrooden spoke for the first time. His voice was soft, but undeniable authority exuded from every word; to question or interrupt was impossible. "You will receive your pay when you produce the girl. Not a moment before."

The clever retort died in Quillan's throat, and he found his head dipping in acquiescence. When he spoke, his words were leaden and monotone, like he was under a spell. "Princess, show yourself."

Melodea stepped forward from her hiding spot, positioned in the brush between Quillan and the army encampment. Even if she'd had the guts to try and escape, she was pinned. A good plan, if Quillan said so himself. And he usually did.

But as Melodea came into view -- so lovely and helpless, jaw set firmly to hide its trembling -- the king's spell was broken, and Quillan's heart started beating again; an erratic, throbbing sensation that left him speechless for an entirely different reason. He found himself unable to even meet the princess's fearful gaze.

Nimrooden snapped his fingers and one of his guards left to fetch the payment. When the guard returned, he unceremoniously plunked the bag on the ground. Quillan didn't bother to check the amount. This was the price for Melodea's freedom, bought and paid; the thought of counting it made him sick.

Slowly, he reached down and grabbed the money bag, tying

it to his belt and fighting down the bile that had risen in his throat. He led Melodea towards Nimrooden without offering so much as a word of comfort. He had none to offer.

"What do you plan on doing with her?" Quillan's question, meant to be casual, came out strained.

"What concern is that of yours?" Gauln scoffed. He grabbed Melodea, roughly binding her and pushing her into the waiting arms of a bodyguard. The guard stood behind her, hand placed threateningly on her shoulder.

Quillan cleared his throat. "Thief's curiosity."

"If you *must* know ..." Gauln raised his dagger, dragging it lightly across Melodea's neck. She recoiled, breathing labored.

A voice in Quillan's head screamed in protest. The scream turned into words – illogical, foolish words, fueled by pathetic sentiment and weakness. After all, hadn't he known exactly what Melodea's fate would be when he captured her? But the voice refused to be silenced, and the words tumbled out before he could stop them.

"I'll buy her." Quillan swallowed, glancing at Melodea. She watched him, equal measures of disbelief and hope etched into her face. "With the sum of my bounty," he added.

Nimrooden eyed him curiously. "You'd pay that much for a girl? She's hardly worth such a price for the ... *pleasures* –" he smirked at Quillan – "you desire."

Mind racing, Quillan adopted his normal, casual air. He pulled a gold coin out of the bag and fiddled with it. "It's simple. I get what I want. You don't lose any money. When I'm done with her, I'll get rid of her – but not before – and the princess of Mieldren will be out of the picture of your expanding empire. Win-win." He tossed the coin, a reminder of the significant sum the king could be saving.

Nimrooden considered for a moment. "You don't want her for pleasure, do you." It wasn't a question, and Quillan found no ready reply. "You actually *like* the girl."

Slowly, Quillan nodded. "I'll keep her away from her

kingdom, all the same. Take her back with me to Tarith."

Something unreadable flashed across Nimrooden's face, and his gaze hardened. "No."

"Please, I'll –"

"I said ... *no*."

The hatred in Nimrooden's eyes spread, consuming his entire body until he began to shake with it. A hatred directed at Quillan. Clutching his sword hilt, Nimrooden's knuckles turned white, as if his very bones were protruding from flesh. "Get out of my sight."

Quillan backed away. Before he knew it, he was running as fast as he could, mounting his horse, gold in hand, to flee.

Leaving his only hope of redemption shackled, awaiting her own execution.

&)

Freedom trudged through another swollen, muddy stream. Any chance of being dry in the near future had long since fled Raven's mind. Rain dripped steadily off her woolen hood and cloak as she squinted at the dark storm clouds gathered overhead ... a herald of her mission's doom, if such portends could be believed. Her mind wandered to Tristan, wondering if he was stuck in the same wretched downpour.

If he was still alive.

She pulled the map out of her saddlebag and verified her progress. If Tristan's drawings were accurate, she was still on course. With luck, she'd arrive at Mossy Falls later that evening.

The wind gusted; Freedom crow-hopped, throwing his head. "Steady, boy!" Raven said, her voice quavering. She'd never been afraid on a horse, no matter how fast it ran or how high it jumped. But she'd never been by herself in the middle of an unfamiliar forest, with wind and rain pelting against her, and no one around for miles. If Freedom threw her, and she was injured ...

She brushed the thought aside. Fear would only make Freedom even more uneasy. The best thing she could do was keep her eyes open and keep going, alert but not afraid. She could do this.

Who was she kidding? If Tristan didn't return, there was *no* way she could do this. And if she didn't … Laynia would perish. She couldn't, but she had to. She didn't want to, but she must.

By nightfall, Raven had reached Mossy Falls. After unsaddling Freedom and hobbling him to forage nearby, she gathered wood and began arranging it, small dry pieces in the center. The dry wood hadn't been easy to find; she'd had to use a dagger – the same one Tristan had taken from one of the dead bounty hunters – to chip some from the center of an old, hollow log. With the aid of her flint and steel, she soon had a crackling, albeit smoky, flame.

"And who said a princess couldn't light a fire?" she said with a smug grin. The smile faded, and she sat back against a tree, pulling her blanket higher around her shoulders. "What am I doing here, Freedom? Alone, in the wilderness, waiting for my – my –" she tried again, "for *Tristan* to return, even though he probably never will?"

She sighed, laying back, and whispered, "I must be a fool to hope that I'll see him again. But if I don't hope … I'd be an even bigger fool. I *have* to believe in him, or what do I have left?"

ନ

Tristan didn't allow himself a moment's hesitation. Whipping his sword out, he severed the arrow tip, sending the bow sailing uselessly into the underbrush. His assailant, however, dodged Tristan's second swipe and drew his own sword. They circled each other, evaluating.

The man wore a mask over his mouth and nose. Brown eyes peered from beneath his hood; Tristan recognized him as one of the men from the inn, and later, as the man who'd ridden away with Melodea. Although Tristan had never seen his face, he was the only thief who hadn't been killed.

"Never hold a bow to someone at point blank range. Don't you know anything?" Tristan taunted. There he went again, critiquing his opponent's fighting style out loud. He'd have to work on that … later.

"Uh, I hadn't counted on you being that fast," the man said. "Actually – oh boy, this is awkward. I never wanted to kill you. Only to talk." He slowly reached up with one hand and removed his disguise, first the hood, then the mask. He looked a few years younger than Tristan.

"You're a bit young for a bounty hunter," Tristan said, lowering his sword slightly. Not that age was necessarily an indication of a fighter's skills – or how many crimes they'd committed.

The man offered a sheepish grin. "Maybe. How about you put down your sword and I'll put down mine, then we'll talk?"

"What, the arrow was a peace offering?" Tristan asked sarcastically.

"I thought you'd listen better at arrow point, but …" He coughed. "Bad idea. Anyway, I'm Quillan."

Tristan raised an eyebrow in reply.

"I … have news of your missing princess," Quillan said.

"You mean *after* you kidnapped her!"

"And here we go," Quillan muttered.

"Where is she?" Tristan demanded. "And why did you take the trouble to find me, if not to kill me?"

"I turned her over to Gauln, and I … well, she …"

"Spit it out, man!"

Quillan threw his hands up. "Because I regret it, alright?"

Tristan shook his head. "Unbelievable. I'm working with a penitent kidnapper." He sheathed his sword. "And I suppose you want my help?"

"That's the general idea."

"And you have a plan?"

Quillan grinned. "Absolutely."

The Plan

The two figures silently crept towards Nimrooden's camp, leaving their mounts tethered to a tree a few hundred yards back. A steady wind masked any noise from the men's approach and blew their scent in the opposite direction. No need to alert the dogs. The sun was only a memory on the western horizon, leaving the forest in deep shadows. A perfect night for a clandestine rescue.

"Any idea where the princess might be held?" Tristan whispered. There were hundreds of tents scattered in the clearing. Hardly an encouraging sight when he was trying to infiltrate the premises.

"Surrounded by guards, I suppose," Quillan said.

"Wonderful – thank you, *King Obvious*," Tristan muttered. They jerked back as a lone patrol jogged past, moving with surprising ease, considering all the armor he wore.

"I sure don't envy him!" Quillan exclaimed quietly. "Can you imagine, having to circle all these louts at a jog? If I were him, I think I'd –"

"Just shush!" Tristan interrupted. "Alright, are you sure about this plan?"

"Of course," Quillan returned with a cocky grin. "I've pulled off stunts like this many times." The grin faltered. "Not with an entire army, though."

"Comforting. We'll fan out and search the – where are you going?" Tristan hissed.

Quillan, who had taken off in mid-instruction towards the sprawling camp, tossed the words over his shoulder, "I'll meet you back here." He slipped down an embankment and out of sight.

Tristan grunted and muttered under his breath. "*Hotheaded*

idiot." While he waited, he studied the patrol patterns, as well as movement within the camp, searching for a path through to … wherever they were holding the princess. Hundreds – maybe thousands – of men milled about, some gathered around campfires, others playing dice for what little possessions they owned. A few were retiring to their tents – but not many.

And no sign of Melodea. *Where is she?*

ଛଠ

Quillan crouched behind the king's tent, waiting for the guards to turn their backs or go relieve themselves. Silently, he congratulated himself on his ingenious plan. *That fool; he must be pretty desperate.* It was so simple. King Nimrooden wanted information about the other princess – Raven or whatever. All Quillan had to do was sell Tristan out, and he'd be as rich as a king. *Say goodbye to the life of a criminal.* He could settle down, start a business with his newly acquired funds, find a woman of his own, maybe even get married.

But could he come home and look his wife in the eyes, knowing their life was bought through someone else's death?

Maybe he'd just stay a criminal. It was easier.

He ducked inside the tent. It was too late to turn back now – he would turn Tristan in and reap the benefits. After all, it was no less than a Laynian soldier deserved. *They certainly know a thing or two about betrayal.* But what he couldn't stomach was that his betrayal would seal not only Tristan's fate, but Melodea's as well. Tristan was her last hope – without him, she'd never escape.

Quillan shook his head. Now was not the time for second thoughts. He had a bargain to pull off.

Striding into the middle of the room, Quillan threw his arms out and put on his most brazen smile. "Good evening!" he said brightly. "Guards as vigilant as ever, I see."

His smile widened as every guard in the room whirled around and gaped at him, followed by their king and general. It took a full five seconds for Gauln to rasp, "Seize him!"

171

The guards grabbed Quillan's arms and dragged him forward, but Quillan made no move to resist. Instead, he rolled his eyes, making sure to clearly convey his annoyance. "I expect such dim-witted behavior from you, General, but surely *his highness* is quick enough to guess: I didn't return here because I have a death wish."

Nimrooden watched with disinterest, leaning back into his cushioned throne. "Then what do you want, clever thief? Is your lust for gold not sated?" His eyes narrowed. "Or perhaps you're here to discuss other lusts."

"Neither, Majesty." Quillan shook free of the guards' grasp, brushing his shoulders off. They were nothing more than irritations, and he wanted Nimrooden to know it.

"Now, if my sources are correct ..." Quillan raised a finger to emphasize his point, "... which they usually are – you planned the capture of a particular Laynian princess. But *I* happen to know she escaped your men in Roehn. So you see, I alone am able to deliver what I promise. My capture and delivery of Princess Melodea proves as much."

"Kirgan already informed us of her escape," Gauln snarled. "And according to *my* sources, you were supposed to bring me Princess Raven *and* the Mieldren brat. Are you trying to excuse your pitiful failures?"

Quillan made a show of sighing, turning to the guard next to him. "Not very bright, is he?" Gauln growled, but Quillan ignored him. "What I *actually* came here to say is this. I've led the personal bodyguard of Princess Raven to your doorstep. With my help, you can capture him, then use whatever means necessary to extract the princess's whereabouts."

The corner of Nimrooden's mouth lifted slightly, and Quillan could almost see the greed burning like fire in the king's eyes. An ugly, repulsive glee. "Excellent. Bring him to me, and we will discuss your ... *remuneration*."

His blood money.

"That's the end of *my* shift. I'm not wasting precious sleep waiting for the infamously late duo on second watch!" Gartin stood, poking a finger at Melodea. "She's nothing more than a useless wench incapable of tying a knot, let alone untying one behind her back." He chuckled. "And she's not going anywhere."

Melodea struggled harder, eyes blazing, but gag still firmly in place. The second time in two days she'd had a rancid cloth shoved into her mouth. Now she had her hands tied around a wooden post planted in the ground, awaiting her execution.

The second guard shook his head, planting himself more firmly at his post. "If General Gauln catches a lapse in watches, then –"

"Then the incompetent fools will find *their* heads on a platter, not mine," Gartin finished. "If you want to wait for those louts, be my guest."

A second later, both guards were hurrying from their post, minds bent on grog and a hot meal, followed by some shut-eye. Melodea worked her fingers at the bulky knot behind her back, but it was too tight. Even if she'd had a clue what she was doing, she doubted anything short of a knife could loosen her bonds. *Useless wench, indeed.*

The most she managed to do was work the gag from her mouth by scraping the side of her face against the wooden pole. Even that offered little comfort, other than her taste buds no longer had such an offending palate crammed against them.

I can't die here. The words replayed over and over again in her mind. But what choice did she have? *After Quillan …* Melodea's eyes squeezed shut. She thought he had the potential to be different! But apparently not. Apparently he was just a common criminal after all.

After a few more minutes of futile struggling, Melodea slumped against the pole, not caring how unladylike her posture was, not caring about how the next guards would jeer at her. Not caring about anything except the mantra she clung to, ringing over and over again in her mind. Without thinking, she spoke aloud, voice lost in the night.

"*I can't die here.*"

And then the night answered back, "You won't."

Melodea gasped. "Tristan! You came!"

"Shh, yes, but it won't do any good if you wake the entire camp." Tristan grinned, drawing his knife. "Now hold still." A moment later she was loose, massaging the feeling back into her tender wrists, hiding a grin of her own.

Tristan shoved a bundle of clothes into Melodea's arms, ordering her to change into them. As she watched, gaping, he grabbed a sack of flour and began lashing it against the pole.

"What are you *doing*?" she hissed, fear making her words sharper than she intended. In the shadows, she slipped out of her servant's dress and into the man's shirt and trousers. "Have you lost your mind? We have to go!"

"Give me your dress."

Melodea tossed it to him, beginning to question his sanity. "I don't see how – oh."

The sack, strung from the pole, wore Melodea's dress in an odd, lumpy imitation of a human figure, and a mass of rope draped from the head like hair. In the darkness, the crude form could be mistaken for that of a person. Especially if the guards were in their cups.

Melodea ventured a smile. "Do I really look that fat?"

"Not a chance," Tristan winked. "Now why don't we get out of here before that pair of delinquent guards decides to make an entrance?"

They crept slowly through the sleeping camp. Only a few soldiers still sat around fires; most were in their tents or sprawled drunkenly on the ground. Hardly model militia material, but Melodea guessed Nimrooden would have them sober and in ranks by the time they reached Laynia. According to Quillan, it was only a few days march away.

Crude laughter sent Tristan and Melodea scuttling for cover.

A trio of men passed, sharing a bottle of spirits and swaying unsteadily on their feet. "That guard'll be speared like a fish in a barrel!" one slurred. He paused to put a hand to his chest and let out a grotesque belch. "No chance he makes it out alive."

Melodea froze. "We've been discovered."

Tristan didn't immediately reply. Instead, he freed his sword, clenching his jaw like he was trying to keep from saying something he'd regret. "Not discovered. *Betrayed*."

He ripped off a piece of canvas from a nearby tent, grabbed a half-burnt stick, and used the end to scribble a few scrawling words. "Take this and run. I'll try and follow –"

A snap sounded next to them, and the drunk soldier appeared from behind a tent. "Well, well ... if it isn't the guard welp himself!" The soldier staggered toward them, companions close behind. "I hope you like pain, pretty boy. Our king's gonna make you squeal!" He reached for his sword.

Before the weapon left its sheath, Tristan's sword was already racing in a downward arc towards the man's collar bone. It shattered instantly, leaving the arm limp as a boned fish. The man howled, drew his sword with his left hand, and began swinging wildly.

"Go!" Tristan shouted, pushing Melodea away.

For a moment she stood, unable to move, watching Tristan ram his sword through the soldier's gut. Then the man's dying scream snapped her out of the daze. She bolted, making for the edge of camp and shoving aside anything and anyone in her way. Wearing standard army garb, few took notice of her. When she reached the wood line, she chanced one last glance at the swarm of men flocking to the fight.

If she left, would she really be any different than Quillan? Abandoning another to die? No, this was different. Quillan had *chosen* to turn her in, *chosen* to leave her. But she had no choice; to stay with Tristan meant certain death.

Resolved that she was choosing the only possible option, Melodea fled.

A hand shot out and grabbed her arm, pulling her off her feet. "Gotcha!" a nasally voice exulted. She screamed, trying to yank her arm free, but the hand held fast. "No escaping, missy ... we figured you'd come this way!" The man snickered, hauling her to her feet and shoving her into the waiting arms of more soldiers.

"Let go of me!" Melodea clawed at exposed flesh, but the men overpowered her, twisting her arms behind her back and clapping her in manacles. One struck her in the stomach, and she doubled over, gasping with nausea.

"Oooh, you're a feisty one, aren't you?" The nasally soldier fingered her hair, leering.

One of the other soldiers slapped his hand away. "Get your grubby fingers off!" he spat, shoving the man to the ground.

The nasally soldier slowly recovered his feet and growled, but he obeyed and kept his distance. Melodea could still feel his ogling gaze; between that and the blow to her stomach, she could barely keep herself from retching.

The next minute she was thrown over someone's shoulder and bodily carried away. She wriggled to free herself. When nothing happened, she sank her teeth into the soldier's beefy neck.

"*Oww*! Why ... you little *viper*!" He threw her to the ground and kneed her in the jaw, sending her sprawling backward.

Pain flooded Melodea's face, and her vision exploded with a crimson flush. Rough hands forced a rope around her mouth, the bristly fibers cutting deep into the corners. The taste of blood was sickening. She was thrown back over someone's shoulder. Her face collided with metal armor, and her world plunged into darkness.

৵

Tristan yanked his blade from the drunkard's stomach. More men were swarming from all directions, converging on him like an angry nest of hornets. His blade hacked in rhythmic blows, downing soldier after soldier. More took their place. A sword slid across his back. His knuckles caught the edge of a knife. Slowly, surely, he was being overrun.

A solid thrust kick to his gut brought him crashing to his knees.

Ropes slid around his neck, hands, and feet. Resistance would constrict the cord around his throat, either strangling him or collapsing his trachea ... fatal options, all. Half-conscious, he was dragged to his feet. Someone swung a hook punch into his jaw, and only the hands supporting him kept Tristan from crumpling to the ground.

"That's enough."

The offender rubbed his fist and sneered. "Feeling guilty, bounty hunter?"

Quillan shrugged. "No, but the king wants to question him. I'm sure he'd be interested to know why his prisoner is incapable of speech." He lifted a shoulder. "Just a thought."

The soldier went quiet.

Tristan managed to lift his head. "I should have known better than to trust *you*." He spat, more blood than saliva, at Quillan's feet.

"Yes, you should have." Quillan stared, face unreadable. He turned to the soldiers. "Take him to the king!"

CAPTIVE

"Ah, so you're the infamous guard that's given Kisby so much trouble. How pathetic." Gauln clucked with disapproval. Behind him, enthroned on his dais, sat a king. *Nimrooden.* Tristan wasn't sure how he knew, but somehow, the name appeared in his mind. The cruelty exuding from this self-proclaimed king was unmistakable. That he was capable of murder – and more – wasn't even a question in Tristan's mind.

He fought to focus. The world was spinning out of control, both literally and figuratively. But slowly, painstakingly, Tristan stood, refusing to kneel before such monsters. He tried to glare, too, but wasn't sure whether he succeeded.

"If it isn't the infamous Nimrooden," Tristan snarled. "Finally daring to show his face after murdering Laynia's queen in cold blood." He couldn't miss Nimrooden's recoil. And something told Tristan it wasn't the omission of his title that caused such a visible reaction.

Turning to the general, Tristan continued. "And his lapdog, Gauln. I hope you enjoyed your trip to Burglar Valley – they say it's lovely this time of year." His words came out closer to a wheeze than anything, but they served their purpose.

Gauln started forward, hand already moving to his knife. "You little –"

Nimrooden raised a hand, halting the general. The king had recovered himself and resumed his distant, almost apathetic gaze. "Bold words for an insignificant apprentice. Kisby told me you were a nuisance – he should have disposed of you sooner and saved me the trouble."

Tristan studied the king, undaunted. "What do you want? I have no information on Laynia that could possibly benefit you, and even if I did, I'd never –"

178

"Tell the likes of you ... yes, we know." Quillan stepped forward, shoving past the assembled soldiers to stand before Nimrooden. "Before you start your interrogation, I want my pay."

℘

It was brazen, this game Quillan was playing. But life never rewarded those who failed to take risks, at least in his experience. Nimrooden respected power. Cowering and begging would only earn Quillan a noose alongside Tristan. The thief spared a glance backward, noticing Tristan had collapsed to his knees, fighting to stay conscious. A stab of guilt shot through Quillan, but he brushed it aside. He couldn't afford to have regrets, not now. Revenge had been served.

"First, I want the princess –" Nimrooden stopped mid-sentence as three guards entered, one with Melodea slung over his shoulder.

"You were saying?" Quillan flashed an impudent grin.

Nimrooden waved his hand, all but ignoring Quillan. "Bring the traitor his coin."

Quillan winced, glancing in Melodea's direction. She hadn't heard – her eyes were just starting to flutter open. A nasty bruise marred her delicate jaw and blood trickled from the corner of her mouth where the rope had dug into flesh.

Once again, the words tumbled from Quillan's mouth before he could stop them. "No."

Nimrooden's eyes darted back to Quillan. "No?" he repeated.

"This time, I take the girl." Quillan's calm, steady tone, so bold in the face of such a powerful king, surprised even himself. Something in Melodea's eyes gave him strength – a strength that defied the will of a king. He nodded, resolute. "Or no deal."

"I have already given my answer. Take your coin and go."

Quillan's gaze hardened. "Final chance."

"Guards, remove this vagrant ..." Nimrooden rapped his fingers on the arm of his throne. "And leave his corpse for carrion."

179

"I don't think so." Quillan launched into a backflip, landing behind Tristan's kneeling form. He kicked one guard in the groin and elbowed the other in the soft part of the temple, knocking him out cold. Holding his knife to Tristan's neck, he forced the prisoner to his feet. "If you want to find your missing princess, I suggest you give me what I want. Otherwise, your key information source bleeds out like a stuck pig." Quillan made a slicing motion with his knife, and Tristan flinched.

Gauln chuckled, nudging the king's arm. "I like him!"

"Be quiet, Gauln." Nimrooden frowned, but a glimmer of amusement played at the corners of his mouth. "Very well, clever thief. But if I ever see you again, it'll be your body dangling from a low branch. You'll die – slowly – with your feet hanging mere inches from the ground."

"Fair enough." Quillan nudged Tristan forward. "I'm sorry," he said, quiet enough so Melodea couldn't hear. "But I'll keep her safe."

"Yeah right," Tristan muttered. "You've shown your true colors, *comrade*."

Quillan didn't reply. He turned to Nimrooden, giving an elegant bow. "A pleasure, Majesty. Don't take this the wrong way, but I hope our paths never cross again." He unlocked Melodea's shackles, swept her into his arms, and gave her shoulders a comforting squeeze as he carried her to their waiting horses. "You're safe now."

She smiled faintly, eyes boring into his with gratitude and ... *trust*. With a dry cough, she mouthed a silent, "Thank you." But her eyes drifted back to Tristan.

Quillan looked away, utterly ashamed.

∽

Tristan's head snapped to the side; gray edged in on his line of sight, blurring his peripheral vision. All he could make out was Gauln, fist raised, bloodlust dancing in his eyes. The brute actually enjoyed torturing him. No surprise.

"You're resilient, *boy*, I'll give you that. You remind me of a soldier I once knew. Self-righteous and arrogant … before he joined my side. Now he's just arrogant." Gauln snickered, revealing red, swollen gums and crusted teeth. They reminded Tristan more of fangs than anything – stained from the blood of his prey. Not a comforting thought.

"Why don't we just kill him?" Gauln asked, turning to Nimrooden. "There are only so many places for a spoiled princess to hide. And this boy's getting on my nerves – all high and mighty and full of noble cause." He spat on Tristan and scowled.

Tristan made a face, wiping the saliva onto his shoulder. "That was disgusting."

"I want him alive. Even a princess can hide in these forests, and we have a schedule to keep." Nimrooden regarded Tristan blandly. "Besides, you may be surprised by her resourcefulness."

"Why, because you thought her mother was clever?" Gauln scoffed. "The way you still worship that wom–"

Nimrooden whirled on Gauln, hand crushing around the general's throat. Gauln gasped for air, clawing desperately but unable to pry the fingers away.

"Know your place, *General*, unless you want a rope on a low branch, too," Nimrooden snarled. He threw Gauln to the ground, where the general cowered like a struck dog.

"Yes, Your Majesty."

It was the first time Tristan had seen Gauln afraid of his master. There was more to Nimrooden than lofty titles and a powerful army. He commanded - no, *demanded* – a respect and terror that put even the powerful general on his knees. And worship what woman? Was Gauln referring to Queen Mariah? Nimrooden had killed her! Why would he –

Nimrooden snapped his fingers and two of his men scurried forward. "We move out at first light. With the princess missing, I don't want to take any chances."

He turned to Tristan. "And as for you, my *noble knight* … let's

181

see if we can't make you talk."

සො

It was still dark out when Quillan finally stopped, easing Melodea out of the saddle and letting her rest while he set up a rudimentary camp. He had put plenty of distance between them and Nimrooden, although no amount of distance was enough for Melodea. In her mind, she could still see the hundreds of torches and the men swarming around Tristan, seeking his blood.

After Quillan had come for her, they had ridden off on his horse, leading Sunflower in tow. By some unspoken agreement, they'd left Tristan's horse. Like there was the slightest chance he could escape. *He'll be dead by morning, and all because of me.*

Melodea absently watched as Quillan coaxed flame from a smoldering wad of dry grass. "Why did you come back for me?" she whispered.

Quillan didn't look up. When he spoke, his words were halting, almost forced. "Because I … couldn't allow you to be killed. Not after I turned you in. Your guard friend offered to help me," he added.

"And now Tristan will be killed instead of me." Melodea buried her face in her hands. "Why do people sacrifice themselves for others? It's not as though the lives of royalty are more valuable than any other!" she blurted. "And I'm probably the most useless royal anyone could have ever chosen to save. My life is *not* equal to Tristan's."

Quillan spun around, seizing her hand. "Don't say that! Your life is precious. You shouldn't regret what Tristan did to save you – I know he doesn't." He swallowed, lowering his gaze. "And if our places were reversed, neither would I."

"Why?" Melodea knelt, forcing him to look her in the eye. "Why would you sacrifice yourself for me? Why did Tristan?"

He laughed quietly; when he spoke, his words held a bitter edge. "Whatever his reasons, they were far different than mine." Quillan withdrew his hand, leaving hers oddly cold and empty.

"Believe me, Princess, I'm no hero ... just a lost man hoping desperately that I've found the key."

"The key – to what? I don't understand, Quillan." Melodea chewed on her lip, peeling away a fresh scab. Blood oozed from the tear. A day ago, it would have been enough for her to send a maid for salve, but now, she couldn't even feel it. "If there's something you're not telling me ..."

Once again, Quillan averted his gaze. "The key to what makes you so different. So good. Like you believe every person in the entire world has a value and a purpose." He threw a stick into the fire; it was instantly enveloped by a thousand sparks. "Then again, maybe you're mistaken. I know I don't have value, and if I have a purpose, it's only for evil."

"You're wrong. Admitting you've made mistakes is the first step to fixing them. The first step to change." She touched his jaw, prompting him to look at her.

He resisted, keeping his face turned away. "I can never change." His voice was strained. Could he actually believe his own words? "I was a fool to think otherwise." He cleared his throat, pulling away. "I'll – go get us some more firewood."

"Quillan –" Melodea pleaded. She reached for him, but he had already vanished into the shadows.

Her hand came back damp with his tears.

ॐ

Tristan awoke, lying prone on hard wood, surrounded by darkness. Iron bars frowned at him, blurring in and out of focus. "Where –" He was seized by a spastic fit of coughing that left him breathless and dizzy from pain.

"You're in the jail cart, kid. You're to be left until dead."

Carefully, Tristan turned his head, not daring to roll over onto his side. A single guard watched him through the bars, seated on a barrel, not bothering to look menacing or particularly vigilant.

"They said you were an ornery one. From the state of you, I don't doubt it. Can't imagine why you'd take such a beating for

183

some hoity-toity princess and her accursed kingdom."

Tristan raised an eyebrow. "Wouldn't you? To save your kingdom – your friends?"

The guard laughed raucously. "I don't care a mite about my kingdom, and my friends ain't worth taking a beating for, either. Not that any of 'em are particularly pretty. I imagine your princess is, though. Is that why –"

"Then why are you going to war?" Tristan interrupted. He didn't care to discuss ladies with this lout – if he insulted Raven, Tristan wouldn't be able to punch him through the bars.

"I didn't want to go," the guard said, frowning. "But Nimrooden enlisted all the able-bodied men in Tharland and the Wilderns. Not that the Tharlanders needed much encouragement – they're a bunch of thieving cutthroats, mostly. For me, though, it was either join or die," he finished with a shrug.

Tristan smirked, laying his head back. "Great predicament."

The guard scowled, ripping into a greasy piece of meat. "All I'm saying is –" he gulped down a large chunk – "if I was you, I'd be a free man."

"If you were me, you'd be dead. Do you really think Nimrooden would let you live?"

"He would!" The guard shook a chicken leg at Tristan, sending fat globules flying. "And what's more, he'd reward me for my cooperation."

Tristan chuckled dryly. "Shows what you know. So, do I get water, or do I just thirst to death?"

"You don't get *nothing*!" The guard waved the meat through the bars. "If ya like, you can smell it," he taunted.

Tristan ignored him and began evaluating his wounds. Nothing life-threatening, but if he didn't get them cleaned, infection was sure to set in. At least he'd die of thirst long before gangrene took him – not that either death was particularly appealing. He tested the bars, but they were solid. No chance out that way.

The guard glowered at him, fingering his sword. "Don't you try any funny business. The last men you outwitted got beheaded … all four of 'em, just for a five-minute lapse in guard duty. I don't fancy joining them."

"Don't worry," Tristan assured him. "When I get out, I'll make sure you're dead long before Nimrooden gets to you."

Tristan heard the guard's nervous swallow, and he hid a smile. *So gullible.*

FLEE!

A gentle breeze whispered through the white canvas of hundreds of tents, past snoring soldiers and foul-tempered men on watch, and between cell bars into Tristan's blood-caked hair. He forced his heavy eyelids apart. Dawn would come soon. After breaking into a bottle of ale – which was prohibited for soldiers on duty – Tristan's guard had fallen asleep. If Tristan was going to act, now was the time.

He grabbed the only useful object within reach ... a pitchfork that had been carelessly left leaning against the prison cart. Using both hands to steady the fork, Tristan inserted the prongs underneath the blades of the guard's battle axe and lifted it out of its sheath.

The butt of the axe made a slight *ding* as it nicked the guard's helmet, then landed without further incident into Tristan's waiting hands. He gave a quiet sigh of relief. After replacing the fork, he pulled the axe through the bars. Oh-so-carefully, he began chipping away at the cart's wooden floor – the only part not covered with metal. By the time dawn had broke, he had created a sizable hole, just enough for one person to fit through.

"Thanks for your help," Tristan whispered, slipping the axe back onto the guard's back. After relieving the man of his sword, Tristan staggered towards the wood line.

Minutes ticked by with agonizing slowness. Every slight noise sent his heart racing, and at any moment, he expected to be set upon by the entire army. But no one ever appeared.

When he finally made it out of the encampment, sweat was running freely down his temples. He slumped against a tree, exhausted, and breathed a quiet prayer of thanks.

And then a snap of a branch sounded from behind.

Rallying what strength was left in his beaten body, Tristan

readied his stolen sword, turned, and leapt from behind the tree ... where a massive figure stood, waiting for him.

§

The moment Melodea awoke, she thought she'd been trampled by a stampeding herd of aurochs. Every part of her body ached, from her jaw to her back to her poor bum, which had suffered three lengthy rides and two nights sleeping on the cold, hard ground.

And then Melodea noticed that Quillan was gone. She stood, scanning the trees. "Quillan?" she called. Nothing. More desperate this time, "Quillan!"

He left me. Stunned, Melodea plopped down next to the fire ring, poking absently at the dead embers. *How could he have left me?* She hurled the poker into the ashes, sending up a gray cloud.

"Are you just now getting up? I thought breakfast would be ready by the time I got back."

Melodea shot to her feet. "Quillan! You came back!" She fought the urge to throw her arms around him. He'd probably take that the wrong way. Still, she couldn't deny the relief flooding through her.

He laughed nervously, kneeling to restart the fire. "Why wouldn't I?"

"No reason." She gave him a reassuring smile.

Quillan grunted, not convinced. "Hand me Nightmare's saddle bag, would you? My horse," he added, grinning impishly.

Melodea frowned, retrieving the bag. "That's an ... odd name."

"Eh, I guess. But it's rather fitting for the *Thief in the Night* to ride a nightmare." Quillan dug through the leather saddle bag, producing a pan and a pouch of biscuits, dried meat, and even a couple of shriveled potatoes. Once they were crudely peeled and quartered, he placed them on the pan to fry, adding a few herbs and spices.

"After we eat, we should keep moving towards … wherever it is we're going." He fiddled with his stirring stick. "In Tarith, there's a village I call home. It's not much, but my mother raised me there, and I think … what are you looking at?"

Melodea held Tristan's crumpled note. Until that moment, she had completely forgotten about it. What message could have been so important that he wasted precious time, and risked capture, to write it? "Tristan gave me this, before …" Her voice trailed off, and she unfolded the message.

Meet Raven at Mossy Falls. Don't trust Quillan.

"What does it say?"

Quillan snatched at the note, but Melodea crumpled the cloth in her hands. Tristan was wrong. She *could* trust Quillan. The very fact that he was still here, and had come back for her, vouched for his character.

Melodea stuffed the note back into the pocket of her trousers. "He said to meet Raven at Mossy Falls, that's all. Do you think you can get me there?"

Quillan shrugged reluctantly. "I guess."

"I'll compensate you, of course," she added.

"No, it's fine – I'll take you." He absently stirred their breakfast. "But if she isn't there, will you go back to my village? Until Nimrooden is defeated, or …" He didn't finish the thought, but they both knew exactly what he meant. *Or Laynia falls. And with it, Mieldren, Roehn, and all of Alarkin.*

"I don't know, Quillan. Tarith is a *long* way, and my father would be overcome with worry."

Quillan nodded slowly. "I understand, you don't have to –"

"But I'll think about it." Melodea smiled.

Quillan smiled back, eyes so boyish and sincere. Was it possible he'd ever been a thief and a bounty hunter? He seemed like a new person, incapable of such heinous acts. Incapable of whatever Tristan had accused him of.

Betrayed.

That was what Tristan had said. He hadn't meant Quillan, had he? Not after Quillan had rescued her. Perhaps Tristan was mistaken, and he'd only thought Quillan had betrayed him. That was it.

That *had* to be it. Because Melodea had placed her life in Quillan's hands. And, if she were being honest, her trust.

Doling out two platefuls of food, Quillan thrust one in her direction. "Eat up ... our princess has a head start!"

ဢ

Raven huddled under the canopy of the trees as rain continued to leak from the leaden sky. Just like it had all last night and that morning. If it weren't for the heavy tree cover, she'd be soaked through and miserable. As it was, she was still fairly soggy and even more miserable.

It was time to go.

"It's past midday, boy. We can't wait any longer." Raven stroked Freedom's wet muzzle, drawing from his strength. "Laynia needs us."

She tossed the saddle on his damp back, packed up her gear, and stamped out the paltry fire. The rain would extinguish any embers within minutes. She had just placed her foot in the stirrup when Freedom's head swiveled, ears picking up noises too faint for her to hear. Raven paused, listening, until she heard it, too. *Hoofbeats.* Her heart leapt into her throat.

It might not be Tristan. But if it was ...

She led Freedom down an embankment into the thick foliage, wet leaves slapping against her face. If she wasn't thoroughly soaked before, she certainly was now. It was all she could do not to shiver as she listened, waiting and watching.

Hoping against hope that Tristan was alive.

Two riders approached and stopped near her abandoned camp; she couldn't see the far horse, but the one closest to her was a gray. Her heart sank. It wasn't Tristan.

"She couldn't have been gone long - the ashes are still warm,"

189

one of the riders said.

"Fool!" Raven growled. How could she have been so careless? For all she knew, these riders could be more bounty hunters!

"I hope not. I think I'm going to lose permanent use of my legs if I ride any longer."

Raven squinted. Although the speaker wore men's clothes, it was a woman's voice she heard. Specifically ... "Melodea?" Raven sprinted up the embankment, spooking the horses with her sudden appearance. Freedom crashed after her, whickering at Sunflower.

"Raven!" Melodea clambered out of the saddle. To Raven's surprise, she threw her arms around her, fairly bursting with relief. Finally, Melodea stepped back. "I'm *so* glad we found you!"

Raven grinned. "I think *I* found *you*, actually." She turned to the other rider. "And who are you?"

"This is Quillan ... he helped rescue me." Melodea beamed at her rescuer, and Raven glanced between the two. Did Melodea actually *like* someone? The thought was almost too much to grasp. Still, she seemed happy enough, considering the circumstances, and genuinely glad to see Raven. If only Tristan could –

Raven's smile faded. "Where's Tristan? Didn't he find you?" Quillan stared at his boots, refusing to meet her gaze. Raven looked at Melodea, fighting to keep her voice calm. "Well?"

Melodea had trouble looking her in the eye, too. "Tristan was trying to free me, but we were caught. Quillan managed to get me out, but Tristan ... he's been captured." She hung her head. "And it's all my fault."

"I'm sorry. I wish I could have done more, but there were too many soldiers," Quillan added.

There was something odd about his expression, almost like he was ... guilty. That was it. Not just because he failed, but somehow, he felt responsible. Raven would have to keep her eye on him. Where had he come from, anyway? He looked like one of the bandits who had kidnapped Melodea in the first place.

One of the men Tristan had gone to rescue her from – and never returned.

Raven threw her boot into the stirrup and hoisted herself into the saddle. "You have to ride to Laynia and warn my father. No one else!" She removed her ring, offering it to Melodea. "This should convince him."

"Wh-where are you going?" Quillan stuttered.

"To Nimrooden's camp."

Melodea grabbed Raven's arm, ignoring the ring. "You can't go back there – we barely made it out alive!"

Raven wrenched her arm free, eyes flashing. "Tristan saved my life. I am *not* leaving him for dead!"

Melodea shrunk away. "Raven, please ..."

Ignoring her, Raven dug her heels in and dropped the ring, hoping Melodea had the sense to take it. But before Freedom could leap forward, Quillan snatched the reins and pulled the stallion to a stop. "You can't go after him! Do you hear me?"

"I can't *leave* him!"

"Do you think I would have abandoned him if there was any chance?" he demanded. "I'd be the first one to go with you!"

"Really?" Raven snapped. "Because I'd be the first to remind you that you're the same criminal who's responsible for his capture in the first place!"

Quillan paled, recoiling. "I didn't – I never meant to –"

"Raven, he saved my life!" Melodea protested.

"*He's* the one who kidnapped you!" Raven nearly shouted. "Why are you defending him?"

Melodea's response was so quiet, Raven barely heard her. "Because I believe he can change."

Raven fell silent. Change. She'd promised herself, after Tristan left, that she would change. Try to make amends with Melodea, and start trusting her judgement. If Melodea was willing to forgive Quillan after he'd kidnapped her, the least

Raven could do was respect Melodea's decision. Obviously, a lot had transpired between them in Raven's absence.

Quillan spoke to Melodea, eyes downcast. "Princess Raven is right. Nothing about me merits defending." He turned back to Raven. "But regardless of what you may think of me, my point stands. To return to Nimrooden's camp would be suicide. And even if you could make it in without getting caught, Tristan is probably –"

"Don't say it. Don't you *dare* say it."

But the implication was clear. Tristan was gone. A rush of emotions coursed through Raven, unlike any she'd ever felt. Breathing was impossible. Had her last hope died at Nimrooden's camp?

Maybe more than just my hope. What had Tristan become to her, anyway? Something closer than a friend. Circumstance had thrown them together, forced them to rely on each other more than she'd ever relied on another human before. And now …

Now, the only thing left for her was to let him go. For the sake of her kingdom. *She didn't want to, but she must.* Raven could almost hear Tristan's voice in her mind, urging her to keep going. And she couldn't let his sacrifice be in vain.

As if he could read her mind, Quillan released Freedom's reins and offered a grim nod. "We need to keep moving. If Tristan were here, he'd tell you the same thing."

Raven murmured a barely audible, "I know." She dismounted and stooped to grab her ring, using the distraction to compose herself.

When she mounted again, her face was void of emotion. "We ride to Caritas."

೫

As their horses plodded westward, absolute silence reigned, broken only by the steady beat of hooves. If there were any forest creatures, they remained hidden; even the birds had forsaken these forests in search of more pleasant nesting grounds.

No traces of civilization – not so much as a crude path – were anywhere to be seen. Unlike the surrounding kingdoms, Tharland was sparsely inhabited. Not that Tharland could be considered a kingdom – how could it? It had no king or political leader of any kind. The entire region was a no-man's-land. To attempt a conquest was unthinkable.

"Just like Burglar Valley," Raven muttered.

"Tharland is far worse than that petty lot of vagabonds," Quillan said, scowling with distaste. "It is filled with the most treacherous criminals, ruled only by their own lust for blood and gold … exactly the type of evil Nimrooden feeds on."

"I'm surprised my father has allowed it to –"

"You think King Wilgaun would stop this? He cares nothing for the lands outside his borders!"

"Like you said, it's *outside* his borders. Why should he?" Raven scoffed.

"Tharland is on his doorstep – what's to stop the criminals here from crossing over and raiding outlying Laynian settlements? But all Wilgaun cares about are his lucrative trade relations," Quillan spat. "Anything that will increase his profit and pad his coffers. Ever since the queen died, he stopped caring, as if the world died with her. To the detriment of his subjects."

"That's my *father* you're speaking about!"

"Let's not –" Melodea started.

"Would you rather I give you all the politically correct nonsense that everyone else does – tell you what a wise and considerate king he is? Why should I bother withholding the truth – to spare the feelings of a spoiled princess?" Quillan shook his head. "I've never had much use for kings, and your father is no exception."

"How dare you –" Raven bit off the insult that was on the tip of her tongue. "You're nothing but a common criminal! You have *no right* to judge my father, or anyone!" Quillan recoiled, but once started, she couldn't stop. "If you think my father is a poor ruler, it's because you're on the wrong side of justice. Men like you who make this world a wicked place. If it weren't for you, Melodea wouldn't have been captured and –" Tears stung her eyes and she faltered. "Tristan would still be alive." She kicked Freedom into a canter, riding ahead.

Raven couldn't totally disagree with Quillan; she knew her father was obsessed with trade relations. Truth be told, he rarely looked beyond his own city to the suffering and unrest that plagued his people. Burglar Valley proved as much.

But despite Quillan's perceptive criticisms, it didn't change the fact that he was to blame for Tristan's capture. That Quillan had escaped when Tristan hadn't. And right now, that was the only thing that mattered to Raven.

A Question of Loyalties

"I need to walk a moment."

Melodea's sudden announcement startled Quillan out of a vicious downward-spiral of dark thoughts. Princess Raven was right, of course ... men like him *were* the reason that King Wilgaun and other rulers were failing. With rising crime and disconsolate subjects, who had time to look to trouble beyond their own borders? In any case, he'd spent far too much time rehashing his hasty words; a walk wasn't a bad idea to cool off. "I'll join you."

"Oh, there's no need – that is, I'd rather – it will only take a moment ..." Melodea continued to stutter, and it took Quillan far too long to realize the source of her embarrassment.

"You need to use the ladies' woods."

Melodea nodded, mortified, and Quillan fought to hide a grin. How did that princess manage to be so utterly –

He stopped himself. Had he really been about to say *cute*? He rolled his eyes. He'd never been sentimental or a romantic. Sure, his statement might be accurate, but it was absurd that he'd allowed such thoughts to surface. Melodea was sweet and kind, and he had even grown to respect her. But settling down? Having a wife? He'd considered it a thousand times, and each time, he came to the same conclusion:

He'd break his wife's heart.

Melodea clumsily lowered herself from the saddle and tromped off into the bushes, positioning herself as far away from the others as she felt comfortable in the eerie woods. Quillan couldn't see her, but he could hear her stop in the middle of a bramble thicket, attesting to her lack of woodsman knowledge in the art of relieving oneself. *She'll get a poke in the behind as soon as she –*

195

A loud yelp confirmed his incomplete prediction, followed by more tromping toward a suitable spot. She'd be a while in finding one. *Now is as good a time as ever.* Quillan cleared his throat. "Uh, Princess, about earlier …"

Raven smirked wryly, appearing to have calmed after some alone time. "Right. About earlier."

It took Quillan a few seconds to form an apology. He was definitely out of practice – something he'd have to work on. *If* he planned on reforming. "I'm sorry for what I said. About your father. You were right … people like me are responsible for his troubles, just as people like him are responsible for me turning to crime. Not your father!" he added quickly, sensing the princess was about to scourge him again. "I mean other rich, heartless nobility who don't give a da–" He stopped himself. "Who don't care about common folk. Not that your father is heartless!"

Raven nodded once. "If we're going to survive this, we all need to be on the same team. No petty quarrels. But," she added, "even if we set aside our differences, it doesn't mean I trust you, and I *certainly* haven't forgiven you. And after this is over …" Her eyes glinted dangerously. "I never want to see your miserable face again."

"I understand." Quillan studied Raven, gauging how likely she was to follow through with her unspoken threat. From her expression, it seemed likely. He had to admit, she was nothing like he had expected, and certainly nothing like the other fawning nobility he robbed for a living.

For a second, Quillan wondered if perhaps, when Tristan had left Raven behind, he was leaving more than a friend. He pushed the thought aside. Princesses like Raven and Melodea didn't look at commoners like him and Tristan. It simply wasn't done. And a good thing, too … if he didn't know better, he'd say Melodea was getting attached to him. And he'd hate to break her heart.

A few minutes later, Melodea crashed out of the underbrush,

cheeks tinged with pink and puffing from the exertion of her hike. "If you're all done making up, shall we be off?"

Quillan looked away, embarrassed, and nodded. A quick glance at Raven revealed a similar reaction. At least he wasn't the only one who felt like a reprimanded school-boy.

They continued riding until nightfall. Not daring to risk a fire, they ate a cold supper and rolled up in blankets, shivering against the frigid air and ground. Melodea and Raven lay back-to-back, sharing their warmth, while Quillan fended for himself a few feet away. He had almost warmed up enough to finally drift off into sleep when a noise pulled him back from the precipice of slumber. It took him a moment to realize it was someone talking quietly. *Raven*.

Staring through the forest canopy into the starry sky, her mouth moved in the darkness, words no louder than the rustling wind. Black hair reflecting the moonlight, deep blue eyes luminous in the darkness, she could have been an ethereal faery being.

"If anyone can hear me, please … let Tristan be alive. Bring him back to me." Too proud to cry, her eyes shimmered with unshed tears. Only after they had closed did Quillan dare to breathe.

He shut his eyes, unable to sleep, unable to stop the steady throb inside his chest. Everything Raven was going through – everything Melodea had gone through – was his fault. Not to mention Tristan. Was he even alive?

No. He was dead. Exactly how Quillan had planned it. All for the sake of his pathetic retaliation, avenging a father who had deserved his noose as much as any other criminal. Now, in Quillan's twisted search for vengeance, he'd sealed the fate of an innocent man who would die a tortured death.

Not as strong – or perhaps as innocent – as Raven, Quillan let the tears flow silently down his face. *What have I done?*

෨

A warm breath caressed Tristan's forehead, and something

197

lipped at his hair. The looming figure – a large, muscly horse – nickered, grateful that someone had come to find him after being left tethered in the middle of the woods.

Tristan exhaled in relief. "Destiny! Boy, am I glad to see you." He sheathed his stolen weapon, untied Destiny, and painstakingly mounted – on the third try. Even moving slowly, his head swam with dizziness, and everything throbbed. *Just like after my first day of sword training.* The thought made him smile – which made him realize he had a painful gash under his eye from someone's fist. It would be ugly and bruised before long, but thankfully he didn't have any upcoming formal occasion that required him to look his best.

Using the supplies from his saddlebag, he quickly bound up the worst of his wounds, packing them with a pungent, leafy ointment to ward off infection. It wasn't a great patch job, but it would keep him alive until he reached Laynia.

Tristan rode hard until dawn, rested briefly so Destiny could catch his breath, then kept pressing south. He found a camp a few miles further, with two sets of hoofprints leading towards Mossy Falls. Was Quillan taking Melodea to find Raven? Even after writing the note for Melodea, he'd never expected to see either of them again. Why would Quillan bother going after Raven, unless …

Unless he meant to turn her in to Nimrooden, too.

He pushed Destiny harder.

They reached Mossy Falls a few hours later. There, he found ashes – not a day old. Three sets of hoofprints rode west. Tristan followed, tracking them. They weren't moving exceptionally fast, not like he'd expect if Quillan was taking them back to Nimrooden. Besides, the tracks still headed west, not north, where Nimrooden's camp was located.

He stopped just as it grew dark. Well, darker. The forest of Tharland always seemed to be in eternal twilight, either lit with gold or silver as the sun and moon traded spots on the ethereal horizon. But the twilight did little to redeem the numerous bogs, pitfalls, and ensnaring vines. If anything, it disguised the treacherous terrain.

After a few hours of broken, fitful sleep, Tristan rose with the dawn and forced himself to press on. He couldn't ignore the weariness that clung to his body, but he could certainly defy it. *Just two more days, then home, and rest. But not before.*

Something glinted in the forest. He pulled Destiny to a stop, listening; a grotesque snore rattled through the morning stillness. A few dozen men were camped, bearing Nimrooden's colors. Tristan edged closer on foot, scanning. *A hunting party. Did they follow Quillan's trail to find Raven?* Whether they had or not, Tristan had to get to her first.

He edged away from the slumbering soldiers, remounted, and kept going. Within the hour he came to another camp, although there was no fire and no one around – only a few blankets and three horses on a picket line. Unsheathing his sword, Tristan quietly approached.

∽

Quillan rapped his knuckles against his thigh. They had to keep moving. It was only an hour past dawn, but he'd woke with an anxiousness that he couldn't shake off. The princesses had gone to fill their canteens at the creek – and whatever else women did in the morning - while he packed up camp. But so far, all he'd done is pace back and forth, listening and scanning the tree line. Something was there, close by, encroaching. If they didn't keep moving …

A snap sounded directly behind him, loud and deliberate. *Closer than I thought.* He twisted, drawing his sword … and was met with an arrow a few feet from his face.

"Look familiar?"

He slowly shifted his focus from the arrow tip to the hooded figure. Quillan lowered his sword, unable to keep the disbelief from his voice. "*Tristan?*"

"Considering I took the precaution of keeping my bow *out* of your sword range."

Quillan couldn't do anything but gape. "But – but … you're dead!"

∞

Despite the warm summer, the water was still icy cold. That hadn't stopped either of the princesses from rinsing the layers of dust and grime from their faces. Shivering, Melodea used the clean underlayer of her skirt to pat herself dry. "How long do you think it will be until –"

Raven shushed her mid-sentence. "I hear voices."

"It's probably just Quillan."

"Then who's he talking with?" Raven peered through the trees, but the foliage was too thick to make anything out.

"Um … the horses?"

Dropping her canteen, Raven sprang to her feet. "Since when do horses talk back?"

After the incident at the Thorn and Thistle, Raven had kept her sword on her at all times, but she hadn't expected to use it. She drew it now, cautiously making her way toward the camp, followed closely by Melodea. The moment Raven broke through the tree line, her eyes locked onto the figure, whose bow was aimed directly at Quillan.

"Drop it!" She strode forward, weapon raised. "Drop it, or I'll run you through!"

To her chagrin, the figure chuckled. "Really?" He replaced the arrow in its quiver. "I didn't realize you were the killing sort, Princess."

The voice … the cloak … Raven whirled to find the large blue roan standing nearby. Suddenly, everything came tumbling together. "Tristan!" she gasped. Her sword slipped from her fingers and fell to the ground. Rushing forward, she threw her arms around the figure before she even saw his face. And then the hood slipped off. "You're *alive*!" she whispered, words choked. "I thought – well, it doesn't matter." She stepped back, suddenly aware that Melodea and Quillan were staring.

"More or less," Tristan laughed. There were dark circles

200

under his eyes, and a bruise across his cheekbone; blood stained his shirt. But he was alive!

Raven reached up, lightly touching the bruise. "What happened to you – how did you escape?"

"Long story." He smiled, but she could see the pain behind his eyes. "Princess Melodea, I'm glad to see you're safe." His gaze settled on Quillan. "I didn't realize you had company."

Before either had a chance to respond, Tristan turned back to Raven. "It doesn't matter – right now we need to move. Nimrooden's army left at dawn, and there's a hunting party a few miles behind us."

He limped towards Destiny, but Raven's hand shot out and halted him. "You are in *no* condition to ride."

"We don't have a choice. Nimrooden's men have found your trail, and they'll be no more than a quarter of an hour behind us."

"He's right," Quillan said. "But," he added, making an allowance for Raven's glare, "we won't make it far with you falling off your horse. We'll take a few minutes to shove some food down you and secure your dressings."

Raven sprang into action. "Melodea, grab some jerky from my saddlebag. Quillan, start tightening his bandages. I'll get the canteens from the creek."

೫

Quillan started removing Tristan's shirt and adding another layer of bandages, carefully avoiding eye contact. Tristan waited until Raven slipped out of view before his hand shot out and grabbed Quillan's arm, stopping him mid-motion.

"What are you doing here?" Tristan demanded. "Tell me, are you conspiring to capture *both* the princesses for Nimrooden, or just for yourself?"

Quillan's jaw worked noiselessly. "Look," he finally said, "I know you don't trust me, and I don't fault you for it, but –"

"Do you even *realize* what's at stake? What happens if we don't get back to Laynia in time?" Tristan's hand tightened, constricting a fistful of Quillan's shirt sleeve. He wished it was his neck. "You could be the downfall of an entire kingdom!"

"I know."

"You know? That's all you have to say for yourself? *You know*!" Tristan released the shirt, shoving Quillan backwards.

"Fine, I've been a fool! Is that what you wanted me to say?" Quillan threw his hands in the air. "There – I said it … I'm a fool! And I despise myself for it. But I'm here to make amends. So take it or leave it."

Tristan grunted and started to reply, but stopped when Melodea returned with bandages, oblivious of the tension passing between them. He shot Quillan an unmistakable look: *I'm watching you.*

Swallowing, Quillan nodded.

Message received.

∽

Tristan's gaze never left Quillan as they rode, like a hawk watching its prey. But Tristan said nothing. There was no reason for the princesses to be involved; any accusations he made against Quillan would only divide them. Melodea may trust Tristan, but Quillan had clearly wormed his way into her affections, although Tristan wasn't sure to what degree. And Raven would probably try to kill Quillan – a tempting thought, but one he didn't have time for.

And then there was Quillan. Why hadn't he turned Raven in, or run off with Melodea? There was no reason for him to help find Raven … unless he *actually wanted* to help Laynia. But then why betray Tristan? The pieces didn't add up.

Quillan turned his horse abruptly and plunged into the foliage, beckoning silently.

"What are you –" Tristan started. And then he heard it. *Voices. Behind us.* He urged the princesses after Quillan. "Go, *go!*" He followed them a dozen or so yards into the dense brush, where they waited in silence, crouched low in their saddles as they listened to approaching men.

"Are you sure they went this way?" someone growled. A voice answered, but it was too quiet and indistinct for Tristan to pick up on any words.

"Fine," the first speaker said, "but if we lose them, you're a dead man. General Gauln isn't far behind, and he has a special way of dealing with incompetence."

Quillan let out a quiet curse. "They're tracking us."

"We already knew that," Tristan returned. "Got anything helpful to say?"

The tracker, whose words had been too quiet to pick up on before, pointed in their direction. "They've left the trail and went that way, Commander Kriptin. It will be more difficult to track them in the brush."

The man called Kriptin rolled his eyes. "And I suppose you'll be wanting extra?"

"Naturally, Commander."

"Just find them, you scum."

Tristan turned to the others. "Time to move. When I say run, we'll –"

He was interrupted by a loud, wet, snort. Sunflower looked at him innocently, nibbling at a pine branch that had, moments before, been stuck up her nostril. Tristan could almost hear Kriptin's head turn in their direction, see his eyes lock onto their position.

"Looks like your services are no longer required," Kriptin sneered. In one swift motion, he swiveled in his saddle and impaled the tracker. "There's your *extra*." Kriptin turned to his men. "FIND THEM!" he bellowed, bloodied sword pointing into the woods.

"Raven, Melodea, go!" Tristan ordered. "We'll hold them off as long as possible."

Melodea dug her heels into Sunflower and fled into the woods, but Raven looked like she was about to protest. Tristan shook his head. "You may have to fight, but now is not the time. We'll be right behind you."

She nodded and took off after Melodea.

Tristan nudged Quillan and drew his sword. Ironic – it belonged to one of Nimrooden's men, and now he was about to use it to kill them. "If you want to prove you're on our side, now is the time."

"Like I have a choice!" Quillan retorted. Still, he readied his sword. "So, do we draw them in, or just wait for them to happen across us?"

"Why would we draw them –"

A soldier pointed. "There they are!"

"Time to go!" Tristan ducked as volley of arrows rained around them. Digging his heels in, he sent Destiny charging into the woods, Quillan following closely behind. Tristan led the soldiers away from Raven and Melodea, dodging between, under, and over fallen trees to dissuade the less competent riders.

"Are we randomly fleeing through the woods, or did you have a destination in mind?" Quillan shouted.

"Nope, just run!"

DIVIDED

Raven reined Freedom in, taking note of the sweat and foam lathering his neck. Somewhere above them, the sun was nearing its pinnacle – another reminder of how little time they had left. Her father would need time to prepare; how would he if they arrived with the army hard on their heels? In her head, Raven knew the army wouldn't arrive for hours, maybe days, after them, but her heart pounded with the fear that all her efforts would be in vain.

"We need to slow down for a little bit," she said. "The horses can't run that hard all day, and we still have another day before we reach Laynia. And truth be told," she added with a frown, "I don't know exactly where we are."

Melodea bobbed her head, barely seeming to hear Raven. "It's like the trees are taunting us," she murmured. "I've never been so tired … so scared … so lost!"

"I know. Me neither."

"How will we ever find them? Tristan and Quillan, I mean?"

"Because we have to."

Melodea looked like she was on the verge of tears. "I can't do this."

Raven reached out and took her hand. "I miss my home. My father. Even when he was scolding me, I never doubted that he loved me. I just wish I would have told him that I loved him. And knowing I might not get the chance …" She shut her eyes, lost for words. She cleared her throat. "But we can't give up. Not on our families, and not on Tristan and Quillan."

"I wish I was home, too. Even when my little sisters drove me crazy, and my mother made me read to her for hours. Or my father bragged about my painting in front of boorish suitors." Melodea's eyes were damp, but she smiled at the memory.

"And when my chambermaid yanked my hair until I thought I would cry," Raven said with a laugh.

"I wonder if we'll ever see any of them again."

Raven's gaze hardened. "Not if we stay here." She squeezed Melodea's hand. "Are you with me?"

She didn't hesitate. "Yes."

A voice sounded from behind. "How touching. A little princess pact. Too bad it's too late."

Melodea stiffened, face draining of color. "General Gauln."

∽

"Did you see their faces when they realized we ditched them? I have never seen such a sight!" Quillan laughed, slapping his thigh. Nightmare's ear flicked backward. "I mean -"

Tristan held up a hand. "Quiet."

"No really, like -"

"Shush!" he hissed. Voices. He scanned, searching for the source, trying to hear over Destiny's heavy breathing.

"What?" Quillan whispered. "I don't hear - oh."

Over a rise, a horse snorted, followed by a man's gravelly voice. "Well, well - if it isn't the elusive Princess of Laynia herself! What coincidence, meeting you here of all places." The man continued, words dripping with sarcasm. "A princess shouldn't be alone in the wilds of Tharland; some men aren't as chivalrous as myself and may wish you harm. Especially with such a timid companion." He chuckled. "What was it again? Melody? Mel-ow-ee-a?"

Quillan jerked on Tristan's sleeve repeatedly. "I know that voice, it's -"

"Gauln. I know." Tristan pulled his arm away. "And he has the princesses." He dismounted, crept up the hill, and assessed the large circle of armored men surrounding Raven and Melodea.

Beside him, Quillan cursed. "That's too many men to fight off."

"No kidding," Tristan snorted. "Do you always state the

obvious?"

"Only around you. I'm always afraid you'll miss some important detail with that noble knight ego blinding you."

"You're lucky I don't have time to argue with you at the moment."

Quillan grinned. "Not lucky. Good planning," he corrected.

Tristan didn't bother to reply.

Below them, Raven urged her horse forward a few paces. "And who are you, *oh chivalrous knight?*" she asked, mimicking Gauln's sarcastic tone.

"A friend, naturally," Gauln said. "Or rather, a mutual friend. I believe you'll recognize Commander Kisbin. Excuse me, I believe you know him as *Sir Kisby*." He sneered, gesturing at the knight.

"Princess." Kisbin stared at Raven, expressionless.

"I don't suppose you're here to protect me, are you, *traitor*?" Raven asked with a defiant lift of her chin. But Tristan could see past her brave façade to the fear in her eyes, the tremor as her hands clenched the reins in a death grip. The desperate searching as her gaze flitted through the trees.

Looking for him.

Kisbin gave a slight shake of his head. "No, I'm afraid not."

Pounding hoofs thudded across the turf as Kriptin and his men crashed into the clearing. "We lost the men. They had too much of a lead," he panted.

Yeah, right, Raven thought. *More like Kriptin's men were too incompetent to keep up.*

Gauln raised his eyebrows, clearly not convinced, either. "How is it that you – who were hot on their trail – lost them, whereas I managed to find the princesses from a half-mile away?"

"I – we ..." Kriptin cleared his throat. "One is fatally wounded – the knight. He won't last long."

Raven recoiled, and the pain on her face was almost unbearable. It was all Tristan could do to keep from revealing himself right then and there.

"Good." Gauln flicked a hand at the princesses. "Take them."

Quillan let out a reluctant sigh. "I suppose we have to stop them, don't we?"

"You don't have to help me." Quillan started to interrupt, but Tristan held up a hand. "Hear me out. We probably won't walk out of this. If you want out, now's the time. But if you mean what you said, and you want to help …" Tristan put his hand on Quillan's shoulder. "It's your choice."

For a moment, Quillan didn't answer, and Tristan thought he might leave then and there. But then, almost imperceptibly, he nodded. "I meant it."

Quillan met Tristan's gaze steadily, something he hadn't dared to do since his betrayal. "Look, it's *my* fault you're in this mess – *my* fault Gauln even found you in the first place. So if you're going to die in some reckless rescue attempt, then you have my word – I'm with you!"

"Great." Tristan grinned. "Because this time, *I've* got the plan."

සො

Raven fought the weight crushing her chest. *Tristan.* Fatally wounded? Won't last long? Instead of the grief rendering her immobile, a fire burned inside her. It wasn't rage. It wasn't vengeance, although both of those clawed for traction in her mind. Instead, rushing through her veins, obliterating any coherent thought, was the will to push on. To fight.

To make sure Tristan's death was not in vain.

Slowly, deliberately, she drew her sword. "They want us alive, so we take down as many as we can."

Eyes wide, Melodea followed suit and drew her only weapon – a small dagger that Quillan had given her. "Alright," she whispered.

If Raven was scared, Melodea was terrified. The weight of Raven's actions, and the extent that Melodea had suffered as a result, sent Raven reeling.

She reached out and squeezed Melodea's arm. "I'm sorry I got you into this. And I'm sorry … I was never the friend I should have been." Raven hesitated, trying to read Melodea's expression. "Can we finally go down together? As friends?"

A smile broke across Melodea's face. "Friends," she agreed.

"Ah, how touching. Don't worry, you can share the same cell … until Nimrooden executes you." Gauln chortled, surveying the scene from the vantage point of his giant destrier.

Sitting back to watch us fight … as if it were some show. Disgusting. Raven swiped at an approaching soldier, eyes still fixed on Gauln. "I'll give you a show," she muttered.

Melodea glanced at her. "What?"

"Nothing."

The soldier raised his sword, and Raven braced herself for the strike – when a loud horn split the air. The entire glade, the princesses included, froze.

And then Raven smiled. "I know that horn," she whispered.

∞

"General – soldiers – princesses." Tristan bowed, easily visible from his position atop the small hill. Raven scanned every inch of him, searching for a wound but finding nothing. *He lied. Kriptin lied, trying to save his own neck.*

Tristan continued. "How pleasant meeting you all here. I really can't stay, but I think that *this* belongs to you." He held up Quillan's bag of gold coins, giving it a purposeful shake. "Why don't you come and get it?" With a mischievous grin, he disappeared on the other side of the hill, leaving the soldiers gawking.

"Don't just stand there – go after him!" Kriptin bellowed, waving frantically. The soldiers snapped into action, and a few kicked their horses into pursuit. Still, too many remained for Raven to make a break for it – especially with Melodea to slow her down.

Gauln's jaw made audible popping noises as he worked it back and forth. He turned to Kriptin, gaze murderous. "I thought you *killed* him."

"I-I did, General. He must be faking, nearly dead from lack of –" Kriptin never finished his sentence. Gauln drew his sword and raked it across the man's stomach. Kriptin slumped, tumbling off his horse and landing in a twitching heap on the ground.

Gauln swung his sword at the other men, spraying them with blood. He was practically foaming at the mouth. "No one, *ever*, lies to me! Or I can assure you … you will meet the same fate. Now bind the princesses, and *find – that – thief*," Gauln snarled, scanning the woods. "He won't be far behind."

"Correction, General. I'm one step ahead of you."

Gauln swiveled in his saddle only to find Quillan's sword plummeting toward him. Gauln dodged, but the hilt still crashed against his jaw, sending him reeling.

"Princesses, we meet again," Quillan said, reining Nightmare in with a lazy smile.

"I really can't seem to escape you, can I?" Melodea asked. She was beaming in a manner Raven could only compare to a love-struck youth.

Quillan winked and tucked a piece of hair behind Melodea's ear. "Not a chance."

"Alright, that's quite enough," Raven interrupted, bringing Freedom in between them. "What's the plan?"

"Just follow my lead and wait for the signal."

Raven frowned. "What signal? That's not even remotely –"

"Kill them!" Gauln screamed, spewing saliva like a rabid dog. With one hand he pointed his sword, and with the other he clutched his broken jaw.

"Not today, General!" Quillan spurred Nightmare forward into the ring of men, sending foot soldiers diving out of the way and horses bolting, rearing, and bucking to evade the stallion's biting and kicking. Even Gauln was forced to give ground as his horse lunged forward, almost unseating its rider before he could pull his mount back under control.

Raven shrugged, unable to hide her grin at the impetuous thief. "I guess that's the signal." She sent Freedom galloping after Quillan, followed closely by Melodea. Behind them, Gauln screeched orders at his men, threatening to have them strung in gibbets if the princesses escaped.

Quillan crested and descended a rise, and the trio were momentarily out of sight from Gauln's men. "Ride as fast as you can to Laynia. Tristan and I will take out as many as we can," Quillan said firmly.

Melodea gnawed on her lip so hard Raven thought she'd draw blood. "Come back safe, alright?" she whispered.

What a typical, princessey thing to say. Still, from Quillan's reaction, Raven guessed Melodea had him wrapped around her little finger and didn't even know it.

Quillan leaned in and kissed Melodea on the cheek. "I could hardly do otherwise." He whirled Nightmare around and shot off toward Tristan, who was flanking from the other direction, pursuers close behind him.

Melodea swallowed, blinking rapidly. "Let's go."

Go. Abandon Tristan and save yourself. You're a princess ... others are supposed to die for you. Exactly what Farah would have told Raven – that she wasn't brave enough to fight. *I'm* done *listening to you, Farah.* Raven set her jaw. "No."

Melodea did a double take. "What?"

"No," she repeated. "We can't leave them again!" She closed her eyes, tone softening. "*I* can't leave *him* again, never knowing ..." Never knowing if he would die because she was too afraid to stand up for those she loved.

Loved? Did she love Tristan? Maybe. Between the adrenaline, believing he had died – twice – and being thrown into an insane adventure together, she couldn't deny her feelings for him were strong. The unfamiliar, uncomfortable surge of emotion that rushed through her whenever he was close. The illogical need to go after him, even when she had been convinced he was dead.

All she knew was she could never abandon Tristan again.

211

Melodea's words were distant, like they were coming through a tunnel or a thick fog. "We don't have a choice!"

"I do." The next thing Raven knew, she had dug in her heels and Freedom was charging after Quillan, leaving Melodea alone, calling for her to come back.

හ

Tristan veered his horse under a low-hanging branch, dipping low in the saddle at the last minute. His pursuer tried to follow, but his reflexes were slow, and he took a branch to the face, unseating him and sending his horse bolting away, riderless. But more were coming, and they were getting too close for comfort.

Out of the corner of his eye, Tristan saw Quillan approaching; Tristan didn't dare slow down to wait for him. Once Quillan had caught up, Tristan pointed at the riders behind them. "We need to break them up and keep them off the princesses' trail until Raven can – Raven, what are you doing here?" Tristan gaped at her. "You need to get to Laynia!"

There was no way the soldiers hadn't spotted her, but if Tristan fell back and clashed blades with a few of them, she might be able to slip away. "Alright, here's the plan. I'll distract them while you go after Melodea and –"

"No." Her tone – and expression – were as unmovable as a five-ton boulder. "If we divide three ways, you and Quillan will have a better chance of escaping. Melodea will take the message back to Laynia."

"But –" Tristan started, but was once again interrupted.

"That's an order!" Raven snapped. She touched his forearm to soften her words. "I'm not leaving you again. And I need to learn to fight my own battles," she added softly.

Tristan finally nodded. "But never fighting alone."

"Never alone," she agreed. And then she was galloping away, shouting taunts at the soldiers to try and keep up.

"Be careful, Princess," he whispered.

හ

Raven's eyes darted wildly through the forest, always searching for the rider she knew was close behind. She had shaken all but one pursuer, who was more skilled than the rest. And Freedom's nearly unlimited strength was failing. "Just a little farther," she urged. She laid a hand on his neck, and wet, sticky lather enveloped her fingers. Heat radiated from his entire body. Either she shook that rider soon, or one of their horses would collapse from exhaustion – and she knew her pursuer would push his horse to the breaking point. The only other option was fighting.

But could she really beat Sir Kisby – no, *Kisbin* – in hand-to-hand combat?

As if he knew this was their last chance, Freedom gave a burst of speed. They were flying, and Raven thought maybe, just maybe, they could make it – when Freedom stumbled. For a moment Raven was weightless, flying through the air. The next, the ground was rushing up to meet her, and half her body exploded in agony.

෴

Black. Everything was black. A loud ringing filled Raven's ears, piercing her throbbing skull and penetrating straight into her brain. Her vision began returning in spotted, distorted fractions, making her head throb even more. Her fingers found a warm, moist spot at her temple. It could have been anything, but the coppery scent was unmistakable. *Blood.*

"It's over, Princess." Out of sight of her spotty vision, Kisbin's footfalls moved across the forest floor, getting closer. "If you come quietly, you will reach Nimrooden alive and untouched. That is my promise."

"The promise of a traitor," Raven growled.

She struggled, using every ounce of strength to lift her head a few inches from the ground. Damp, musty leaves stirred with the effort. She was still mounted, sort of – Freedom lay on his side atop her right leg. His head was erect, but he was breathing heavily; if he hadn't broken or strained something, it'd be a miracle. In fact, it would be a miracle if *she* hadn't broken something.

Even if Raven could stand, she was pinned.

Up, Freedom. You have to move, she silently pleaded. The heady scent from the moldy leaves was making it hard to concentrate. Or was that caused by whatever her head had collided with? She'd heard of internal damage to the brain. The victims could lose sight, thinking capacity, even sanity. Some never woke up ...

"Then you leave me no choice." Kisbin rounded Freedom right as the horse shot to his feet, yanking Raven's leg from the stirrup and leaving her on the ground, breathless and queasy from the pain.

Kisbin drew his sword. She scrambled to her feet and made a desperate swipe at Freedom's saddle to try to grab her sword, but the instant she put weight on her leg, the world faded back into blackness. Her last thought was wondering how Nimrooden would choose to execute her, and of her father when he learned of her demise at the hands of his enemy.

I'm sorry, Father ... I wasn't able to make it back and set things right. How will you know that, despite everything, I loved you?

&

Tristan nearly decapitated Quillan when he materialized out of the woods. "What are you doing here? We were supposed to split up and meet back at Laynia!" Tristan shouted, ramming his sword into its sheath.

"We *did* split up." Quillan gave an exasperated snort. "Gauln and his men herded us back together."

Herded? "Why?"

"How am I supposed to know? I'm not a mind reader," Quillan retorted. "If we keep heading in this direction, maybe we can –"

Nightmare and Destiny locked their front legs, necks dropping as their riders flew over their heads. Tristan landed on his back, breath gone. In front of him, the ground simply disappeared. He clawed forward until his face reached the edge, revealing a sheer drop-off into a deep ravine. Far below was a river.

"I don't suppose now would be a good time to go cliff-diving," Quillan wheezed, barely audible over the raging water.

The hoofbeats, which had been a few hundred feet behind Tristan for the past few miles, came crashing behind them. Destiny and Nightmare bolted into the forest, leaving their riders on foot – trapped between a cliff and fifteen armed men. "Talk about a rock and a hard place," Tristan muttered.

"A valiant effort … and a waste of my time." Gauln dismounted, something between a smirk and a scowl warring for dominance on his face.

"That bruise on your jaw really adds flair to your smile, General. All the ladies will love it." Quillan stood, crossing his arms and regarding Gauln casually.

Gauln chuckled. "I'll almost regret killing you, Thief. Perhaps I'll keep your humor alive … once you're dead."

"I don't remember listing you in my will," Quillan returned with a cocky grin.

Giving a shrug, Gauln signaled his men to load their weapons. "Well, I'm afraid this is goodbye. I hope your afterlife is secure." He sneered at Quillan. "But there's no place in heaven for scum like you."

The soldiers began winding their crossbows.

Quillan turned to Tristan. "I'd better double check that will. Looks like it'll be put to good use soon."

An unexpected tightness formed in Tristan's throat. "Quillan, I want you to know –"

"No … no last words." Quillan gave a half-hearted grin. "I hate goodbyes."

"Fair enough." Tristan paused. "And I don't care what Gauln says. Heaven is made for men like you."

"Thieves?" Quillan asked wryly.

Tristan shook his head. "Men who choose to turn and do the

215

right thing – no matter the cost."

"No matter the cost, eh?" Quillan repeated, staring into the distance.

"Take aim," Gauln ordered.

Tristan clapped a hand on Quillan's shoulder. "Until tomorrow?"

"I'm afraid it will be a bit longer than that," Quillan said. At Tristan's questioning look, he added, "What I mean is ... I'm sorry. For everything. But we both don't have to die today."

"There's no way out, Quillan."

Gauln's hand raised. The second it dropped ...

"There is for one of us."

No sooner had Gauln's hand started to move than Quillan lunged forward, knife in hand, and tackled the general to the ground. "Go, Tristan!" Quillan yelled. He kneed Gauln in the gut as they wrestled for control of the knife.

The soldiers, recovering from their shock, searched for an opening.

Tristan's blade pierced the nearest man. "I'm not leaving you!"

A crossbow fired. It took Tristan a second to focus on the bolt piercing Quillan's side.

Quillan staggered away from Gauln, knife slipping from his fingers. His face drained of color, but something flashed through his eyes that made Tristan take a step backward. "Yes, you are." He dove forward, ramming his hands into Tristan's chest.

Tristan stumbled off the edge of the cliff, arms flailing, grasping at a handhold. Nothing. Above him, a dozen shots fired – at him, or at Quillan? He had just enough time to see the blood trickling down the cliff when something slammed against his back, expelling every last bit of air in his lungs.

Then everything was engulfed by water.

STRENGTH TO CARRY ON

I'm still alive? Raven lay perfectly still, wondering if this was some trick, or if she was actually dead. What happened when someone died, anyway? Was it the end?

The question didn't seem relevant. She was in far too much pain to be dead.

Something cold and wet caressed her face. She flinched, and it stopped. Slowly, painstakingly, she pried her eyes open. Kneeling beside her, Kisbin anxiously watched her face, a bloodied cloth in his hand.

"You must get to Laynia before you're seen, or we're both dead." He reached for her, ignoring her recoil, and grabbed her hand, removing her ring. "Evidence of your death," he explained briefly. He rose, walked to his horse – Freedom was nowhere to be seen – and mounted. "Farewell, Princess."

"Why are you doing this?" Raven rasped. Sandpaper was a good analogy for the state of her throat.

Kisbin hesitated. "Because you reminded me that I used to be a better man."

Raven drifted back into the dreamworld. It was filled with the echo of hoofbeats, growing distant as they faded into the mist.

೮०

Tristan coughed water out of his aching lungs. He lay prone on the riverbank, where he'd managed to drag himself before blacking out. *Quillan must be dead by now.* Tears stung in his eyes, mixing with the river water. There had been nothing he could do. At least, that's what his mind told him. But he still couldn't help wondering if, somehow, there was a way both of them could have made it out.

Tristan stood, fought to control his ragged breathing. It was too late to save Quillan, but Raven was still out there, pursued by half a dozen of Gauln's men. And there was no way he would let her share Quillan's fate. He couldn't.

He started at a walk, then a jog, then a slow run, but a sharp pain shot across his back. The fresh scabs had broken open, and blood was seeping through his bandages. *Not now.* He couldn't afford to slow down. Gritting his teeth, Tristan pushed through the pain and kept running – one step at a time. One step closer to Raven.

If she was still alive.

ော

Melodea pulled back on the reins, halting Sunflower. Everywhere, the dark forest surrounded her. Every tree looked the same, every winding path led deeper into the gloom. The sun was undetectable through the thick canopy; it was barely light enough to see, let alone tell direction. *If I knew how to tell direction. Have I even been going in a straight line?* So that was the real trick of the forest … endless wandering, until starvation or despair took you. Brilliant end.

How had her life come to this?

Just weeks before, she had been sitting in her room, sewing and reading and doing all the things demanded by her status and sex. Now, she was lost in an endless forest, pursued by a forgotten army, and left to fend for herself, all the while trying to warn a kingdom of its impending doom. The situation was so absurd, she might have laughed, but any emotional outbreak might set her crying again. And she didn't have the strength for tears.

She mumbled something about resting – she wasn't quite sure what she said, or if any words came out at all – before half sliding, half falling, out of the saddle. Curling up in fetal position, she fell into a deep and troubled sleep.

ော

It seemed only seconds ago that she'd fallen asleep when the distant neigh of a horse sent her scrambling to her feet. But it wasn't from behind, where her pursuers should have been – it was ahead. She snatched Sunflower's reins, interrupting the mare mid-chew, and dragged her toward the sound. *What if I'm caught?* She scoffed aloud. So what? She was dead here anyway.

Ahead, the ground sloped sharply downward. Melodea draped Sunflower's reins carelessly over a tree branch, dropped into a sitting position, and scooted quietly down the incline. Ahead, she heard more snorting, and more horses moving than the hunting party should have had. The trees began to thin. She reached the bottom of the hill and crawled up an embankment, then peered over. *The end of the forest!*

A cold, sharp piece of metal touched her neck.

"*Got you.*"

ॐ

Tristan had lost track of the amount of time he'd been wandering. He was heading in the right direction, but the chances of stumbling onto Raven in the vast forest were slim to none. And he couldn't go on foot much longer. *Regium, I need you now.*

A few snaps sounded ahead. It only took a moment to place the noise as animal, not human. Tristan cautiously approached. *There had better not be bears in this forest.* A loud snort sent him sprinting forward, heart racing. Had he found her?

Her horse. The empty saddle. The blood on the stallion's leg.

Tristan thought he would collapse then and there. Was he too late? Had Raven already been captured, or killed?

Freedom jerked his head up, pawing the ground and tossing his head repeatedly; the reins were snared on a branch. Tristan inched forward, extending his hand. There was no telling what an angry stallion could do, especially to someone who wasn't his normal rider. Some horses were trained to only respond to one master and unseat or attack anyone else who attempted to mount. Still, Tristan had to try.

"Easy there, boy," he murmured. His fingers tentatively brushed across the stallion's neck. Ever so slowly, the stallion

219

lowered his head, finally sticking his muzzle against Tristan's shoulder. Tristan untangled the reins and flipped them back over Freedom's head. *Here we go.* Sticking his foot in the stirrup, Tristan swung his leg over the stallion's back, and sat.

Freedom remained motionless.

"Find her. Find Raven," Tristan whispered. They bolted forward, and Freedom ran like the north wind set free.

He knew where she was.

༄

Raven rocked back and forth on the ground, willing herself to stand. Working up the courage. The last time she'd put weight on her leg, she'd collapsed instantly and was left with a throbbing pain. A large bruise was forming across her thigh, and her knee ached, but nothing was broken as far as she could tell. Still, that didn't make anything feel better.

Before she lost her nerve, she pushed herself to her feet, avoiding putting weight on her right leg. She was dizzy, and blood pounded through her head, but she managed to remain upright and not pass out. It wasn't much, but it was progress.

She scanned the dark forest, but her horse was nowhere in sight. She cupped her hands to her mouth. "Freedom!"

A nicker came from behind her, and Freedom trotted up. But he wasn't alone. She started to call Tristan's name when she stumbled forward.

He vaulted from the saddle just in time to catch her before she faceplanted. Good thing, too – she wasn't sure she could take another fall.

Tristan gently lowered her into a sitting position on a log. He looked worse for the wear, too … blood seeped through his clothes, and a new gash had opened on his forehead. His clothes were damp, which didn't make sense, but Raven dismissed it as the least of her concerns. "How did you find me? And where's Destiny?"

"Another long story." Tristan laughed lightly, but it didn't reach his eyes. They were serious, almost pained. "I found

Freedom wandering riderless. I thought you were dead," he said softly. He touched the dried blood in her hair, sending shivers down her spine.

As a distraction, Raven told him about Kisbin and how he'd spared her. She glanced around. "Where's Quillan?"

Tristan looked away, struggling for composure. "Quillan stayed behind. Sacrificed himself so I could escape."

Quillan. Dead. And Melodea ... who knew where she was, or if she'd escaped? "I'm so sorry," she whispered. "But we have to keep moving."

Tristan gave a quick nod of assent. "To ensure his death was not in vain." He smiled tenderly, fingers finding hers and folding around them. "Let's go home, Princess."

UNEXPECTED MEETINGS

"Let go!"

Hands roughly pulled Melodea to her feet. She flailed, trying to break the hold, but the man crushed her tighter against his armored chest.

"Don't touch –" The words died on her lips. The silver armor. The russet plume. The insignia of a lion. "You're from Roehn!" she gasped.

The Roehn soldier raised an eyebrow, unimpressed with her detective skills. "I am. And you are now my prisoner. I'll take you to my captain – he'll decide what to do with you." He muttered something under his breath about Tharlanders and magic.

"I – I need to speak to Courtney!" Melodea stammered, barely matching his stride as he dragged her toward the large encampment.

The young soldier glared, giving her arm a shake. "You will address her highness with due respect under *my* watch. And I won't bother the princess with Tharland witches. You'll be taken to the captain, and that's final."

"Witch?" Melodea sputtered. "I am *Princess* Melodea, heir to the throne of Mieldren. You *will* unhand me."

He started laughing ... and then stopped, studying her face for any trace of falsehood. Finding nothing, he slowly shook his head. "You're either crazy, or a good liar. Princess Melodea, you said?" He guffawed nervously. "That's a good one."

Crazy? Did she look crazy? Perhaps, she admitted. Covered in dirt, stinking of horse, and emerging half-alive from Tharland. But she was no liar. "I could be crazy, or I could be lying. But you forgot a third option ... I could be telling the truth." She narrowed her eyes. "Are you willing to risk that possibility?"

For a long time, he did nothing but stare. Then he gave a hesitant, almost imperceptible nod. "Very well."

A sigh escaped her lips before she could stop herself.

"*But*," he added, raising a finger, "if you try to harm Her Highness, I will dispatch you with my own hand – trial or no. Understood?"

Melodea pursed her lips. *Not quite the welcome I was expecting.* Still, she dipped her head in agreement. "Understood."

"Good. This way."

After sending a stable boy after Sunflower, the soldier – who introduced himself as Hawk – led her to the center of the tents. Melodea couldn't help comparing it with Nimrooden's camp. Certainly, it was cleaner, crisper, more organized. But the underlying structure was the same, with the king's tent located in the center. *Where Tristan almost died … and Quillan rescued me.*

Two guards standing at the tent's entrance intercepted them.

Hawk stepped forward and saluted. "I found this young woman while out scouting. She claims to be Princess Melodea, and requests to speak with Her Highness."

One guard ducked inside, then emerged moments later. "Princess Courtney will see you."

As Melodea followed her escort inside, the guards watched her, not bothering to hide their stares. She shrank away, ashamed of her rags and dirty face. Was this what it was like for a pauper being presented to royalty? Vulnerable, with no fine dresses or servants, no assurance that you wouldn't be thrown back into the gutter that you came from?

A flutter of gauzy curtains preceded the arrival of Roehn's Princess. Courtney glided into the room, bedecked in an exquisite emerald gown, hair falling in delicate ringlets around her face. She stopped inches away from Hawk, tapped his breastplate, and grinned. "How may I help you, Soldier?" she purred.

Hawk cleared his throat, face turning red. "The Princess of –

or at least she claims to be – of Melodea – I mean Mieldren. That is, she says she's the princess –"

"Melodea!" Courtney exclaimed, sparing the poor soldier any more embarrassment. To Melodea's surprise, the princess sprang across the room and practically tackled her to the ground with a hug. "How in Alarkin did you get here? I thought I might not see you again – and I've been so lonely, surrounded only by soldiers – and my father is such a bore, always planning strategy. I've positively been *dying* for suitable company. But I suppose that's too much to ask for on a war march." She crushed Melodea in another hug, and it was all Melodea could do not to squirm.

Of course, she should have known Courtney was only glad to see her out of loneliness. Melodea carefully extricated herself from Courtney's squeeze. She was feeling light-headed – when was the last time she'd eaten?

Taking Courtney's hands, she led her to a sofa, perching on the edge to avoid soiling the fine material. "War march?"

Hawk was still in a daze, mouth hanging open. "You – you know her?" he finally managed. "I mean, you know her, Your Highness?"

"Know her? She's the reason we're marching to Laynia! Actually, Raven is, but Melodea was there, too. Of course, *I'm* the one who told Father," Courtney added with a smirk.

Melodea's head swam with the onslaught of information. Told her father – King Albastan – what? About Nimrooden? "But I thought ..."

"What, that I would let Raven fight some maniac alone?" Courtney snorted. "Small chance of that. When I sent my servant to fetch your horses, I secretly had him inform my father. I returned from the labyrinth to find the armies mobilizing to march out, with a message on its way to King Taungan. We would have sent word to Tarith, too, but it was too far – our rider would never have made it in time." Her delicate nose crinkled. "Besides, Tarith has never been a close ally to anyone. They might not have come."

The last few sentences merged into a jumble in Melodea's mind. "My father – he's here?"

Courtney acknowledged her with a brief '*mhm*' before continuing her tirade. "My brother stayed back in Roehn, along with a portion of our soldiers, in case Kirgan came back. We couldn't catch him, or the others; they must have found out about Raven's sick-in-bed ruse and fled. Cowards."

Melodea smiled wryly. "I know. The man we knew as Sir Kisby has been hunting us for the past few days, along with Nimrooden's head general." The smile faded. "I don't know where Raven and Tristan are. Or Quillan …"

"Who's Quillan?"

Thief. Betrayer. Rescuer. She closed her eyes, remembering their parting. The kiss. "He's –" Melodea cleared her throat. "He's a friend."

Courtney shrugged. "Well, there's nothing we can do. Finding them in that forest is impossible, even if we knew where to start looking."

"Nothing?" Melodea recoiled at the coldness in Courtney's voice. "They could be lost – they could be dying!"

Hawk, finally recovering his wits, sighed. "Princess Courtney is right. All we can do is warn Laynia and pray that your friends arrive before the assault."

"No, it's too late to warn them." Melodea's voice broke. "Nimrooden's army is already on its way. We'll never make it in time."

RIDERS OF DELIVERANCE

"You have to leave me here."

Never again. That's what Raven had promised herself – that she'd never leave Tristan behind, no matter what. And he had the audacity to suggest he stay behind at the border between Laynia and Tharland. "We continue together or not at all."

"You have to get to Laynia before Nimrooden, and you can't do that if I'm slowing you down." Tristan continued in a softer tone. "We've been riding for hours. Freedom can't get us both back to Laynia – not in time." As if attesting to Tristan's words, Freedom's body heaved beneath them, head hung low.

Raven's arms tightened around Tristan, like she could hold him in the saddle. Like she could keep him here – with her. "You're not leaving. That's an order." She hated the way her voice quavered when she spoke.

Suddenly, his arms were around her, swinging her into the saddle in front of him. She found herself trapped in his gaze, powerless to look away, to breathe. Tristan brushed his knuckles across her cheek. "And who's going to make me, Princess?" he murmured. His eyes flitted to her lips, but all he did was give her hand a gentle squeeze. "You have to let me go!"

Her nod was a death sentence. Tristan would be caught in the open fields between Laynia and Tharland and overtaken by Nimrooden's men. And Gauln wouldn't give him another chance to escape.

Raven swung her leg over the pommel and took the reins, unable to meet his gaze any longer. "I'll see you back in Caritas."

"Farewell, Princess." Tristan kicked his feet out of the stirrups, started to dismount.

And then Freedom bolted.

Raven slammed into Tristan's torso. Only her balance and his arms around her waist kept them both from flying out of the saddle. "Easy, whoa!" She pulled back on the reins, but Freedom didn't respond. He'd gripped the bit between his teeth, and even Tristan's attempts at stopping the stallion were ineffective.

Freedom ran on. Foam began to lather his body; his muscles trembled. Every time he stumbled, Raven thought it would be a repeat of what had happened in the forest – a fall, the crushing weight on her leg, and finally a blow to the head that meant lights out. But it never came.

Instead, they crested a foothill, crossed a stream that was so familiar, and raced through a field dotted with wildflowers. And then Raven laid eyes on something she hadn't dared to hope she'd see again.

The gates of Caritas.

∞

He awoke to the flicker of a small fire, the smell of warm bread, and waves of heat and cold that raced through his entire body. His head was hot, his chest was cold, and every part of him was shaking. There was a sharp pain in his side that should have made him remember something, but it didn't.

He remembered nothing.

Hours, days, or minutes? As he drifted in and out of sleep, he wasn't sure how much time had passed. An old woman filled his dreams – or were they his waking hours? It was impossible to say.

When he finally managed to stay awake for more than a few seconds, he was able to discern that the woman was, in fact, real – although you wouldn't know it to look at her. She was more forest creature than human, with moss and twigs in her hair and a dress made from a thick, curly wool. Even her eyes were a muddled mixture between green, gray, and brown, like the colors of a murky pond.

"He's awake," she croaked.

Was she talking to him, or about him? He didn't see anyone else she could be addressing. "I think so," he replied. "Where

227

am I?"

"The forest of Tharland. In my cottage, I might add."

He eyed her curiously. "Who are you? And where did you find me?"

"Meera's the name." She stared at the wall, head tilted sideways and eyes focused on something distant. Not altogether there, he thought. "By the gorge," she added. "He had some nasty wounds. We fixed him up. Almost died, though. Slept for days." The old lady cracked a toothless grin. "He had nice horses. They like the nanny goat."

Horses. He had horses? "What did they look like?"

"A big gray. And a blue roan. Stallions, I think, though gentle as lambs. He must have trained them well. They would feed us all winter, what with the price they'd fetch at market."

A blue roan ...

He sat bolt upright. "I need to get to Caritas!"

Meera eyed him quizzically. "And why would he need to do that?"

"I – I have to set something right."

Meera smiled. Like she'd been talking to him the whole time, she said, "I'll help you pack."

℘

"We made it," Tristan whispered.

Freedom had stumbled to a halt, head almost bent to the ground, trembling, blood flecking his nostrils. Both Raven and Tristan dismounted, practically pulling the stallion forward. He was favoring one leg.

The eastern gate – which led directly into the castle grounds – was kept shut; any visitors would enter through the city at the southern gates. But they didn't have time to go around, so Raven marched straight up to the gate and glared at the watchtowers, waiting for someone to announce her presence.

When no one immediately appeared, Raven banged on the wood with her fist. "Open up!"

"Who goes there?" An old, roughly shaven man peered

through a viewing window in the gate's side door, rubbing sleep from his eyes.

Raven bristled. *Who goes there?* Did no one recognize their princess? She'd come in mud-specked, bedraggled, and late enough times that her own guards should be able to recognize her. "Open this gate, or so help me, I will have you hung for treason!"

"Now, Miss, there's no reason to –"

"Do what she says, Brogan," Tristan ordered, stepping forward. He placed his arm in front of her, a physical barrier to keep her from strangling the man, no doubt. She probably needed it; the thought had crossed her mind.

The gatekeeper, Brogan, squinted. "Tristan?" He opened the side door, chuckling, and clapped Tristan on the shoulder. "I thought you were off in Mieldren somewhere. What are you doin' back in these par– oh, Princess!"

Brogan dropped to his knees hard enough to leave a bruise. From his grimace, it most likely would. He glared over his shoulder. "Open the gate, you fools!" he shouted. The gates swung open, followed by the raising of the portcullis.

Raven rushed inside, snapping her fingers at the nearest soldier. "Take him to the stables," she said, thrusting Freedom's reins forward. "See to it he's attended to – immediately!"

The soldier jerked his head up and down. "Yes, Princess!"

She leaned her head against Freedom's forelock. Tears stung her eyes. "My brave, brave boy." Then Tristan's hand was on her elbow, urging her to move, and Freedom was led, limping, away. She blinked rapidly, stumbling forward. Next thing she knew, she was in a full-out sprint towards the great hall, every part of her body numb. Her leg no longer throbbed; her head no longer ached. All she knew was an all-consuming desperation to find her father.

Bursting into the throne room, Raven shoved her way past observing courtiers to the front of the crowd. Gasps and murmurs of outrage followed in her wake, but it didn't matter.

Only one thing mattered now.

"King Wilgaun, I need to speak to you!"

Wilgaun's head shot up, scanning the crowd. She elbowed her way to the front, and his eyes found her. They took in the dirt, the tears in her dress, the blood. Finally, they came to rest on her face.

She expected scolding, shock, horror. Even surprise. Expected him to say anything and everything. But Wilgaun simply stood, threw his crown and scepter aside, and enveloped her in his arms.

"*Tell me everything.*"

Everything. About her betrayal. About how she'd been hunted, bound, left alone and bleeding. How she'd watched her friends as they risked their lives to save her. Breeanah. Courtney. Melodea. Quillan. And Tristan.

Only one of them had made it back with her.

"I will," she whispered.

∽

"Nimrooden is marching on Laynia. He will be here with his army from the Wilderns before nightfall tomorrow." Tristan paced the length of the room – back and forth, back and forth. He was tired, exhausted, but to sit down would mean to sleep – and he couldn't afford that. Besides, being in the king's private chambers made him uncomfortable.

Wilgaun rubbed a hand across his face, processing the wild tale Raven – with occasional input on Tristan's part – had told. No longer did he look like the grand, powerful king Tristan had caught glimpses of when he was growing up. Instead, Wilgaun had grown weary and tired, aged beyond his years. A king who was nearly broken. "I can't believe after all this time … the years I spent hunting him, only to have him show up at my doorstep with another army at his back."

Raven placed a tentative hand on his shoulder, ready to pull away in an instant, but the king smiled at her and – for a moment – the weariness seemed to lift from his shoulders.

As Tristan observed Raven and her father, he couldn't help but compare their relationship with the relationship he shared with his own parents. They'd always been kind, loving, never hesitating to offer affection – and Tristan had been eager to reciprocate the affection. And yet from the exchange, it looked like Raven had rarely dared to get close to her father, and visa-versa. Maybe Raven's near-death experience could bring them together.

But if he'd learned anything from his parents, it was that no family could be complete without the High Regium. Raven didn't even know who He was ... and the king had long since abandoned his faith in the old ways. No, there would need to be something more to heal the wounds between father and daughter. Some*one* more.

Tristan stepped forward, regaining Wilgaun's attention. "With all due respect, Your Majesty, we must ready the army. They will be here soon."

Wilgaun nodded absently. "Of course." He waved at a servant boy. "Find Captain Illan – tell him to assemble the war council immediately."

The servant boy, whose job was serving food and wine, could do little more than gape. He'd probably never had a personal order from the king, especially one as important as finding the second-in-command of Laynia's army.

Tristan raised his eyebrows at the lad, hoping it would prompt the return of coherent thought. "Well? You heard your king. Off you go!"

The boy snapped to attention with a loud, "Yes, Sir!" followed by a "I mean, yes, Your Highness!" before he bolted out the door. Tristan chuckled; he'd been a boy like that once, too, all eagerness and legs. How time flew.

Wilgaun clapped Tristan's shoulder. "Go and clean yourself up. Both of you. If your estimates are correct, we have until nightfall tomorrow before Nimrooden's army arrives. When you're finished, meet me in the war council ... we have much to discuss."

℘

Raven knocked on the infirmary door, where her father's physician had left Tristan after seeing to his wounds. When she entered, bandages were strewn everywhere, and the air was heavily infused with the pungency of herbal ointments. A few healers were assisting him, pulling a tunic over his freshly bandaged chest.

She grinned, perching on the edge of the counter. "You'd be a spoiled royal. It's only been a few hours since we got back, and you won't even bother putting a tunic on by yourself!"

Tristan returned the grin. "Hey, I'm only imitating you. I heard it takes royal ladies no less than *three* maids to help them into their gowns."

"Not true!" she protested. "And if it was, it's only because they have the most cumbersome amount of under layers, outer layers, and – and ... middle layers!" Maybe not the most technical term, but it got her point across. "Besides," Raven added smugly, "I put this on *all by myself.*"

The dark red tunic – replete with brown leggings and half gloves that went up past her elbows – was the most practical thing she'd worn in her entire life. Being injured and attending war councils had their advantages. Besides, most of her stylish wardrobe had been left in Roehn. Thank goodness. Most of the dresses were positively suffocating.

One of the healers interrupted their banter with a lecture. Her tone was almost reprimanding – like Tristan had a choice whether or not to take a sword to the back. "You're fortunate. Gangrene is all too common, and even a small cut can lead to putrefaction and death. Make sure you keep the bandage clean and *don't* do anything strenuous."

Raven bit her tongue to keep from spouting out a lecture herself. Don't do anything strenuous? She wanted to scream, *don't you realize we're about to go to war?* But no, the healer had no idea. No one did, except her father and his closest commanders.

232

Speaking of which. "My father wanted me to remind you to report to the ... *council*. Something about numbers and strategy. You know, men talk."

"I hadn't forgotten, thanks."

Raven watched the healers cleaning up. A few minutes later, a messenger would arrive, telling them to re-stock supplies and set up a full-fledged medical station. Blood, screams, and death would fill these halls in a matter of hours. And she would be expected to help, to stay with the other women and ease the soldiers' last hours in this world, while the men fought and died for their kingdom.

She grabbed a knife, made a game of sticking its point into the wooden table. The healers would be furious when they noticed, but so far, they were too preoccupied with disposing of bloody bandages. "Melodea didn't arrive before us. I checked." The words left her mouth before she could stop herself. It made everything too real to speak out loud, but Tristan had a right to know. And maybe she thought he could make it better – tell her *why* Melodea hadn't made it, *why* she could have been delayed. Maybe, he could quiet the voice inside of her that said Melodea was already dead.

Instead of making up a lame excuse, however, Tristan slipped his arm around her shoulders. "Wherever she is – whatever she's going through – the High Regium will watch over her."

"Who is he – this *royalty* you keep talking about? See, I learned something from my Latin studies," Raven said with a faint smile.

"He is ... the *true* king. He created the world – the stars – the galaxies. Life itself." Tristan gave a short laugh. "He created everything!"

Raven shook her head. Tried to ignore the excitement flaring in her heart. "My father never taught me to believe in any god. He said we make our own destinies."

A mysterious smile played at the corners of Tristan's mouth, which meant he knew something she didn't. It was infuriating.

"You should ask him about the High Regium sometime. You might be surprised at what he says."

She raised an eyebrow. "And you would know this how?"

"Oh, you know – I have my sources," Tristan said vaguely.

What was the word she'd used when she first met Tristan? Ah, yes. *Insufferable.* She was considering bringing it back into her vocabulary.

"Yes, well, anyway," she sniffed, "I'm skeptical. Besides, gods are like kings – always asking for something, always demanding perfection. And I think you've figured out my deplorable secret – I'm not perfect."

"I think I may have figured that out," Tristan said with a wink. "But you're wrong. The High Regium is different. He doesn't require perfection, or anything. Just your heart."

"Hm. I don't know about that." Raven stood, offering Tristan a hand down. "My father's waiting for you."

A brief flicker of disappointment crossed Tristan's face, but he took her hand with a smile. "Best not to keep a king waiting."

Had she brushed him off too quickly? Clearly, Tristan cared deeply about his *high ruler.* And he wasn't pious or self-righteous like the few religious men she'd met. She'd thought they were all cut from the same cloth, no matter what god they served – but as with most things, Tristan broke the norm.

And could she deny the feeling – however brief – that this Regium was different than the others? Was that where Tristan got his sense of honor and loyalty from? She remembered a few of the soldiers mentioning Tristan's father; he'd served under King Wilgaun, where he had been respected for his courage and devotion to his family. Tristan was no different. Did they both owe this to their god?

The questions were too much to contemplate, much less answer at the moment. Nimrooden was on his way, and she didn't have time to fantasize about gods and family devotion. Maybe later. After Laynia was saved, and she'd had a minute to think without fear hanging over her head like a dark cloud.

After her world was put right.

When Nimrooden was hanged for his crimes.

DRUMS OF WAR

Tristan followed Raven through the winding hallways, barely aware of the scurrying servants and healers as they rushed through the castle, bandages stacked high in their arms. Had he gotten through to Raven? Or had she shut down as soon as he'd mentioned giving the Regium her heart? She certainly hadn't given him much hope, the way she'd closed the conversation so abruptly. But maybe, after this was over, she'd be ready to listen. *If it isn't too late.*

When they entered the war council, Laynia's commanders had already assembled, listening to Wilgaun's briefing on the situation. From the looks on everyone's faces, they were resigning themselves to the next twenty-four hours without sleep. *Yeah, well, join the club.* He couldn't remember the last time he'd had a full night's sleep. Back in Roehn, actually.

"... the northeastern wall, where the fighting should be heaviest," Wilgaun was saying. When Tristan and Raven entered, he beckoned them forward. "Good, you've come. We've much to discuss."

Gone was the weary, despairing old man. In his place was someone younger and robust, more grim and determined, bearing all the authority granted by his station. A true king.

Tristan dipped his head and joined Wilgaun at the circular table, Raven hovering closely at his shoulder. It was strange, but it was almost as though she trusted him more than anyone in this room. A high compliment – and a heavy burden. Raven would have to learn to rely on more than just him, or her father. One day, she would rule this kingdom.

But for now, he was grateful to have her by his side.

"I've ordered the women and children to evacuate into the catacombs beneath the castle," Wilgaun explained. "If the city is attacked, I want to minimize citizen casualties in the initial onslaught."

"All due respect, Sire, but will it really come to that?" The speaker, who Tristan recognized as General Altin, couldn't keep the skepticism out of his voice. "The walls have never been breached, and a full-scale evacuation could take us –"

"A day? A few hours?" Wilgaun raised an eyebrow. "Thanks to my daughter and this young knight –" Tristan started to correct the title, but the king held up a hand, "– we will have enough time. And I'll use every spare second we have if it means less lives will be lost. I will not gamble with the lives of my people – not with Nimrooden. Not again. Enough people died because I didn't take him seriously the first time. So tell me, General. *Now* do you think this evacuation order unnecessary?"

Altin's swallow was audible. "No, Sir."

"Indeed." Wilgaun turned to Tristan. "I would like you to brief my commanders on the size of Nimrooden's army, as well as their last known location and any other information that may be useful."

Tristan snapped to attention. He recalled everything he could – even down to the weapons they used and the number of mounted calvary he'd seen. "These men are not just Nimrooden's army. They're a fighting force coerced and recruited from the Wilderns, the criminals in Tharland, and who knows where else," he concluded. "To counter their brute strength, we'll have to have superior tactics, and try not to engage on a level playing field as much as possible. Utilizing our advantage on the castle ramparts with bows, crossbows, and catapults will be essential."

He cleared his throat, aware everyone was staring at him. These men were trained in the art of war – they didn't need some novice telling them what to do. "At your discretion, Commanders. I was only thinking out loud."

"On the contrary," Wilgaun said, eyeing him. "Any input is welcome. In fact ... I would like you to serve as one of my tacticians on the battlefield, since you seem so adept at planning."

At first, Tristan wasn't sure if he was being mocked, but enough time passed without anyone laughing that suggested the king was entirely serious.

Tristan jerked into a bow. "Thank you, Your Highness."

Another hour was spent discussing individual strategies for each of the commanders' units; a record amount of time, Tristan was sure, but it seemed like ages. With a hot meal in his belly and fresh clothes on his back, he was ready to crawl into bed and sleep. Raven yawned enough times that he felt a little better about his own exhaustion.

Finally, Wilgaun dismissed the meeting, with each commander branching off to their specific stations to prepare. Before Tristan could leave, Wilgaun caught him on the shoulder. "I've laid a heavy responsibility on you ... but only because I believe you're capable. Can you handle it?"

Could he? Although he would have other, more experienced commanders to keep an eye on him, serving as a tactician was no small job. But he couldn't deny that strategy was one of his strong points. And with the Regium on his side ...

Tristan straightened, nodded once. "Yes, Sire, I believe I can."

Wilgaun smiled grimly. "Good. Now get some rest – you've earned it."

⁊

The next day – which, by the time she woke up, was very late morning – Raven headed straight toward the stables. She spent the day sitting with Freedom, talking to him. Trying not to believe that he was dying.

The stallion had suffered severe dehydration, gone completely lame in one leg, and who knew what kind of internal damage. He wouldn't stay on his feet and refused to eat. If he didn't get better soon ...

When she finally forced herself from Freedom's side, Raven intercepted Tristan on his way to his post.

"I see they gave you a new sword." She pointed. "And a fancy emblem."

Tristan shrugged, but seemed pleased that she'd noticed. "I'll be stationed with Captain Illan and General Altin on the northern wall, where Nimrooden will focus his attack. We're finalizing preparations to secure the gates."

"Be careful out there." Be careful – was that the best she could come up with? There was no lasting impression, no hope or encouragement. Just a reminder of the obvious. "And don't do anything foolish." She inwardly kicked herself. Why couldn't she say what she really felt? That she'd be lost without him – that she cared about him? *That she loved him*?

She had to admit it because it was true. Now that there were no more perilous forests, kidnappers, and death hanging constantly between them, the idea of marriage should have been as foolish and childish as ever – especially marriage to a commoner. Once they returned to Caritas, she thought all her feelings would evaporate, or at least lessen to a manageable degree. But with an imminent war, they had only grown stronger. If she let Tristan go without revealing anything of her heart, and he died, it would tear her apart.

But no words came.

Tristan smiled, running a hand through his hair. "Since when have I ever done anything foolish?"

For some reason, his words rubbed her the wrong way, especially with all the emotions wreaking havoc inside her. She whirled around, staring into the distance, arms crossed. "I don't know, like when you almost got yourself killed? Or when you teamed up with a bandit? Or –"

Tristan appeared in front of her, leaned in, and silenced her with a kiss. Gentle, barely brushing her lips, but enough to send a bolt of lightning through her entire body.

It was a lifetime before Tristan spoke. When he did, his words had a breathless quality. "I'll come back. Always. As long as you're waiting for me."

All Raven could do was nod.

§∂

It was near midnight when Raven heard it first. Echoing through the halls, vibrating the foundations of the castle, and beating just louder than her heart. *Drums*.

Raven was flying through the halls, racing to the castle overlook, slamming against the parapet railing. Beyond the wall, they stretched for what seemed like miles … soldiers, marching row upon row, bearing swords, spears, maces, anything that could cause another man tortuous pain. Flaming torches gleamed off their black armor and giant catapults; thousands of horses, screaming and pawing, already anticipating the stench of blood.

Regium, I don't know if you exist. But if you do … save Tristan. Save us all.

But only her doubts answered her.

§∂

Tristan watched in dread fascination as the encroaching ranks of men drew closer. Tinier than ants from this height and distance … but just as numerous. Drums beat out a hideous chant. *Boom. Boom. Boom.* Could Raven hear them? If she didn't now, she would soon enough. The entire city would. The catacombs would quake – the castle itself would shudder at the drum's call.

But the armies would *not* pass through these gates. Not while Tristan was alive. *Which might not be for much longer*. He dared a smile at the irony.

A lone horseman came galloping forward, brazenly exposed. Tristan could see red running down the man's sword – or was he just imagining it? The rider removed his helmet, and while it was too far to make out distinct features, the crown on his head was unmistakable.

"Wilgaun – and all the fools who follow him – hear me!" Nimrooden shouted. He jabbed his sword at the ramparts. "I will purge the fields of Laynia with your blood. Surrender will mean death. War will mean death. And victory …" He paused, voice dropping to a growl. "There is no victory."

"Stand your ground!" Altin ordered. But his words were drowned out by the chants, a predator's song to its prey. "*Death! Death! Death!*"

THE RISING DAWN

"Hold those gates!" Wilgaun paced the ramparts – closer to the battle than any of his commanders felt comfortable with. He only wished he could get closer. Close enough to run his sword through Nimrooden's black heart. "Don't let them fall!"

A loud cry. A burst of flame. And a dozen fiery projectiles careening through the air, aiming to decimate the city, the castle, the walls … and everyone on them. The faint glow of dawn had spread across the eastern horizon, matching the angry orange of fire licking the stones of Caritas.

"They've started firing the catapults!" General Altin shouted.

"I'm not blind, Altin," Wilgaun replied. "Return fire."

"Return fire!" Altin bellowed. Archers sent a volley of arrows raining into the field. A few ballistae also fired from the parapets, taking out multiple targets per arrow. Almost all found their mark – more a testament to the sheer number of forces amassed, rather than the archers' accuracy – but fell short of the soldiers manning the enemy catapults.

"Incoming!" With no further warning, a soldier slammed into Wilgaun, sending them both crashing onto the flagstone as a fiery projectile smashed into the wall beneath them. Oil and flame immediately engulfed the stones.

The soldier who had saved Wilgaun was dead.

Tristan hauled Wilgaun to his feet. "Are you alright, Your Highness?"

Wilgaun nodded stiffly, brushed away the ashes. With a dismal twist of his mouth, he regarded the dead man at his feet before turning to his commander. "Captain Illan – when should we deploy ground forces?"

Illan snapped a salute. "Your Highness, Nimrooden isn't concerned about losing numbers. We can't fight him on the

242

battlefield – if we trade lives, Nimrooden's larger force will overrun ours and he will prevail. I suggest we send word to our allies and try to outlast the siege. The only problem is those catapults."

"Since they are the bane of our existence at present, what do you suggest we *do* about them?" Wilgaun asked sardonically.

Tristan grinned. "Actually, Sire, I have an idea."

ॐ

"Aim catapults and ... *fire!*"

At Altin's command, the air was suddenly filled with giant boulders. They flew onto the battlefield, crushing a path through the men and beasts before rolling to a stop. Minutes later, a second volley fired from the walls.

"King Wilgaun, we have the boulders landing within a hundred feet of the enemy catapults," Altin said. "Shall we load the canisters?"

Wilgaun raised his eyebrows at Tristan. "This is *your* plan. What do you say – are we ready?"

Tristan surveyed the field. It may not have been explicitly communicated, but this was a test. *His* test. The king was evaluating him as a soldier, leader, and tactician. For the moment, he was just glad Wilgaun wasn't evaluating him for son-in-law potential. That *would* make things more stressful, if such a thing were possible.

"Have one catapult fire to make sure the accuracy is adequate – before we launch all the canisters," Tristan said.

"Very well. Altin?"

Altin relayed the order. A wooden canister launched towards an enemy catapult, landing a few dozen feet away. But instead of rolling through the soldiers, the canister exploded in a fiery inferno, licking across the brittle grass and devouring the catapult with oily flames.

Wilgaun smiled briefly. "Hit. Proceed to fire all other canisters."

The enemy soldiers, after watching the destruction of their

243

first catapult, started hauling the others back out of range. But it was too late. As one, the rest of the canisters of burning oil were loosed. Few hit their targets directly, but the spray radius of the oil ignited the majority of the catapults, instantly kindling the bone-dry wood. Those that didn't burn to a crisp were dragged out to the edge of the field, smoking and badly damaged. A chorus of cheers sounded from the wall.

Tristan stumbled forward as Wilgaun slapped him on the back. "Congratulations – it looks like your plan worked," the king said with a note of admiration.

Tristan grinned – maybe a bit too enthusiastically. Wilgaun was the king, not his best friend. Wiping the grin off his face, Tristan cleared his throat. "Thanks, Your Highness."

"Alright, there'll be time for slapping yourself on the back later, soldier," Captain Illan said lightly. As one of Wilgaun's oldest, most loyal commanders, Illan was rarely seen on the training grounds anymore. His blond hair had long since faded to gray, and he had grown a full moustache that only added to his imposing presence. Still, he was friendly enough – when he was feeling magnanimous – and was unmatched in strategy. He'd been the primary factor in implementing and refining Tristan's catapult plan.

Illan pointed to the field. "We've got company."

With the war machines out of commission, Nimrooden's soldiers were re-forming ranks and marching toward the walls. Laynian archers kept up a constant hail of arrows to slow their advance. But as Illan had predicted, Nimrooden had men to spare. Wanton death meant nothing to him compared to the glory of his self-acclaimed, impending victory.

Under the cover of shields, soldiers surged forward with a battering ram to break through the gates. Even so, they took heavy casualties from the archers overhead. The dead began to form a pile at the foot of the wall, but the gates held fast.

"How infuriating – expecting an easy kill, only to find their prey has teeth." Altin smirked.

"Thanks to my daughter's warning," Wilgaun said with a meaningful look.

Altin coughed into his glove. "Yes, of course, Sire."

"With help," Illan added, elbowing Tristan smartly in the ribs. Apparently, the captain was feeling magnanimous. It was almost worth the burning that spread through Tristan's injured ribcage.

"Let's hope –" Tristan rushed to the edge of the wall. "Siege ladders!"

Altin frowned. "Why would we hope for siege – ah, I see."

Across the breadth of the wall, soldiers were hoisting up giant ladders. The moment one was secure, men swarmed up the rungs, weapons in hand.

"Knock those ladders down and send the vermin straight to the pit!" Illan bellowed.

෮

Tristan yanked his sword from someone's chest, making a wet sucking noise. He'd lost track of how many he'd killed – and no matter how many went down, or how many ladders they pushed off the wall, more took their place.

"Hold the ramparts!" Altin shouted. "We lose the wall, we lose the gate!"

The siege ladders were becoming harder and harder to deter; areas of the wall were running thin on troops. No riders had been able to make it past the enemy army, which meant no help was coming. The soldiers of Laynia were losing heart – and without that, the battle was lost. Laynia was lost.

As if their prospects weren't bad enough, the lone cry of a battle horn sounded behind the enemy forces. "Nimrooden's reinforcements," Tristan muttered, slamming the stone wall with the heel of his hand.

Altin's sword lowered a fraction.

Illan squinted against the rising sun. "If they belong to Nimrooden, why are his rear defenses collapsing?"

Tristan looked closer. Sure enough, the approaching army

was cutting down Nimrooden's forces from behind. Fresh swords stabbed and sliced tirelessly, each stroke a killing blow.

"It's Roehn ... and Mieldren!" Tristan exclaimed.

"But – but how did they know?" Altin sputtered.

"My best guess is at the bidding of another headstrong princess," Tristan said, grinning. "*Yes!*" he cried, pummeling the rampart with the hilt of his sword.

"Commanders," Illan yelled. "Order any troops *not* defending the wall to assemble at the eastern gate. We will attack Nimrooden on two fronts. Archers, double your efforts and cover us from the ramparts!" He slapped Tristan's chest. "Boy, you're with me. King Wilgaun, I advise you to wait until we've completed the initial charge before joining the fight."

Wilgaun grunted in disapproval but nodded his compliance.

Seconds later, Tristan was mounted and charging onto the battlefield. Laynia's cavalry formed a flying wedge formation, splitting the hostile forces down the center with the force of a full-speed gallop. The combined armies of Mieldren and Roehn followed suit from the opposite side of the field, meeting Laynia's troops in the middle. Within minutes, they had successfully divided Nimrooden's army into two equal parts.

Most of the time, Tristan was hacking at any enemy that came into range, rarely having to use more than one or two blows. Nimrooden's army was mostly on foot and were mercilessly trampled under the horses' shod hooves. Brutal, but killing was killing. And it was better than taking a blow, only to survive and lay in agony, waiting for the final slaughter.

They repeated the flying wedge maneuver twice; when the enemy had thinned, Illan ordered his men to break formation and fight at will. After that, they dispersed across the field to hunt down stragglers.

Tristan had just executed a slice to a man's throat when he heard someone approaching from behind. He turned a split-second too late and caught the flat of a blade to his back. The ground rushed to meet him as he was sent lurching off his horse.

Coughing and gasping for air, he stumbled to his feet.

And nearly caught Gauln's fist with his face.

Tristan dodged to the side, putting distance between them so he could recover his breath. "You again," he wheezed, spitting blood.

Gauln sneered. "I told Nimrooden we should have killed you when we had the chance." They circled each other, testing the waters. Neither had fought the other -- Tristan had only taken Gauln's hits while tied and half-conscious. But could Tristan win this fight, even with a level playing field?

As if reading his thoughts, Gauln advanced, sword lashing out with a barrage of powerful blows. Tristan scrambled backward. He knew that to stand a chance, he had to take the offensive. But Gauln's constant onslaught was making any counterattacks difficult.

Tristan managed a quick downward slice, pausing the one-sided attack, but Gauln batted the sword to the side and slammed the pommel of his own into Tristan's skull.

Tristan reeled, tripped, and did a sloppy block that earned him a slice across his bicep. Still, the split-second occupied Gauln long enough for Tristan to kick him square in the knee.

"You'll pay for that," Gauln growled. He lunged forward and stabbed at Tristan's chest; Tristan batted it away, but Gauln rammed his knee -- the one that hadn't been kicked -- into Tristan's solar plexus.

Breathe. Just breathe and stay alive. Those were Tristan's only objectives, but trying to do both at the same time was too much. After deflecting only a few blows, he took the flat of Gauln's sword to the jaw. The next thing he knew he was sprawled on the ground, the taste of blood filling his mouth -- *again*.

"It's over!" Gauln panted. His eyes were pulsating with hatred, fingernails digging into the hilt of his sword as he raised it over his head, flipped it backhanded. "Time for you to die, cur!"

Tristan didn't have time for last thoughts before Gauln's

sword was driving toward his heart.

And then it wasn't. A blur, a grunt, a wet ripping noise as metal parted flesh. Gauln's jaw worked noiselessly as he stared at his own sword hilt protruding from his gut.

Kisbin snarled as he released the handle and shoved Gauln's corpse to the ground. "I should have done that *long* ago!" He wiped his bloody hands on his pantleg and helped Tristan to his feet. They studied each other in silence, Kisbin searching for words, Tristan – for the second time – reevaluating the knight-turned-traitor-turned-friend.

"I believe I owe you my life," Tristan finally managed.

Kisbin lowered his gaze, scanned the valley of corpses.

Most of the battlefield had gone silent as Laynia and her allies hunted down and captured the fleeing survivors. They would be tried in court; some would be indentured to undo the damage Nimrooden's army had wrought, then return home when their servitude had been fulfilled. Tristan knew firsthand many of these men were victims of unfortunate circumstances and poor judgement. Others, however, would be hung as punishment for the path of hatred and death they had chosen. Like Kisbin. Would he have any chance of escaping the noose?

"Hardly." Kisbin forced himself to meet Tristan's eyes. "That was one small step in repaying a large debt I owe you and this kingdom – in earning my forgiveness. Tell me, honestly." He licked his lips. "Do I have any chance of earning yours?"

A voice whispered in Tristan's mind. *He tried to kill you. He tried to kill Raven. He deserves death.* "No one can earn forgiveness."

Kisbin's face fell. "I understand."

Hate him ... "But the High Regium gives it freely. He forgave me for every wrong I've ever committed." Tristan smiled, clapping Kisbin on the shoulder. "You can't earn my forgiveness, because it's free, too."

A shaky breath left Kisbin's mouth. "I can never thank you enou – *ugh*!" He coughed, faltering.

Warm blood splattered Tristan's face.

"No!" Tristan tried to grab Kisbin's arms, but the knight collapsed.

Farah stood over him, dagger dripping red. Golden-white hair blew wildly around her face; the white hem of her dress was stained with dirt and blood. Her lip curled in disgust. "How pathetic. But Kisbin always was weak."

Tristan frantically scanned the ground for his sword. It lay a few feet away – out of reach. "Yes, he was. Until today. To defy the sins of your past takes strength." He inched towards the sword, voice dropping menacingly. "More strength than a witch like you could ever have."

Farah shrieked an otherworldly curse and lunged, slashing her dagger towards Tristan's throat. But too slow. He grabbed her wrist, twisted it, and wrenched the weapon from her hand, driving the hilt into her temple. She collapsed, unconscious.

Tristan fell to his knees, cradling Kisbin's head in his lap.

Blood trickled at the corners of the knight's mouth; his skin was deathly pale. But his eyes were bright, looking up at Tristan with unfathomable peace. "Thank you … my friend," Kisbin wheezed. His breath came in short, labored gasps, but Tristan could find no trace of fear in the man's face. "I was never – a good man. But you've reminded me … that the Regium … always … forgives …"

His gaze shifted out of focus to the sky above. To a world with no more death.

Tristan gently closed Kisbin's eyes, letting his hand linger.

When he returned to Farah's unconscious form, her lips were parted, but no breath stirred inside her lungs. She, too, had met her demise, fate sealed by the hilt of her own dagger.

Tristan found himself alone, adrift in a sea of death.

৪০

"Sire, we've found Nimrooden. My men are in pursuit."

Wilgaun had been on the battlefield only a matter of minutes. As soon as he'd been able to convince Altin, the two – along with a contingent of Wilgaun's personal guards – had joined the melee, only to receive Illan's report that they were hot on Nimrooden's tail.

Clapping his captain on the back, Wilgaun gestured for Illan to lead the way. *Finally.* The murderer would be brought to justice, *finally.* Laynia would be safe, *finally.* And Wilgaun would take his revenge, *finally.*

After joining with the rest of Illan's soldiers, the party of thirty men ran their horses through the scattered woodland to the north of the castle. From his position protectively jammed into the middle, Wilgaun couldn't see the fugitives, but it was clear his men were gaining on them.

Less than a quarter of a mile later, the soldiers reined to a sharp halt as contingents from Roehn and Mieldren headed off Nimrooden's escape route. Surrounded, the Wildern soldiers formed a tight circle around their leader.

"It's over!" Altin shouted for all to hear. He spurred his horse forward. "Surrender, and you *will* receive a fair trial."

What happened next was too fast for Wilgaun to react. The soldier, screaming curses at Laynia's king. The arrow, impossibly finding its mark. The pain piercing his chest. The thud as his body hit the ground. And the blanket of stillness, where he felt and saw nothing, as he succumbed to shock.

∞

The next few minutes were a blur. Faces fading in and out of view. Someone begging for him to stay awake. The flowering blossom of fire spreading across his chest. The panic as his body gasped for air, unable to pull enough into his lungs, and the steady ache of his racing heart. Beads of blood broke out on his forehead. Or was it just sweat? He wasn't sure, and he didn't have the strength to find out.

Laying on a soft bed, surrounded by furs, Wilgaun found Illan standing over him, saying something about the dungeons. Healers and physicians hovered over his form like so many vultures, poking this and stuffing that and ripping the arrow shaft out of his chest. He watched numbly as his own blood seeped out of him, staining his bandages an ugly crimson. Was this what it was like to die?

"…Understand me, My Liege?" Illan gave his king a slight shake, which prompted a string of swearing from the physician that Illan pretended not to hear. "We caught him. We caught Nimrooden."

Nimrooden. Mine at last. But at that moment, the thought of revenge seemed hollow and pointless. All Wilgaun wanted was to see his daughter, one last time … make things right …

"Well done." The weak congratulations had barely passed Wilgaun's blue lips before he slipped back out of consciousness.

GRIM REAPER

Blue lips. Cold sweats. Blood everywhere. The physician said this limp, nearly lifeless husk of a man was all that remained of her father. The king, left to slowly suffocate, or die from the air inside his chest cavity – the healers weren't optimistic. Of those with punctured lungs, few survived.

Raven glared at the physician, who she had literally backed into a corner. "*Wait*? There's nothing else you can *do*? You're supposed to be the best healer in the land – you're supposed to *save* him, not watch him die!"

"Your Highness, I –"

"Enough, Princess." Illan stepped between her and the cowering imp of a man who had the audacity to call himself a healer. "There's nothing he – or any of us – could have done."

"I don't believe you."

Illan growled, running his large hand across his face. The warning in his voice was unmistakable; he wasn't used to being crossed, even by royalty. "Princess ..."

"No." Raven held up a hand. "Tell me how it happened."

The captain shifted uncomfortably. "I don't think that's a good –"

"Tell me, or I will personally see every man in your battalion whipped for failing to protect their king!" Raven's eyes flashed, and the captain stepped backward. She was behaving irrationally – foolishly, even. And no one knew it better than herself. But her father was on his deathbed, no word had come from Tristan, and Freedom ...

Oh, her brave stallion. Tears sprang to her eyes, but she didn't relent. She *couldn't* relent or she would crumble. Her brave stallion, who had fought harder than any man, was lying lifeless in the stables, his beautiful body awaiting burial. The horse who

252

had given his life for his mistress, and his country.

"Well?" she demanded.

Illan grunted and eased his giant form into a chair. It creaked under his weight. "Nimrooden was on the run. We were in pursuit, and had him surrounded, but one of his men fired an arrow – a single, lucky shot. He managed to hit your father, knocking him from his horse. We killed the soldier, but it was too late – the damage was done."

"And Nimrooden?"

"Princess, I really don't think –"

Raven's hand shot forward and clasped Illan's jaw, forcing him to meet her gaze. "I am Laynia's heir, am I not?" He nodded reluctantly. "Therefore, in event of my father's absence or inability to function as monarch, I am your queen. Yes?"

Illan sighed. "Yes."

She released his jaw. "Then as your queen, I order you to tell me where Nimrooden is being held." Her voice softened. "I have as much right as anyone to his life. Trial or no."

Illan stared mutely; perhaps his mind wandered back to that fateful day – the day his queen was murdered in cold blood. Perhaps he blamed himself, or he felt compelled to answer her as his sovereign. Or perhaps, deep down, he knew she was right. If anyone deserved to end Nimrooden's life, apart from the king, it was Raven ... and thanks to Nimrooden, her father may never have the chance.

Reaching into his chest plate, Illan removed a single key. "He's being held in the high tower – in shackles, so you needn't fear him escaping."

Raven's mouth twisted into a grimace, voice dropping into a snarl. "I don't fear him *at all*. He hides behind women and armies and thinks that makes him powerful. But I won't allow him the credit of being anything more than that."

"Careful, Princess," Illan snapped. "He may not risk his life unnecessarily, but he's dangerous. Don't underestimate him." His face fell. "Your father did ... as did I." He touched her cheek gently, almost fatherly. "Don't make the mistake of doing the same."

She jerked her head once. "I understand. But I'm still going." She started to leave.

"Princess."

Raven turned to find Illan offering her a dagger with a beautiful, jeweled hilt and a razor-sharp blade, narrowing to a tip.

"This was hers. Your mother's."

A wave of emotion strangled any words she might have said.

Illan pressed it into her hands. "You deserve your revenge."

"Thank you," she whispered. Then she was gone, darting up staircases and flitting through abandoned hallways.

Clutching her mother's dagger to her chest.

ꙮ

He smirked, not looking away from the window. The glass was scrubbed spotless. Outside was a stormy gray; the bright rays of morning had turned to an overcast afternoon. Somewhere below, the armies were slogging through heavy rain and mud, tracking down the last of the enemy forces.

"I almost didn't hear you. Impressive." He rested an elbow on the sill, sending a series of metallic clanks through the chains running from his wrists to the iron ring on the floor.

She stood in the doorway, easing it shut but not advancing any further. "That was my intention."

For a moment they stood in silence. Then he shifted, looking at his guest for the first time and taking one step from the window. His straight black hair fell to his shoulders; a day's growth of stubble protruded from his square jaw. Pale blue eyes watched her, trying to see beneath her cloak.

"I assume your father knows nothing of your visit." It was a statement, not a question.

She returned with an equally flat tone. "Of course not. You saw to that, didn't you?"

"Princess, why don't we cease with this game and get down

to business, where you tell me why you're here and I tell you how much I really don't care. Shall we?" His gesture set off another series of noises from his chains.

"Fine." Raven stepped away from the wall and removed her hood. "I'm here to kill you. Still don't care?"

For the first time since she'd entered, Raven actually elicited a reaction from Nimrooden. Ever so subtly, his eyes widened, and the confident poise slipped. He shrugged. "Maybe, maybe not."

"Afraid to die?"

He didn't grace her with an answer. "You look like her, you know."

"Who?"

"Your mother. Mariah."

Now it was Raven's turn to give pause. Then she advanced on him, knuckles going bloodless as she squeezed the hilt of her dagger. "You have *no right* to even say her name –"

"Because I killed her or because I loved her?"

Raven gaped, unable to move or speak.

Nimrooden smirked, but without the grating self-assurance and demeaning edge this time. "No doubt this surprises you. I'm sure your father failed to mention, but your mother and I were betrothed." He tilted his head. "Sort of. She loved me, and I –" An afflicted groan slipped through his lips. "I worshiped the ground she walked on."

Raven recovered enough of her wits to reply. "Until you killed her?"

An emotionless mask fell over Nimrooden's face, and he began pacing, filling the room with the sound of his shackles. "She wasn't royal. Just the daughter of an insignificant nobleman. I was a young commander in Tarith's army. We'd known each other since childhood – I wasn't rich, and neither was she, but that didn't matter to either of us. We made plans to marry."

He glanced at Raven but didn't seem to care if she were

listening. But how could she do otherwise? This was a side of her mother she'd never heard of – a side her father had never dared mention. *Did he even know?*

"But her family disapproved," Nimrooden continued. His eyes flashed murderously; a reminder of who he really was. Why she had come here in the first place. Raven stepped back, holding her weapon tighter.

"Her father threatened me. Said he'd call in a favor with my commander and have me discharged." He threw his arms in the air, pacing faster. "So I asked Mariah to run away with me, get married in secret. And she would have – if it weren't for *him*."

Raven asked, voice barely audible, "Who?" But before the word had passed her lips, she already knew the answer.

Nimrooden spun and advanced on her, until his face was mere inches from her own. He reached the end of the chains, keeping his arms locked behind him, or Raven might have backed away.

"Your *father*!" he spat. He turned away, allowing her to breathe again.

"He came visiting in all his pomp and glory, bedecked in an extravagant display of his riches – furs, silks, rings of pure gold. Mariah's father had little wealth, but he had titles and land, and the ear of Tarith's throne … enough to tempt the mighty *King Wilgaun*," he taunted.

"Please –" She cleared her throat weakly; it was dry as cotton and threatening to choke the life out of her. "He's my father." But Raven's protest went unheard.

"He thought he could snatch her from me. What was a lowly soldier in the face of such a grand king?" Nimrooden's words tumbled over each other, each syllable spewing hatred. "He tried to sweep her away with decadent balls and glamorous parties. Got her father on his side. But it wasn't enough – Mariah never would have been bought. Until …"

Nimrooden's tirade faltered, and Raven wasn't sure if he would continue. He reached out, clutching the chain in a death squeeze, as if to strangle the life out of it. There was no doubt he was imagining it was her father's neck.

"Until Wilgaun set me up." Nimrooden released the chain, letting it drop to the floor. "Somehow, he uncovered an assassination plot on Tarith's monarch – something I had *nothing* to do with! Conveniently, I was found guilty by association with one of the noblemen who had birthed the plot – unbeknownst to me."

"And ... my mother?"

Nimrooden fixed his gaze on Raven, blue-gold eyes lifeless, face and tone slack. "Mariah bought Wilgaun's lie. Naturally, I had no choice but to desert, but when I came to her, asking her to flee with me, she refused. *She betrayed our love.*"

Raven shook her head, willing the story to end.

"Oh, but that's not all. The next thing I knew, I was a fugitive in the Wilderns, and she was wed – the new Queen of Laynia." He sneered, daring Raven to correct him. Daring her to justify what – in his mind – were the unjustifiable actions of a corrupt king ... her father.

Raven remained silent. What could she say? No one could convince a madman.

"But you are wrong, Princess." His gaze drifted out of focus. "Even when my sword pierced her side, and her eyes widened in terror and hatred, I *never* stopped loving her. But she stopped loving me."

He stepped closer, and Raven fought to breathe. His fingers played with her hair – the same way Tristan had. But instead of the warm, pleasant shivers, Nimrooden made her want to turn and flee, to wash away the defilement his hands had wrought.

"One of us had to die, don't you see?" he murmured, releasing her hair. The strand fell limply against her collarbone. He let out a low hiss. "And Wilgaun was too much of a coward to kill me."

She inched the dagger out of its sheath.

℘

Raven's fingers brushed over those of the motionless king. His skin had taken on a deathly pallor from blood loss, and his eyes were shut tightly. Although the blue had faded from his lips, and his breathing had evened, it was too late.

King Wilgaun would not wake again.

"I'm sorry, Father," she whispered. "I'm so, so sorry."

In her mind, she could almost hear him asking, *"Why are you sorry?"*

"Because I never told you that I loved you. Because I let my fears and doubts about myself – about my ability to rule – hold me back from becoming the woman you wanted me to be. And then I blamed you for trying to make me overcome those fears."

His voice replied, *"But aren't I also to blame for letting my fears and doubts get in the way of my love for* you? *For never telling you how much I loved you?"*

"It doesn't matter who's to blame." The tears poured silently down her cheeks. "It doesn't matter because I'll never get to tell you, and you'll never get to tell me. It doesn't matter because you're dying, and you're going to slip away, and I'll never get the chance to tell you …"

"You just did."

"I know, but it's not the same –"

"Raven, I heard every word you just said."

Raven's eyes shot open, and she gasped, "Father?"

Against all hope, Wilgaun's gray eyes had opened, and were twinkling merrily at the shock that must have been written across her face.

"You're still here!" she murmured. She sunk her face into the uninjured side of his chest, the warmth enveloping her face.

"Is there anywhere else I should be?" There was a note of his old gruffness in the words, but he chuckled lightly. It broke into a wet cough.

Raven sat back, dabbed at the blood flecking the corners of his mouth. "Shh, save your strength."

He pushed the cloth away. "No. While I still have strength

left, I need to make things right. With you. You've had your turn, and I refuse to die until I've had mine." He struggled to sit, but ended up short-winded and wheezing; instead, he satisfied himself with the pillow Raven propped behind his back.

Taking her hand, Wilgaun gazed solemnly into his daughter's eyes. "Illan told me what happened."

Raven started to look away, but he cupped her face with his free hand. "No, listen. I can't blame you – I had similar plans. Well, at least until I took an arrow to the chest." He smiled ruefully, and Raven slapped his hand in playful reproach.

He went serious again. "But I must know. Did you do it?" He searched her face like he was reading an ancient scroll, probing its hidden secrets. "Is Nimrooden ... *dead*?"

Raven didn't answer. In her mind, she was once again in the high tower, fingers locked around the dagger, ready to bury the steel deep into Nimrooden's heart.

ℰ

"Go on. Finish it. Put the dagger between my ribs – do what your father was too weak to do." Nimrooden flashed a sickly smile, placing his hands over hers on the dagger hilt and aiming it at his chest. "I'm dead anyway. It would be a sweet sort of revenge, knowing Wilgaun would have to live on, knowing his daughter was stronger than he could ever be."

A thousand rationales burst into Raven's mind. How her father would understand, if he ever found out. How Illan would grow in respect for the future queen. How her mother would finally rest in peace – avenged.

But then Tristan's face came to mind, with the words he'd spoken before riding off to battle. "I'll come back. Always. As long as you're waiting for me." *Would he be proud of her, knowing she had taken it upon herself to be Nimrooden's judge, jury and executioner? To bypass the laws of justice and replace them with savage vengeance? Somehow, she couldn't see him being pleased.*

And then there was this Regium Tristan had spoken of. Would this god accept her, knowing she had killed a man in cold blood – no matter

259

how justified?

Raven brushed these thoughts aside. What did it matter what some deity thought about her conduct? He'd never been there for her; when her mother died, and she and her father had fallen apart, he was silent. When she fled for her life across the wilderness of Tharland, he was nowhere to be found.

Her muscles tensed, preparing to sink the dagger into Nimrooden's chest.

And then her words – whispered in the emptiness of Tharland, when she thought Tristan was certainly dead – came back to her. She'd asked for someone, anyone who could hear her, to bring Tristan back to her. And they had. He had.

But now Tristan was lost again, somewhere in a blood-stained field – dead or alive, she didn't know. All because of Nimrooden.

"Give in," Nimrooden growled. "End it all! What are you waiting for?"

What was she waiting for? Nimrooden deserved to die!

Setting her teeth, Raven thrust the dagger downward … and halted, tip resting over his heart. She slowly backed away. "No. I won't do it."

Nimrooden's eyes flashed. "Kill me!"

She shook her head. "I refuse to become what you are – twisted and warped by hatred and the need for revenge. I have every right to stick this dagger into your chest, but I won't. And it's not because I'm weak. It's because I'm strong. I don't need revenge to make me feel powerful, or hatred to solidify my convictions. My father loves me, and I know – in life and death – my mother loved me, too. More than anything."

Raven rammed the dagger into its sheath. "And you're wrong. My mother didn't marry Wilgaun because of his riches, or position, or because she was deceived about you. They married because – despite their differences – they loved each other. Maybe not as passionate as your love for Mariah, but a love where she could feel safe, and protected. A love that led to me." She smiled sadly. "And that is a love that you will never know."

Raven turned to leave, then hesitated. She glanced back at the shell of a man who was all but begging her to end his failed existence.

"I refuse to hate you anymore."

಄

"No. I didn't do it." Raven squeezed her father's hand. "I didn't kill Nimrooden."

Wilgaun slumped back, releasing the breath he'd been holding. "Thank the Regium."

The Regium. Had *He* a part to play in her sparing Nimrooden's life? He'd certainly been a consideration, albeit one she had tried to ignore. But who else could have been responsible for that quiet nagging in her heart, the one that stopped her from becoming the executioner? In the end, it wasn't Illan, or her father. It wasn't even Tristan, as much as she thought about him in that moment.

Could it be that the Regium had stilled her blade?

"Tell me about Him."

Wilgaun glanced up in surprise, wondering that she'd taken his expression literally. "The Regium?"

Raven nodded, and Wilgaun fumbled for words. "Well, He's – I guess He could be called – that is to say ..." He paused, a wry smile twisting his mouth. "He is a King that I stopped serving a long time ago, in a time of despair. And I was too proud to go back afterward."

"So you *did* believe in him once?"

"Once?" Wilgaun stared off thoughtfully. "I still do, I suppose. I just stopped surrendering. I was so full of bitterness that I couldn't accept Mariah's death was *my* fault, not *His*."

Raven touched her father's grizzled cheek. "It wasn't your fault. It was Nimrooden's. He was so caught up in revenge ... he lost his way."

Wilgaun sighed. "Yes, I suppose."

Raven played with the blankets, debating. In the end, her curiosity won out. "Did she – love him?"

He thought for a moment. "Perhaps ... once. But even before I came along, Mariah realized there was a darkness in him she couldn't overcome, no matter how much ... affection she felt for him. When your mother helped me expose Nimrooden's part in the assassination plot – when she chose me over him – that was when I realized I loved her." He smiled faintly. "Though I did a poor job showing it at times."

"*She* exposed him?"

"Yes. Although I don't think he found out until years later – maybe never. It doesn't matter now." Wilgaun tightened his grip. "What matters is what we do with the short time I have left."

Raven started to protest, but he put a finger to her lips.

"Don't bother denying it, daughter. I can feel it here," he touched his chest lightly. "It's only a matter of time. But before I go, I want to set things right. First with you – then with my King."

She smiled through her tears. "So do I."

℘

Raven would always remember those last moments with her father – the tears, the laughter, the memories they shared. The moment when they both pledged themselves to the High Regium – how her father, eyes closing, whispered that his King was waiting for him.

Now Wilgaun lay still, face peaceful, all pain gone.

Eyes and throat stinging, Raven kissed his forehead. "He was waiting for us both."

Suddenly, the king's chest rose and fell.

AFTERMATH

Raven's black dress billowed across the wet grass. She knelt, alone, in the middle of a green field, where the gray sky stretched on forever and the north wind sung laments of bygone ages. The cold seeped straight into her, but nothing compared with the pain inside her chest. Nothing compared to the aching.

The soft ground was dark and moist, recently turned. All around the grass was green, but not here. Here, the ground was dead soil. Here, it marked Freedom's grave.

Tears poured silently down Raven's cheeks; the tightness in her throat threatened to strangle her, body and soul. She thought maybe, if she just pretended this had never happened, she'd find him in the barn, waiting for her like always – find he wasn't gone. But no; this was goodbye. Forever. For the rest of her life. She'd never canter across the fields on the stallion's sturdy back, never hear his eager nicker when she entered the barn. His stall was empty – as was his place in her heart. And she knew nothing could ever fill it again.

Raven's fingers clawed into the damp earth. She wanted to say a thousand things – to say she was sorry, that she was grateful, that'd she'd miss him. Things she'd never get to tell him again in this life.

But maybe in the next.

"Run free, my beautiful boy," she whispered. "In fields where you'll never grow tired, and sickness and death are fleeting memories. I'll meet you there … one day. But not yet." She smiled faintly. "I still have a lot left to do."

Clutching a braid of his mane to her heart, Raven walked away.

Freedom was buried in the meadow, where a myriad of wildflowers beckoned, and the brook ran crystal waters over

263

stone. Where the stallion could run forever in eternity, waiting for his princess to join him.

༚

After the last of Nimrooden's army had been captured or killed, Tristan returned, weary but alive. He held Raven, neither speaking, each mourning their losses and thanking the Regium for those who had survived. That *they* had survived.

Shortly after, Melodea and Courtney joined them. Raven was overjoyed to see Melodea alive, and equally surprised to see the princess of Roehn so far from home on the fringes of a battle.

Now, two days after the battle, the three princesses stood silently garbed in black as King Albastan lay prepared for his final trip to Roehn, where he would be buried among his ancestors.

Courtney silently traced her father's coffin, tears spilling from her eyes, words a gravelly whisper. "This is my fault."

Raven wrapped her arm around Courtney's thin shoulders. "You didn't fire the arrow, Courtney. The only one to blame is Nimrooden and his men, and they will be brought to justice."

When Albastan's body had been discovered among the dead, no one could say when he had died or who had killed him. All the soldiers saw was the arrow protruding from his heart – a quick death – and the faint smile on the king's lips.

Courtney whirled around, breaking Raven's hold. "Justice? You want to talk about justice? Both our fathers are shot by Nimrooden's assassin. My father is found dead. And yours? He's brought back to the castle alive, where you get to say goodbye."

"Courtney …" Melodea warned.

Holding up a hand, Courtney stopped her. "But no. Instead of goodbye, the Regium heals your father. *Heals him!* With not a scratch left! And my father –" her voice broke, and she pointed at the coffin – "by some cruel twist of fate, is dead. Forever." Her eyes blazed, her jaw quivering with fury, face inches from Raven. "Where is your so-called justice?"

Raven opened her mouth to answer, but couldn't.

Courtney straightened, voice going flat. "You were right. This wasn't our fight. I should have let Laynia fall."

∞

Raven watched as Roehn's armies trickled across the battlefield – past the mass, nameless graves created for Nimrooden's fallen – vanishing into the southern horizon. She turned to Melodea, suddenly light-headed. So much needless death. So much sorrow.

"Will you be leaving, too?" The thought of losing her friend, after all they'd been through together, left an empty pit inside of Raven. In the end, she realized that Melodea – not Courtney – was the true friend. And now …

"Actually, I thought I might stay a while. I can't imagine returning home, not after everything. And now that Quillan is gone …" Melodea's eyes drifted toward Tharland. "You and Tristan are the only ones who understand the hardships I endured. That *we* endured," she amended, squeezing Raven's hand.

"Do you regret it? Coming with us, I mean?"

"No." Melodea smiled. "I don't regret it. I never want to go through something like that again, but …" She paused, lost in thought. "It changed me. I can't go back to being the same timid princess I used to be. And I don't think I'll miss *her* one bit."

Raven returned the smile. "We've both changed. For the better, I think. And I never thought I'd hear myself saying it, but I'm *so* glad you're staying."

"Good." Melodea quirked a brow. "Because I already told my father, and I would hate to waste the half-hour he spent trying to talk me out of it!"

∞

The new apprentice gate guard almost turned the man away. After all, he reasoned the stranger could easily be one of Nimrooden's leftover assassins, sent to kill the king when the arrow had failed. But the senior gate guard, Brogan, recognized one of the horses – a blue roan. The stranger was allowed to state his case, and – after a flurry of messages and inquiries – permitted entrance.

The stranger strode casually to the castle courtyard, waiting under the watchful eyes of half a dozen guards. *She'll come,* he thought. *She has to come.* Sure enough, the princess emerged a few minutes later, holding the rather cryptic note the stranger had sent her.

"You wanted to see me ..." Melodea's voice trailed off as her eyes locked on the stranger. For a moment, neither spoke, neither moved, each rendered speechless by the sight of the other.

Then the note fluttered to the ground as Melodea ran into Quillan's waiting arms.

QUEEN OF ROEHN

Roehn, a few days later ...

Courtney paced the length of her room. The hem of her dress swept in a wide arc across the floor, collecting any remaining dust the servants had missed and catching on the occasional piece of furniture. She ignored it. She ignored everything.

Taelon was missing. When she'd returned from Laynia, her father's corpse in tow, she had expected to find the one person she could count on to share her grief. Her mother would lock herself in her room, and the noblemen would start calling in favors and forming alliances to claim the throne. But Taelon – carefree, good, kind Taelon – would sympathize with his only sister. They'd never been friends, but they'd always been loyal. Even when they fought, they made up. Even when they disagreed, they never let the outside world know. Only father had guessed how often they quarreled; Mother was never informed anymore since she only feigned a headache and scolded her children for immaturity.

Recently, Courtney and Taelon had ceased almost all dissention. Taelon was engrossed in his politics and hunts, Courtney in her tutelage and suitors. Maybe, in a few years, they might have even called themselves friends as well as allies.

But not now.

The last anyone had seen of Taelon was the day of Raven's departure. He'd ridden out to see the armies off, then set back towards Roehn, alone. Nothing to be alarmed about, nothing to arouse suspicion. Even Mother thought it was good for the prince to have some time to himself, to consider his plan of action during his father's absence.

But Taelon had never returned. Evening had come and gone;

night had fallen twice. A search party had been deployed. They found nothing – not the smallest trace of him. They had followed his mount's hoofprints to the old bridge before losing them in the stream. By the time a tracker had been found, any trace of the prints were long gone.

Her brother was long gone.

Leaving her to deal with a dead father, a distraught mother, a missing prince, and a kingdom in political shambles. Alone.

Courtney seethed, steps increasing in speed and force. Her heeled boots made hollow clacking sounds that echoed through the chamber and into the hallway, frightening off nearby servants.

How dare he? How dare *any* of them? That traitor, Kirgan – Nimrooden – Raven – her brother – even those two Laynian servants who'd gone missing from her castle a few hours after Taelon! How could they leave her like this? How could they tear her kingdom apart and think they could get away with it?

Nimrooden had been hanged. That was a small comfort. Whichever of his minions had killed her father, Courtney was glad to know the orchestrator had been brought to justice, no matter how merciful the quick death had been. But Kirgan was nowhere to be seen. Perhaps he was responsible for Taelon's disappearance – perhaps the runaway servants were. It didn't matter. She would find all of them, somehow. And if she didn't, she would make sure someone paid.

Someone had to pay.

And it wasn't going to be her.

"Guards!" Courtney's screech brought in two soldiers, stumbling over one another in their haste. She sneered. At her beck and call, ready to report to her. Their future queen. "Call a council meeting."

The guards glanced at each other uncertainly. One ventured a humble protest – Hawk, her personal guard, whom she'd appointed the position to after her brother's disappearance. He wasn't as much of an eyesore as the other brutes, and actually had some wits about him.

"Your mother has called for a time of mourning," Hawk said. "The steward will rule in the king's absence, and the nobles will reconvene when the queen sees fit to –"

"Do I look like I need your advice? I know what my mother ordered! But I am ordering *you* to disregard her orders and obey me. Your princess." Courtney leaned back, allowing the fire to ebb from her words – just a little. Too much anger, and she'd frighten the guards beyond submission. Not enough, and they'd treat her like a princess. A girl. A weak, helpless girl who didn't know the first thing about politics. And they'd be wrong.

"My mother is not fit for rule," Courtney continued calmly. Composed, as a queen ought to be. "Her judgement is clouded by the grief of losing her son and husband in a matter of days. I will bring this matter before the council for due consideration."

Hawk tried once more, words carefully measured and infused with respect, as if he knew better than to incite the wrath of his princess. "Exactly, she is clouded with grief. And with all respect, as are you, Princess. Which is exactly why you should allow the steward to fulfill his duties until such a time as you are ready to take up –"

"*I am your princess!*" The words that came from Courtney's mouth were nearly a shriek. She didn't care. Let Hawk – and all her men – think what they wanted. It was the nobles she had to convince, and in order to do that, she had to meet with them. A task which Hawk was interfering with.

"You *will* do as I say –" Her eyes glittered dangerously. "Or I will remember. When I am crowned queen, I will remember your disloyalty. Your lack of respect." Her face was inches from Hawk's, her words a deathly whisper. "Your ... *insurgence*."

She whirled around, gown brushing across the guards' feet, and rested herself in a fetching poise against the windowsill. "Do I make myself clear?"

The other guard snapped a salute. "Yes, Your Majesty!"

Hawk's reply was a second slower, a mite less enthusiastic.

269

His sullen glare was even less so. "Yes, *Your Majesty*."

"Good." Courtney smiled, running her fingers along the pane. "I quite like the sound of that. *Your Majesty*."

She flicked her wrist dismissively and the timid guard shuffled out of the room. Hawk lingered a moment before giving a smart half-bow. When the princess failed to acknowledge, he too left.

Her words were spoken into the still room, a murmur that resounded like the rumble of thunder. "*I* will be queen. And Laynia will pay."

Epilogue

Two years later…

Raven brushed her nose against his, her eyes sparkling, a smile fixed on her face. "Who's my beautiful boy? You are! Yes, you are!" Her crooning voice might have sounded ridiculous, but who cared? She was a princess – any servants who overheard would keep their thoughts to themselves, or gossip to their fellow workers over lunch. If she provided them a bit of harmless entertainment at her expense, she wouldn't judge.

After all, *they said* a mother's time with her child was short. Best make the most of the time and hang the criticism. Babies were made to be fawned over.

Melodea rocked her own little girl, Elehna, on her lap. "Who would have thought that, in a few short years, we would go from discontented, helplessly-flawed princesses to … *mothers!*"

Raven laughed. "It suits you – I always knew you'd be a perfect little wife, holding a perfect little child and living the perfect life. I, on the other hand …" She clucked her tongue. "Let's just say it's a wonder my little boy hasn't found himself suffering in the hands of a perfectly *incapable* mother."

"*Wonder?* More like you have a nursemaid to thank for that."

Raven feigned a scowl. "You incorrigible little imp!"

"Did someone say my name?" Quillan popped his head through the doorway, grinning.

"You certainly are an imp," Melodea teased.

"I'm wounded." He flashed his wife an audacious wink. "Come now, ladies … your carriage awaits. And Liberty is giving me a headache with all her impatient stomping." He disappeared into the hallway.

Raven rolled her eyes. "That girl could run all day and still

271

want to go."

Melodea gave a pointed raise of her eyebrow. "It was *your* choice. And I daresay you'd die of boredom without her."

"Tristan coerced me!" Still, Raven couldn't suppress a smile. She hadn't been able to resist the black filly from the moment she set eyes on her. And that Freedom was Liberty's sire made her all the more special – the stallion's first and only offspring.

"We should head out soon," Melodea advised. "Although I don't see what the rush is – the sea will certainly wait for us."

Raven smirked. "Yes, but our husbands may not."

৪১

Tristan took a deep breath of the fresh air, almost imagining he could taste the salty tang of the sea. Wilgaun had built his daughter a seaside manor for her wedding, and this year, Quillan and Melodea were accompanying them from Mieldren.

It was one of the few times Tristan could escape from royal life. While he'd grown used to being waited on hand and foot, every once and a while, he liked to swing an axe and chop his own wood.

He and Quillan were loading the last bit of luggage onto the carriage, battling each other in an unspoken competition of who could lift the heaviest bag.

"Ready to get away from Trythe yet?" Tristan asked, nudging Quillan.

"You have *no* idea. My in-laws are driving me crazy." A grin spread across Quillan's face. "But what's a man to do when he's married to such a good-hearted princess? I blame you entirely, you know. I swear, you're just trying to get back at me for turning you in to Nimrooden."

Tristan chuckled, heaving the last suitcase onto the carriage roof. "All part of the plan, old chap."

Wilgaun ambled into the courtyard, eyeing the haphazard pile of luggage. His hair had more gray than it used to, and his girth was a touch wider, but otherwise Tristan's father-in-law was in excellent health – a living reminder of the Regium's influence in their family's life.

And if that wasn't enough, the fact that Wilgaun hadn't skinned Tristan alive when he asked for Raven's hand was a miracle unto itself. But he was a knight now – and elevated to status of prince. That *did* take some getting used to.

"Take care of my grandson," Wilgaun reminded. "Too much excitement at such a young age isn't good for him – he may turn out more headstrong than his mother."

Raven emerged, holding Rinnian on her hip. "Father!" she admonished, eyes sparkling with amusement.

"I'll be sure Rinnian doesn't get into too many adventures," Tristan laughed. "But he's bound to find some, especially with such an adventurous mother."

Wilgaun harrumphed, kissing his daughter and grandson. Rinnian giggled as the king's whiskers brushed his face, and a deep rumble filled Wilgaun's chest.

෨

After a flurry of goodbyes – most of them repetitive and accompanied by well-meant words of caution – the carriages rolled out of the southern gate. Raven couldn't erase the smile from her face. In many respects, that day was much like the one two years earlier, when she'd embarked on her life-altering journey. Leaving Saush – now older and a bit stiff – waiting at the gate, with Smokey off chasing mice in the kitchen. Her father kissing her goodbye. The carriage bumping over the dirt roads.

But things had changed. *She* had changed. Tristan was right beside her, not on his blue roan. Quillan and Melodea sat across from her with little Elehna. There were fewer guards outside. And instead of Freedom tied behind the carriage, Liberty pranced and snorted, more than ready for an adventure of her own.

And in place of Breeanah, Synthia accompanied Raven as her chamber maid. Faithful, grumpy Synthia, who had adopted little Rinnian as her own. Raven couldn't help but wonder what would have happened if things had been different – if Breeanah had come with her, instead of remaining in Roehn, along with Drin. But she had disappeared, leaving no evidence that she was anything more than a memory in Raven's past. *Who knows? Maybe Breeanah is off on an adventure of her own.*

But that was all in the past. This was the present. Raven had been given a life she'd never dreamed was possible. In this new life, Tristan's arm rested across her shoulders. Quillan and Melodea fawned over Elehna. The rocking carriage was lulling Rinnian to sleep. And somewhere ahead, the sea was beckoning.

Raven brushed her lips across her son's forehead and quietly began to sing:

> *Return to me on a starlit night,*
> *When the moon hushes the sea.*
> *I cannot bear to see the dark,*
> *When you, my light, are gone.*
> *Will you return and sing to me,*
> *When the moon hushes the sea?*

Acknowledgements

First, I'd like to thank my amazing family. I couldn't have done it without you. Especially, though, I'd like to thank my mom, who read through this book no less than *five times* over the course of its six-year journey. Mom, you are my critic, my editor, and my cheerleader (who happened to catch an error in my acknowledgements page). *Mom rocks!*

I'd also like to thank all my readers. All the notes, comments on my blog, and in-person encouragements have pushed me to keep writing and keep making my work better. Writing wouldn't be nearly as fun or fulfilling without all of you to appreciate it!

Lastly, thank you to my favorite authors out there; you'll never know how much your stories motivated me to write! They say imitation is the sincerest form of flattery. I hope I didn't imitate you *too* much, but I can't deny, this story has been inspired by so many others.

ABOUT THE AUTHOR

 J. H. GATES is the author of multiple prize-winning short stories, along with her upcoming novels *Threads of Darkness*, the fourth book in the Prophecies of Berinfell, and YA primeval fantasy, *The Hinterlands*. She lives in the mountains of North Idaho where she finds her own adventures and writes her own story, one which has just begun. For more about J. H. Gates, visit her at www.jhgates.com